Blaze

Praise for the Midnight Fire Series

Blaze

Midnight Fire Book Three

Kaitlyn Davis

All Works By Kaitlyn Davis

Midnight Fire
Ignite
Simmer
Blaze
Scorch

A Dance of Dragons
The Shadow Soul
The Spirit Heir
The Phoenix Born

A Dance of Dragons – The Novellas
The Golden Cage
The Silver Key

To my family for their unconditional love,
my friends for their overwhelming support,
and my fans for their incredible enthusiasm.
Thank you from the bottom of my heart.

Chapter One

Kira ripped another page from her notebook and crumpled the thick paper between her fingers. Frustrated, she threw the ball into her wastebasket.

Quite the collection, she mused as she glanced down at the paper pyramid by her feet. Kira had been sitting at her desk for nearly an hour, but still the right words had eluded her. How could she explain it to Luke, her best friend and ever-faithful protector? No matter what, he would be angry. No matter what, he would feel betrayed. But it was the only way to keep him safe from Aldrich.

Kira sighed and leaned back in her chair, slowly swiveling it from side to side as she thought back a week and a half ago to the night of the Red Rose Ball. Kira could still picture it perfectly—the fear on the vampire Diana's face when she realized she was about to die. The way both of Kira's arms lit entirely on fire, pushing her power further than it had ever gone in order to break through Diana's immunity. The moment Tristan's maker, Aldrich, burst into the room only to be interrupted by a swarm of conduits exploding through the windows. The minutes Aldrich spent calmly evaluating her without any hint of fear, knowing his power to move objects with his mind was unbeatable. And of course, the feel of his hand when he slipped her a note with his address, promising that her birth mother would be there, waiting for the daughter who had been taken away from her more than seventeen years ago.

Kira remembered watching the mansion collapse in on itself after the conduits had set it on fire, remembered holding both Tristan and Luke's hands while the three of them observed in silence. She remembered how the note Aldrich had given her seemed to burn a hole through her pocket and the moment a plan popped into her mind. Most of all, Kira remembered the moment she had decided to act on it.

After destroying the mansion, the conduits retreated to a safe house to question the vampires they had captured. Luke followed, but Kira stayed behind feigning exhaustion. True, she had desperately wanted a shower and a soft bed, but the promise of a few hours alone with Tristan was what she had really needed. That night, while Luke was off on official business, the lie had begun—the lie that made this letter to Luke so difficult to write. Kira and Tristan were going to fight Aldrich, and they were leaving Luke behind.

Kira dropped her pen and glanced at the photo of her and Tristan that sat on the corner of her desk. Taped to the back, hidden behind the blue plastic frame, was the note Aldrich had slipped her before he had escaped. Kira didn't need to look at it to know what it said—she had the address memorized by now. Her mother was waiting in some cold castle in England, and Kira needed to find her. But it wasn't that simple.

When she first told him, Tristan had been furious. It was the night of the ball and they had just gotten back to the hotel room after ditching Luke. Kira tried to casually let it slip that his maker, Aldrich, had invited them to his castle, but Tristan wasn't fooled by her light tone. His eyes had flashed an ice-cold blue that stabbed at Kira's heart and he yelled at her for the first time. Kira knew it was his own fear and insecurities that fueled the outraged response—his own issues with Aldrich—but Kira suspected Luke's response wouldn't be any better, which was why she had decided to keep it a secret.

After calming Tristan down and firmly stating that she would be going to England with or without him, he had finally started listening to her. They worked out a plan to get her birth mother back, but it was a two-person plan. And tomorrow Kira would be ditching Luke at the airport to secretly fly to England with Tristan.

Oh yeah, Kira thought, *this will go over very well… not!*

She had reached for her pen again, ready to finally

write a coherent note, when strong arms enveloped her from behind, circling her shoulders and sending a chill down her spine with the suddenly cool touch.

"Hi," Tristan whispered in her ear as he pressed his cheek against hers and placed a soft kiss on her neck.

"Hi," Kira said, letting her head fall back against his shoulder. Perfect timing, she thought, thankful for the break from writing this note. A little procrastination never hurt anyone.

"Ready for your party, birthday girl?" he asked.

"Crap—no!" Kira shot up, suddenly energetic with surprise. "What time is it?"

"Almost five."

Tristan laughed under his breath, not at all surprised that Kira was running late. Never one for shorts, even in the middle of summer, Tristan had on his classic dark blue jeans and a crisp white button-down. Kira didn't have time to admire how the stark ivory brought out the twinkling blue of his eyes, she was too concentrated on being on time for once in her life.

"No, no, no…" Kira buzzed while pulling her T-shirt off and reaching for the yellow cotton dress hanging on the back of her door. She had been so focused on writing the note that she had completely forgotten about her birthday barbecue—the one happening in roughly five minutes. The only reason she was still at home in Charleston was her birthday, otherwise Luke would have shipped her back to

Sonnyville already. Kira knew he was eager to keep training her in order to see what her stronger powers meant. He had already forced her to light the wooden table in his backyard on fire, so she didn't even want to know what he was preparing back in Sonnyville.

"Don't worry. No one's here yet," Tristan said while he watched Kira tug her shorts off and smooth out her dress. Had Kira been less pressed for time, she may have felt a little self-conscious about changing right in front of her boyfriend, but as it was, she didn't have any time to be insecure.

"Are my parents outside?" Kira asked and bent over to pull the fuzzy socks off of her feet.

"Your dad is starting up the barbecue, and your mom is setting plastic plates on the table with Chloe."

"Perfect," Kira said, yanking one last time on the stubborn sock. Tristan put a hand on her back to keep her from falling over, and she slipped her feet into a pair of sandals. "How do I look?" Kira said while twirling around a few times.

"Beautiful as always," he said, catching her hand and guiding her toward him. Kira spun right into his arms and quickly kissed his lips, loving how familiar yet exciting his touch was. The slow exploration of her body, sexy in its restraint, made Kira feel delicate—something she direly needed when most of the time she felt too powerful, too uncontrolled, too…everything.

Tristan pulled back, breaking the kiss, to say, "I hear Emma's car out front."

"Just when we were getting to the good stuff," Kira cursed, making both of them smirk. Her best girlfriend was nothing if not prompt.

"I'll go get everyone to the backyard." Tristan slipped free of her arms. "You still need to put your contacts on." Kira grimaced, thinking of the bulky, itchy lenses that had become part of her daily routine. She nodded regretfully and pushed Tristan toward the stairs while she stepped into her bathroom.

Only Luke and Tristan knew about the change in her eyes. On their way home after the ball, Kira bought color contacts and had been using them ever since. It wasn't the perfect solution, but it was something.

Looking in the mirror, Kira still had trouble recognizing herself. Bright cobalt blue irises stared back at her. Orange-yellow flames danced around the edges, pushing into the cooler color and fighting for a place, but the shockingly saturated blue overwhelmed everything else. Sometimes, Kira liked how the blue popped against her red-blonde hair, but mostly she missed the warm, comforting green that used to be there. Her hair was already over the top with its bright hues and voluminous curls, she didn't need even crazier eyes to get noticed in a crowd.

Nothing else had physically changed about her since the night of the ball, but something stirred inside Kira, making her feel stronger. Luke and Tristan had no explanation for her new eye color, and Kira didn't want to harp on it when there was so much more to worry about. She had barely used her power since that night, only practicing when Luke forced her. She was more in control of her body and her fire, but the flames she commanded had changed. It was more than just the difference between her softer Protector powers and her rage-filled Punisher flames. Everything was stronger. All of her fire burned brighter, scorched hotter, and practically exploded with heat. When Luke had challenged Kira to light his wooden table on fire, it had come easily, like flipping a switch. The destruction was almost too welcome, too natural to her.

A high-pitched screech pulled Kira from her thoughts.

"Kira!" Her younger sister Chloe yelled from the bottom of the steps, "Where are you?"

"Yeah, Kira, where are you?" A deeper voice laced with mirth called after. *Luke*, Kira thought, hearing his laughter mix with Chloe's a second later.

"Coming!" she yelled and quickly pulled on her eyelid to slip in one contact. More squeals echoed down the empty hallway, and Kira followed the sound after quickly putting in her second contact.

When she looked down the steps, Kira saw the source of the noise. Luke had trapped little Chloe in his arms and was tickling her mercilessly while she giggled and squirmed to get away. Kira raced down the steps two at a time to free her sister.

"Kira!" Chloe yelled again before bursting into a new round of giggles. Kira smiled to herself. She knew exactly what to do. Reaching for Luke's stomach, she squeezed her hands against his abs and gave him a taste of his own medicine.

"No!" Luke laughed against Kira's attack and released Chloe, who followed Kira's lead and jumped on Luke to tickle him. He fell to the ground in mock surrender, chuckling helplessly and begging Chloe to stop.

"I win!" she screeched and raced out the back door, leaving Kira and Luke alone. Suddenly, Kira didn't know where to look. Between his confession of love the night of the Red Rose Ball and her plan to go to England behind his back, things were more than a bit strained. At least, it felt that way to Kira.

She offered her hand, doing her best to ignore the electric jolt his touch caused, and helped pull Luke to his feet. He dusted his khaki shorts off and tugged his navy T-shirt back down below his waist.

"Happy birthday," he said after a moment.

"Thanks," Kira responded, briefly glancing at his disheveled blonde locks and slightly strained gaze.

"So, Sonnyville tomorrow? I challenge you to get through an entire meeting with the council without burning their completely wooden dais to the ground," he joked, trying to lighten the mood.

"Yeah, can't wait," Kira hurriedly replied before heading for the door. She couldn't stand lying to him. At least that would end tomorrow. Even if he hated her for it, at least the lying would finally end. "Everyone's waiting, I better get out there." Kira nodded in the direction of the kitchen window.

Luke followed her gaze to the spot where Dave, Emma's silent but lovable boyfriend, and Miles, their geeky on-his-way-to-Harvard friend, stood next to her father around the grill.

"Yeah," Luke agreed and walked outside behind her.

"Happy birthday!" everyone shouted when Kira stepped into the sunlight. It was a small party, but it was perfect. Kira smiled at the streamers hanging in the trees surrounding her backyard and the freshly painted sign wishing her a happy eighteenth birthday. Chinese lanterns hung from the porch railing, ready for the sun to set so they could sparkle in the darkness, and raspy strains of the local radio station struggled to be heard from an old boom box sitting on the table.

"Thank you!" Kira smiled and stepped lightly down the porch stairs, practically dancing with her movements.

"Now, Kira, we know you're the chef in the family but tonight the men are making steaks," her dad said while standing beside an already smoking grill. Even though Kira knew he was really just her uncle, not even related by blood, the familiar image of him behind their family grill made it seem like old times, before Kira had known anything about the conduits or her real parents. "Luke, did you grab the aprons?"

"Got 'em, Mr. D!" Luke said, stepping past Kira to rush over to the grill.

Kira was more than happy to let the men do the work tonight. She loved cooking, but on her birthday she was allowed to relax. Especially since all she had been doing since she got home was make food—cooking was a serious stress reliever and all of the lying had her pulling her hair out. The Dawson family fridge was currently full to the brim with praline pecans, chocolate mousse, patience-trying risotto, and one of Kira's favorites, homemade spaghetti. Her fingers needed the night off.

Kira turned toward the foldout table her adoptive mother had put up in the backyard. She was really her aunt, her birth father's sister, but Kira tried to forget that sometimes. Especially on a day like today, with everyone around, Kira wanted to feel happy, not anxious about how much her life had changed in less than a year. She had gone from being a normal teenager to a mystical half-breed conduit who could potentially mean the end of the world. And the recent events at the Red Rose Ball had changed her again—she felt that in her bones even if she didn't know what it meant yet.

A moment later Kira blinked, pushing old memories

to the side to look back at the table where Emma was setting out the silverware and her mother was arranging a vase filled with fresh flowers. She stepped forward to help.

"Luke, you didn't!" Kira's mother gasped and put a hand to her mouth to cover her laughter. Kira stopped walking and turned just in time to see Luke finish tying an apron around his waist—the apron no one in her family ever used, the one her mother bought her father as a joke years ago, the one that had a life-sized photograph of Michelangelo's *David*... in the nude.

"Luke," Kira whined with a grimace, but the semblance of a smirk tugged at her lips.

"Just trying to get this party started." Luke grinned. He reached for the raw steaks and started dropping them on the grill.

Kira shook her head, but couldn't shake the small curve of her smile.

She looked around for Tristan, noticing he wasn't grill-side with the other men, and spotted him at the far side of the yard with Chloe. The two of them sat in the middle of a ring of Barbie toys, and Tristan was pretending to listen intently to whatever Chloe was trying to explain about her dolls. He looked up, as if sensing Kira's gaze, and flashed her a dimple-filled grin followed by a roll of his eyes.

"Should we go save him?" Kira's mother whispered in her ear, but Kira shrugged.

"Let him suffer." She laughed and out of the corner

of her eye, she saw Tristan shake his head at her. He had definitely overheard. *Good,* Kira thought, *let him know I'm totally calling the shots.* But her brief moment of power passed when a wad of napkins was shoved in her face.

"I'm going inside to work on the potato salad and coleslaw. Can you girls finish setting the table?"

"Sure, Mom," Kira said and took the napkins from her mother's arms before walking over to Emma.

"How is it possible that I'm wearing a dress and you're not?" Kira asked, eyeing her blonde friend's relaxed shorts and polo shirt attire.

"You're allowed to out-dress me one day a year— consider it my gift to you." Emma smiled and sat down in one of the vacant seats around the table. Kira sat next to her and dropped the napkins onto an empty plate.

"Want to learn how to fold these?" Kira asked. Years of working in a restaurant had taught her this nifty trick, and she quickly folded the first napkin into a simple, yet elegant, pyramid. Kira spent a few minutes showing Emma the steps, but it became obvious that there was something on her friend's mind.

"Is everything okay, Emma?"

"Of course," she said, but Kira didn't buy it.

"Really?" she pressed.

"Yeah... I was just thinking about how sweet it was that everyone came back for your birthday. I mean, Tristan came all the way back from backpacking around Europe just for the weekend—talk about dedication! I'm going to miss this…you know, having the gang together." She ended softly, concentrating on her napkin rather than the people around her. Kira pulled the linen from her friend's fingers, forcing Emma to concentrate on her words.

"I thought we got all of that talk out at graduation! We're still going to be 'the gang' no matter what."

"I know, but it won't be the same. You and Luke were only gone for what? Three weeks? And still, things felt off. Sometimes I just don't want things to change, you know? Like I don't really want to grow up."

You're telling me, Kira thought but quelled her inner monologue. Emma was almost never like this. Sure, she was emotional at times. But normally she was the calm, collected one—not the vulnerable, nervous one. Only one thing would bring this side out in her.

"Did something happen with Dave?" Kira asked, taking Emma's hand to comfort her. Dave and Emma were the perfect couple—they were classic southern sweethearts and they would both be going to college in Texas come fall. Kira couldn't even imagine them apart.

"No…I don't know. I'm just nervous I guess. People always say that when you grow up you grow apart, but what if I don't want that to happen?"

Kira couldn't suppress a sidelong glance at Tristan, who was still trapped by her sister, Chloe. She couldn't deny that her birthday had made her think the very same question—for her and Tristan, growing up literally meant growing apart.

"If you don't want to grow apart, you won't," Kira urged, turning her attention back to Emma and leaving her own thoughts for another time. "Nothing will change if you don't want it to. I mean, Dave is head over heels for you! You're all he ever thinks about and that won't change."

Both girls took a moment to look toward the grill where all four boys—yes, including Kira's fully adult father—were taking turns dropping lighter fluid into the flames to make them explode. Definitely Luke's idea, Kira assumed. "Well, when he's not playing with lighter fluid, all he does is think about you…"

"I know that," Emma said, "it's just that we'll be going to different colleges… they're only two hours away from each other, but still, it'll be different. And people always say that high school relationships never last, that they are sort of your first taste of love before the real thing comes around."

A sudden tingle stirred at the base of Kira's neck and she knew, before shifting to meet his gaze, that Tristan was watching her. His eyes were hidden beneath the shadow of his hair, but the tense muscles in his neck told Kira he was listening—waiting to hear what her response would be. She loved him and he her, but both of them had sensed the change in their relationship. He was a vampire. She was a conduit. They were supposed to be enemies, and the more prominent Kira's powers became, the more impossible their future seemed. That wasn't enough for Kira to give up on them and forget her feelings, but it was enough of a crack for a few small, almost imperceptible doubts to seep through.

"I don't believe that," she finally answered her friend. "Love is love, no matter how old or young you are."

"You're right," Emma said and let a slow smile spread across her face, lighting her features. She broke her long stare in Dave's direction, ready to tackle napkin folding again, but saw the gloomy expression on Kira's face. "Oh god, I've totally ruined your birthday! I don't know what came over me!"

"You haven't ruined anything," Kira said, casually waving the air away. "It's my party and I can cry if I want to!"

"Cry?" Luke's voice interjected from above Kira's shoulder. Kira spun in her seat, completely forgetting the apron Luke had on, and came face to face with the exact part of a nude male she did not want to be staring at.

Quickly shielding her eyes, Kira muttered, "Can you take that thing off? I can't take you seriously."

"You never take me seriously." Luke laughed, stepping even closer to Kira, who leaned further away. *Do not blush*, she thought, *do not blush*.

"Luke."

"Fine, fine. Ruin my fun," he said and untied the

apron before slipping it over his head. "I came over here to talk anyway."

"And that's my cue," Emma said, ducking out of the way and over toward Dave and Miles by the grill. Luke took her vacant seat and Kira instantly felt the space around them thicken. Her throat tightened and she took a deep breath, letting the air out slowly to calm her speeding pulse. She felt nervous around him—something she had never felt, not even since the first time they had met.

"What's up?" Kira said, hoping her voice had come out calm and strong.

Luke reached into his pocket and pulled out a small black box decorated with a white satin ribbon. "It's not much, but I got you a birthday present," he said and clumsily shoved his arm in her direction.

Slowly, Kira reached out and lifted the box from his hand. Using the power Kira had only discovered a few weeks before, she skimmed his thoughts, unable to stop the impulse to dip into his mind. The buzz of his nerves calmed her. His mind was hesitant, stopped on a breath and waiting. An expectation hung in the background, surrounded by a glimmer of hope and a tinge of excitement. But Kira could tell by the bright green hint in his eyes that he was energized—she didn't need the mind reading for that, and she retreated from his thoughts to tug the ribbon free from its bow.

Kira lifted the lid and sitting inside, gently resting on a

white satin cushion, was a tiny golden sun sparkling in the daylight.

"Luke," Kira said, breathing the word out like a sigh.

"I saw it in a store and thought you might like it." He shrugged.

"It's perfect," Kira said and set the box down on the table. Reaching around her neck, she unclasped the thin chain holding her father's wedding ring, an heirloom her adoptive mother had given her months ago when Kira had found out the truth about her star-crossed parents. The locket with her family portrait was still with her grandmother back in Sonnyville and the chain had felt uncomfortably light recently.

Kira untied the charm and slipped it through the chain, letting it fall to the bottom where it easily landed inside her father's ring. The two golden trinkets fit together perfectly, one slightly more aged than the other, but both brilliant against the late afternoon sky.

"So, you like it?" Luke asked quietly. His head was bent toward the ground and he looked at her under hooded eyebrows.

"I love it," Kira told him and pulled him in for a hug.

Maybe things can get better between us, she thought hopefully.

He wrapped his arms around her, holding her close, and breathed deeply into her hair. Kira willed herself to ignore it and not ruin the moment, but when she opened her eyes they met a hard, blue stare and she instantly retreated from Luke.

Kira knew Tristan couldn't help overhearing. His magnified senses were hard to turn off, but sometimes she wished he wouldn't listen in on conversations he knew would hurt him. The downturn of his eyes and straight line of his mouth told her all she needed to know, even if they disappeared a moment later when Chloe pulled him back to her toys.

"Food's ready!" Kira's mother called from the kitchen.

"The steak is being taken off the grill as we speak," her father added.

Luke quickly stood and put the apron back on to help her father, and Tristan walked over to take his place. She grabbed his hand, lacing her fingers through his, and pulled him down into the seat next to her.

"Everything okay?" she whispered.

Tristan nodded, turning away from her to smile at her mother who had just plopped a bowl of potato salad on the table in front of him. "Looks delicious, Mrs. Dawson."

Kira grinned at the formal use of her mother's name. He was a hundred years older than her, but he still wouldn't call her by her first name.

"Delicious enough for you to eat?" her mother asked hopefully.

"Not today," he apologized. "I ate before I came.

Special gluten-free diet and all." Tristan peered at Kira in his peripheral vision, meeting her gaze with a grin. It still amazed Kira that her mother didn't realize what Tristan was, having grown up around conduits. But it seemed like she had truly blocked out that entire part of her past and was choosing not to notice what was right in front of her.

"One of these days you will eat something I cook, Tristan, one—"

"Mom," Kira interjected, changing the topic.

"Right, right. Let me run inside to grab the coleslaw."

"She might force feed you, you know," Kira joked once her mom was out of earshot.

"I can handle it," Tristan said and placed his arm around her, hugging her to his chest.

Kira let her head rest on his shoulder. Soon enough, things would go back to normal between them. There was no telling how long they would be in England and some time away from Luke would be good, even if it was in Aldrich's castle.

She missed being alone with Tristan. He made her feel at peace and helped her step away from the conduits. With Luke it was always about conduits—teaching her how to be one and teaching her about them. He was a constant reminder of the future she couldn't walk away from—one supposedly full of death and destruction. But with Tristan, even though he was a vampire, she felt human. He let her escape her powers, so that even if only for a small moment in time, she was just a girl with a boy—nothing more, nothing less. *And when you're seventeen*, Kira thought, *sometimes that is all you need.*

But she was eighteen now, and Kira wasn't quite sure what that meant yet.

Chapter Two

"Go, go! Before they make me hug them again," Kira said to Luke while she clipped her seatbelt securely into place.

"Relax." Luke revved the engine to life. He was right. Her nerves were on overdrive right now and she felt jumpy. Maybe it was the note burning a hole through her pocket or the fact that she would be leaving for England in an hour, but Kira couldn't sit still. She opened her window to let some fresh air inside Luke's truck and called goodbye to her family. Sticking her hand outside, she waved one last time before Luke swerved around the bend.

"Lots of memories in this car," Luke said and Kira knew exactly what he was referring to. Their last drive to the airport had been a little different, more so than Luke realized. Last time, they had been running away together, but this time Kira was running from him. She tried to stop overanalyzing and instead managed a reply.

"At least a hoard of blood thirsty vampires isn't on our tail."

"You can't deny it—that was sort of fun."

"If you think getting thrown around the bed of a truck is fun…" Kira trailed off, goading him.

"You know what I mean—the rush of using our powers, the thrill of the fight. I know you've felt it," he said, taking his eyes off the road for a moment to look in her direction. "I'm going to talk to the council about letting you join me on a mission this summer—a full-on Protector mission with a team and everything. I know you're ready."

"Luke," Kira said with a strained voice.

"I know you're a little scared of your powers right now, but you can trust me even if you can't trust yourself—you're ready."

Kira turned away from him to look at the trees flying by the open window. She didn't want to listen to him talk about Sonnyville and all of the plans he had for her—no, for them. Late last night, after Kira had amazingly finished packing and Tristan was fast asleep on her bed, Kira had returned to the note. All of her previous drafts—the pile of trash now below her desk—had been drawn out goodbyes, full of explanations and apologies. But Kira had realized none of it would matter. Whatever she wrote would make him hurt and angry. There was no way to explain her actions on paper, but she couldn't tell him to his face even if it was the right thing to do.

Instead, she wrote him a short and to the point note saying she was sorry for ditching him, but it was just something she needed to do. When she arrived in England, maybe she would call Luke and try to explain herself. When she was all the way across the Atlantic, Kira might be far enough away that his pain wouldn't invade her mind and cut through her resolve like a knife.

Worried that her eyes were beginning to water, Kira prematurely rubbed at them. Crying would get her nowhere—she just had to believe that Luke would eventually forgive her.

"Kira? You okay? I don't think I've heard you this quiet since you stopped talking to me in protest of my short-lived popped-collar phase."

"Oh god, don't even mention that ever again." Kira rolled her eyes. Preppy douche-bag was not a good look for Luke. Clean cut polo shirts were fine, but the popped-collar had to go.

Kira shifted in her seat, pulling her gaze from the window to Luke's side of the car. She needed to act like everything was normal or he would definitely be on to her.

"It's just these contacts. They're itching my eyes."

Luke shrugged. "Take them out."

Kira eyed him quickly, watching the bob of his Adam's apple as he swallowed a nervous gulp, before reaching up to follow his instructions. Luke still wasn't completely comfortable with her new look. But Kira understood it. Her eyes had been the one thing that was exactly the same as every other conduit—the one thing Luke probably considered relatively normal about her.

No going back now, she thought and popped one lens off of her eye. Once done with the other, Kira flicked the small discs out the window.

"Wait!" Luke called just a second too late.

"What?" Kira asked. She was just following his instructions.

"Aren't you going to need those in Sonnyville?"

"I have more," Kira said, quickly covering her tracks. The truth was she wouldn't be needing them again for a long time. Aldrich already knew her secret—there would be no reason to cover the color in England.

"Since we're alone," Luke started and Kira immediately tensed. "There's something I've been meaning to ask you."

Please, she prayed, *nothing too serious*. Kira couldn't handle it now. Any intense conversations and she might just blow her cover. Her palms were already sweating and they hadn't even reached the airport.

Hesitantly, Kira asked, "What?"

Luke took a deep breath and his tan hands tensed around the driver's wheel. "Would..." he began but paused to glance at her. "Would you rather fart in front of me or have me fart in front of you?" And then he burst out laughing as Kira shoved him into the door.

"Luke," she said, totally exasperated. "You scared me."

"That was the point." He smirked. "Answer the question."

Kira wanted to yank his pretty blond hair from his head. A bald Luke—now that would be funny.

"Well, since I've smelled your farts, I would rather fart in front of you and give you a taste of your own medicine!"

"Touché," he said and leaned back into his seat, relaxing with the low-key conversation.

"My turn," Kira said, following his lead. She lifted her feet to the dashboard and tried to think of an equally annoying question to ask him. "Would you rather…see my grandfather's old wrinkly butt or accidentally flash our entire senior class?"

"Hey now, your grandfather is a fine looking older man—"

"Council suck-up," Kira muttered under her breath.

"Okay, okay—I'd rather our entire class see me in the nude. My turn again!" he said, and Kira smiled because for the first time in a long time things felt almost normal between them. Strange that having a conversation about her grandfather's behind would bring their friendship back around.

The two of them continued pestering one another with ridiculous questions until Luke pulled around the airport and dropped Kira off curbside with the bags before parking the car.

Kira took the free moment to check her ticket to Atlanta and the connecting flight to London. She and Tristan had checked in online the night before, and he should already be inside the airport waiting for her. *Terminal B, Gate 3*, Kira thought, *that is where it will all go down.*

After memorizing the flight number, Kira stuffed the ticket back into her purse, grabbed her duffle and Luke's, and walked inside. Checking the flight statuses, she saw the Atlanta flight was on time and boarding in half an hour. She would have to act fast to figure out a way to ditch Luke before security. Last time, the private jet had left from Terminal A—her entire plan hinged on that happening again.

"No need for that," Luke said, sneaking up behind her and grabbing both of their bags. "Our plane won't be on the departures list."

"Are we flying the same one?"

"Kira," Luke said, turning around to stare at her with a "do you really doubt me?" expression on his face. "Of course we're flying the same one. Rule number one—okay, maybe not rule number one—but remember, conduits fly in style."

"Right, cause we're so secret-agency," Kira said while elbowing his side.

"Hey, the name's Bowrey... Luke Bowrey," he said

and wiggled his eyebrows in what Kira could only assume Luke thought was a sexy way.

"Come on, double-oh-seven." Kira grabbed his arm, pulling him forward. They continued walking through the small airport until Kira spotted the pre-security bathrooms.

Halting her step, she took a deep breath and realized the point of no return had come. So, right outside the ladies room, she whined to Luke that she had to pee. Throwing her duffle in his direction, she told him to wait for her. Before he could answer, she jumped inside and left a shell shocked Luke behind her.

Inside the restroom, Kira splashed a little bit of cold water on her face and pulled her cell phone free of her purse to text Tristan.

"In the bathroom—phase one is complete."

A second later, she got his reply. "I'm sitting outside the gate with all of our stuff. Love you and see you soon. Good luck."

"Love you too." Kira texted back and clicked her phone off. She took one last look in the mirror, trying to will the nerves away. Then, like in an old Victorian era movie, she pinched her cheeks to bring some color back to her face before drying her hands.

You can do this, Kira told her reflection, *you are strong and you have to do this.*

"Your turn," Kira said to Luke when she emerged. "I'll watch your stuff for you."

"I don't really need to, you know, go." He shrugged.

"Just get inside," Kira said and pushed him in the direction of the men's room. Luke looked at her with raised eyebrows, but slipped through the door anyway.

Quickly, Kira knelt down and unzipped his bag. Pulling the letter from her pocket, she dropped it through the opening and shut his duffle. Her hands were shaking the entire time, and Kira forced herself not to envision the crumbling of his face when Luke discovered the note. Breathing deeply, Kira stood up and pushed her shoulders back, trying to display a calm exterior even though her insides roared.

No turning back now, she thought as Luke reemerged.

"Okay, ready to go?" he asked, shouldering their bags once more.

"Actually," Kira said in one drawn out syllable, "I had another idea."

Luke cocked his head to the side impatiently, and Kira sensed that he was starting to realize something was going on. Thankful that the airport was compact enough that all of her excuses were in the same place, Kira pointed to the newsstand.

"I could really use some gossip magazines and candy. Why don't you go ahead and make sure the plane is all ready to go, and I'll stock up on munchies for the trip?"

"I could use some Good'n'Plenty's," Luke murmured and Kira wrinkled her nose at the mention of that candy.

Black licorice… even as a chef she didn't understand why Luke adored the stuff. "Okay," he finally said, "See you in ten minutes?"

"Perfect!" Kira said. He turned to leave, but suddenly stopped and dropped his bag.

"Wait!" Kira jumped on the zipper to keep him from opening it. His hand was trapped below hers, and Kira's heart began to thud in her chest. Was it his touch or the precarious moment hanging in the air? Kira blamed the fear of discovery and looked into his warm green eyes, praying he wouldn't notice her rapid pulse.

"What?" he asked, looking at her like she was a mental patient, "I need to give you your ticket. Are you sure you're feeling okay?"

"Yeah, of course." Kira shook her head to refocus. "I'll grab them."

"It's fine," Luke said and freed his hand from hers. The sudden cavity created by his absence felt cold against Kira's palm, but Luke continued talking, completely unaware of her tumultuous thoughts, "I kept all my personal stuff in the side pouch."

He opened the side pocket to pull out her ticket. Letting a heavy sigh escape her lips, Kira sat back on her heels and accepted the piece of paper. *Keep it together*, she cursed.

Luke stood up, smiling at her and shaking his head. In that instant Kira knew he had no idea what was about to happen. He knew she was acting a little strange, but he never once imagined she was about to leave him. Why did the nice guys, the trusting ones, always seem to be the ones who got hurt? Kira asked herself, but quickly stopped that line of thought. It would only lead to the one question she didn't want to answer—why did she need to hurt him in the first place?

"Thanks." Kira finally stood up. "See you in ten!" Cheerily, she waved goodbye and turned around to continue her cover by walking into the newsstand.

Once inside, Kira held her hands out in front of her and watched the tips of her fingers twitch uncontrollably. She tried to breathe, pulling resistant air into her lungs, and fell back against the wall for support. The hard part was finally over. Soon, the lie would be up and she would just have to deal with the consequences. Now all she had to do was make it to the plane on time.

Kira pulled out her phone and texted Tristan. "Luke is gone. I'm on my way."

Her phone buzzed almost immediately. "Handicap passengers just boarded. Get over here quickly."

Peeking around the entrance, Kira surveyed the hallway that led to the security for Terminal A. There was no one in line, which had to mean Luke was already through the check and headed for the gate.

"I'm sorry," Kira whispered, almost afraid her voice would fail her. Something about staring down that empty, sterile hallway felt like the end—the end of what, she didn't know, but definitely an end. "Goodbye," she said one last time, trying to ignore the shell encasing her heart. Luke would never trust her the same way again. She had abused his faith in her, she had used their friendship as a weapon against him, and there would definitely be a cost to that. But growing up meant making choices and she couldn't always please everyone.

Kira flipped her body in the opposite direction and made for Terminal B, ready to start her journey with Tristan and ready to finally retrieve the answers about her mother, the ones that had so long eluded her.

The walk was short, but each step felt heavier and heavier until her shoes practically dragged along the floor. When Kira reached the line, only one woman was waiting in front of her. After a minute, a security guard reached out for Kira's passport and scanned her ID before waving her through. She piled her handbag on the conveyor belt, took off her shoes and waited. A new security guard signaled her over to the x-ray machine, and Kira lifted her foot to step through, but a voice stopped her dead in her tracks.

"Kira?" Luke called. His voice sounded faint and far away.

"Kira!" A little stronger now and laced with panic.

Taking a deep breath, Kira plopped her foot down and finished crossing the short distance. She was officially in Terminal B—the decision had been made.

"Kira! Stop!" Luke's voice was closer now. Were those footsteps or was she just imagining it?

Quickly, Kira slipped her shoes back on and reached inside her purse for her headphones. They weren't attached to anything, but she zipped her bag to make it look that way and kept walking past the security check, trying to ignore the voice calling after her.

"Kira! You went the wrong way!" The frustration in his voice was obvious, but that was all there was. He still didn't get it. He just thought she was lost.

Hard as it was, Kira continued to amble down the walkway toward her gate. Trying to act nonchalant, she bobbed her head as if listening to real music and pretended to look around as if searching for Luke. He shouted her name once or twice more, but she kept shuffling her feet farther and farther away from him, using her headphones as an excuse for deafness.

There was a bend fifteen—no ten—now five—feet away. Kira rounded the corner, safe from Luke's eyes, and pulled out the earplugs. It was go time. Her plane to Atlanta was boarding and she didn't have a second to spare.

A vibration tickled her arm and Kira knew Luke was trying to call her. She kept walking and looked for Tristan's sleek black hair in the crowd.

He saw her first and stood up, waving Kira over to the seats he had secured.

"Are you okay?" he asked once she sat down.

Concerned deepened his blue eyes and Kira could tell he was worried for her. It was her plan after all—her plan to go to England, her plan to keep Luke safe and out of the loop, and her plan to ditch him in the airport. Tristan was following Kira's rules now, which meant Luke's reaction was completely her fault. She couldn't blame anyone else for the hurt he was about to feel.

"He thinks I'm just in the wrong terminal," Kira said and shook her head. "He's too trusting."

Or I'm too heartless, Kira thought before smashing the thought down with the rest of the emotions she was suppressing. Too many were bubbling beneath the surface and at the moment, Kira didn't want to feel anything. Once they were in the air, and there was really no turning back, she would feel better about the whole thing. At least she hoped so…

"Doesn't he know security wouldn't let you through the wrong terminal?" Tristan reached into his bag, searching for something.

"I don't know. I didn't turn around to check." Kira leaned back in the seat, completely deflated and drained of energy.

"I had a feeling something like this would happen, so…" he kept rumbling through his bag for another minute before pulling out a grocery bag, "I came prepared. We have salt and vinegar chips…" He pulled the single serving from his bag and kept speaking, "some double chocolate chip cookies, cheesy popcorn, a diet Coke, a regular Coke if it's really serious, and of course, me." He finished with a wink, and Kira smirked subconsciously. Then she ripped open the salty chips and started munching.

"We should be boarding in a minute or so, first class was just loaded onto the plane and I think they called zone one," Tristan said and zipped the rest of his goodies back inside his bag. Kira knew she would pull those out later.

He rested his arm around her shoulder, and Kira relaxed under the weight of his muscles. Leaning in, Tristan whispered, "Everything is going to be fine," into Kira's ear and she willed herself to believe it. But, she was too busy enjoying the potato chips to formulate a response. It didn't matter though because Tristan kept talking to her.

"We'll land in England, go to Aldrich's castle, and demand to see your mother. She'll be there, healthy as can be, and we'll work some sort of deal out with Aldrich," he said softly. While he spoke, Tristan rubbed her arm with his thumb, gently soothing Kira. "Before you know it, we'll be back here and everything will go back to normal. I'll finally get you surfing those big waves down at Folly Beach, and we'll take a trip down to Savannah like I promised we would this summer. Next year, you'll find a restaurant job, you'll cook for all three of your parents and you'll forget all of this nonsense ever happened. You can leave Sonnyville and the conduits behind and have the life you always dreamed of having. You'll see."

Kira sighed as Tristan hugged her even closer. His words were a dream, a complete fantasy. She could never go back. Neither Tristan nor Luke fit into that plan, which meant it didn't work for her anymore. But Kira had no idea what her new plan should be.

"Attention, can Kira Dawson please pick up a yellow emergency phone? Passenger Kira Dawson to a yellow emergency phone, please."

Tristan and Kira jumped up at the same time.

"Luke?" Tristan asked.

"Almost undoubtedly," Kira responded. "Let's just ignore him."

"Kira," Tristan said gently, "He's your best friend, and I can't believe I'm the one who's saying this, but he deserves better than a hastily written letter."

"I know. I just can't face him yet. I'm—"

"Attention all passengers on flight 2963 to Atlanta, Georgia," a female voice spoke over the loudspeaker. "All passengers in zone three are welcome to board. Again, that is all passengers in zone three."

"That's us," Tristan said and stood up. Kira followed him to the line and each of them handed the gate attendant a ticket. They followed the slowly moving progression of passengers until crossing into the plane and sliding into their seats.

Kira pushed her handbag far under the seat in front of her, burying her phone with it. Tristan placed his heavy hand on her legs to keep them from bouncing. Kira stopped fidgeting and took his hand—they were almost in the clear, but she wouldn't feel totally free until they were thousands of miles in the air.

The flight attendant was walking down the aisle, closing overhead compartments and checking people's seatbelts. He stilled in front of Kira and Tristan, reaching behind his back for a fake seatbelt and life jacket. Kira turned to the side, ignoring the security protocol to look out the window at the airport. The plane started moving, gently easing away from the brown stone building. For a moment, Kira swore she saw Luke with two hands pressed firmly against sweeping glass windows, searching the grounds for her. She blinked and the image was gone—a mirage formed from her worry.

Shaking her head, Kira squeezed Tristan's hand and leaned back to shut her eyes and sleep. The steady thud of her heart sounded loud in her ears and Kira counted silently, hoping to bring her body to rest.

Just as her pulse seemed to slow, a piercing cry broke the calm and sent a shooting pain down her spine, from her brain to her heart. The pressure in her skull grew, as if her blood were thickening and pushing against her bone. Sharp needles pierced the spots behind her eyes, and Kira brought her hands to her temples trying to calm the storm. She kept her lids closed, breathing deeply, trying to quell the pain spreading from nerve to nerve. A fierce burn started in her heart, spreading to her limbs with each pump of blood, and her ears began to ring in fury. Pain and anger intertwined, braiding together in an unbreakable knot, and Kira knew exactly what it meant.

Luke had found the note. There was no other explanation for the sudden onslaught of emotions, but Kira forced her body to still—Tristan couldn't know. She had never told him of her bond with Luke.

It was all mental, Kira reminded herself and pushed against the overwhelming flood. None of this pain was truly hers, but it was really Luke's, and Kira couldn't breathe for finally realizing what she was putting him through.

Reaching shaking hands to the ground, Kira fumbled for her purse and pulled out her phone. She needed to call him. She needed to explain. Of course a note wouldn't suffice—it couldn't explain everything she needed to say. That this wasn't about choosing Tristan and it wasn't completely about saving her mother—it was about keeping Luke safe and out of harm. Aldrich had invited Tristan, but had made no mention of Luke. Aldrich would have shown no mercy with Luke, would have taken no pause in killing him. And Kira would never take that chance with Luke's life. Diana had almost killed him once, and she wouldn't let something like that happen ever again.

Kira flipped her phone open, ignoring the concerned expression Tristan was throwing her way.

Before getting the chance to dial, an onslaught of

alerts popped up on the screen. Five missed calls from Luke, and then text messages:

"Kira, you idiot, you went the wrong way."

"Kira—seriously? You're listening to music right now. Turn around and go to Terminal A."

"Did you hear that? They're saying your name over the loud speaker."

"You should have told me you lost your hearing, I would have gotten you really spiffy aids for your birthday. Bedazzled and everything."

"Okay, this is no longer funny, what is going on? Where are you?"

"You left. With him. Without me. Didn't you?"

"A note. Really?"

"So that is all I get?"

"If you don't call me right now, I'm done. I swear. I'm done."

Blank.

"Miss?" Kira turned to sound of an unfamiliar man's voice. The flight attendant. Her eyes burned and she couldn't focus on his features. The blurred image was motioning to her phone. "The captain said to turn off all of electronics. I'm sorry, but that includes your phone. We're about to take off." Kira looked back down at the screen. "Miss?" he said, concern filling his voice.

Tristan's cool fingers pulled the phone free of Kira's hand, and he shut it for her before thanking the flight attendant. Kira couldn't turn her gaze from the empty spots between her fingers. Done, was all she could think, he was done.

"I need to call him," Kira said, coming to life again. "Tristan, I need to call him."

Sensing Kira was on the brink of falling apart in her seat, Tristan handed her the phone. The plane was moving faster, shooting down the runway, as Kira began to dial Luke's number.

It rang once before the plane lifted off the ground.

Twice before the plane soared even higher.

"Kir—" Luke's voice began, but he was interrupted by a beep and the line went dead.

"Luke?" Kira said into the receiver. "Luke? Luke!" Her voice was panicked. She pulled back to look at the screen. No service. They were out of range, flying away from Luke just as she had planned—leaving him behind and all Kira could think was "done."

Chapter Three

Kira felt like a zombie following Tristan as he led her through passport control and customs. She watched the conveyor belt spin suitcases around baggage claim, but the metal blades lost focus in her glazed-over gaze.

Tristan had spent the entire flight to Atlanta reassuring her that in no time at all she could call Luke and fix everything. When they landed, Kira tried calling Luke over and over again, but each ring went straight to voicemail, and she couldn't bring herself to leave messages. She didn't know what to say in only thirty seconds—there were no magic words she could speak to make him understand.

Tristan had spent the entire flight to England reassuring her that Luke would eventually forgive her. When they landed, Kira called him again but once more there was no answer. As the realization that she had probably lost her best friend finally hit, Kira shut down. Tristan saw the transformation—saw the fall of her shoulders, the hunch of her back, the downturn of her lips, and the disappearing light in her eyes. More so, he faintly heard her heart slow and felt the normally churning heat in her body recede.

So, he took her hand and led her out of the airport into a foreign city, trying to find some way to bring her back. He brought her to the Thames, the furiously churning river that cut right through the heart of London. In an odd way, it reminded Kira of the choppy waves that cut along the shore of Folly Beach, the same ones that had calmed her the day Luke had told her what she really was. Perhaps it was the memory of Luke helping her through one of the hardest days of her life, but something about the speeding water pricked Kira to life, giving her one final idea.

Stepping away from Tristan's sturdy body and the arms holding her upright, Kira collapsed onto a bench and dialed Luke's family, praying he had followed through on his plans to fly to Sonnyville.

"Hello?" A woman answered, voice light and musical.

"Mrs. Bowrey? It's Kira. Is Luke there?"

"Oh, one second." Kira heard the scuffle of a hand closing over the receiver. Luke was definitely there—the only question was if he would admit it.

"Hello," a deep, hollow voice answered after a minute. Kira barely recognized the hard sound—it was scratchy and unforgiving.

"Luke." Kira sighed with relief. "I tried calling. I swear, I called you a thousand times. The plane took off and then you wouldn't answer any of my calls. I'm so sorry. I'm so, so sorry, but—"

"My phone broke," was his curt reply.

"Oh?" Kira sat up straighter, hoping this would be easier than she thought.

"I threw it at the wall."

"Oh," Kira said while sinking back down in her seat, totally unsure of herself. Did he throw it at a wall before or after she'd tried calling him?

"Luke—"

"Kira—"

They both quieted.

"I did it to keep you safe," Kira pleaded in a voice barely above a whisper.

"No, you left without me to keep me safe. Abandoning me in the airport, leaving me with a note, lying to me for more than a week—all of that was just...was just...just..."

"Fear?" Kira supplied.

"I was going to say cowardice," he responded and Kira winced at the word, but she couldn't deny it.

"You're right. I was afraid to tell you the truth. I was afraid of how you'd react and afraid I wouldn't be able to leave without you if you knew."

"I don't forgive you," he finally said. His voice still

sounded strained and dark—completely different from the lighthearted tone Kira was used to.

"Can you forgive me?" Kira asked.

"I don't know," he muttered. Kira hung on the pause in his voice.

"That's enough for now." Kira sighed, a sense of light was finally returning to her voice. Her fingers began to warm, and the fuzz around her brain began to clear. Hope. It was enough to bring some fight back into her senses.

"Where are you?"

"England," she said, not giving up any other information.

"That's a pretty big place," he trailed off, inviting her to finish his thought.

"If I tell you where I am, where Aldrich is, all of this will have been for nothing. So, I'm sorry again, but I won't tell you where I'm going. I did this to keep you safe and that means keeping you out of the loop."

"Fine," he said, the hardness returning to his voice, "but I'm coming to England. I'll stay with the Protectors in London."

"Luke," she said sternly. Why was he so stubborn?

"Once I tell the council where you are, they'll send me to London anyway."

"Fine," Kira said. He was annoying, but he had a point.

"I have to go," he said curtly.

"Before you do, you have to understand. This wasn't about choosing Tristan over you, or trying to hurt you, it was about saving my mother and keeping you away from Aldrich's power. You have to understand that. You do, don't you?"

"Goodbye, Kira." He sighed heavily into the phone before clicking it off. Kira stared at the blank screen, knowing that was the best conversation she could have hoped for, but feeling unsatisfied with the outcome. Still, he had talked to her and he was coming to England for her— eventually, Luke would forgive her. He was too nice and too good not to.

Kira stared at the water, letting that belief sink in before glancing at Tristan. He leaned against a lamp pole with his arm crossed, eyes focused on the horizon where the river disappeared around a bend and the city turned to nothing but fog. But for his piercing blue eyes and jet-black hair, he could have been a marble statue. His stance was unflinching. His mind was focused inward and not on the streets around him.

Her attachment to Luke clearly stung, and Kira realized her damage control duties weren't finished yet.

Sidling up next to him, Kira threw her arms around Tristan and leaned against his body.

"Ready to have some fun?" she asked and placed her chin on his chest to look up into his face.

"Shouldn't we be heading to Aldrich's?" He eyed her

warily, unsure of the change in her mood and what really caused it.

"Well, I've never been to London, and I don't think a few hours alone with my boyfriend will make much of a difference. Let's explore." Her words were half-true. Kira was anxious to get to Aldrich and to figure out the mystery of her mother, but she had a feeling the problem wouldn't be solved in one night, and she needed the alone time with Tristan. Too much had happened recently, and they needed to form a completely united front if they were going to defeat Aldrich.

"Where to?" Tristan asked, still slightly rigid. His lips curved into an almost unnoticeable smirk, but Kira was determined to get him really smiling again.

She looked down the river and saw a huge white dome in the distance—some sort of church for sure. It might be interesting, but Kira continued scanning the horizon. Shifting her gaze to the left, Kira spotted houses, a sweet waterside walk. Gazing further, the Parliament building popped up behind a stone bridge and then a giant white Ferris wheel and—*wait*, Kira thought, *what?* A gigantic white Ferris wheel with pods gleamed against the afternoon sky and reflected into the water of the river. It was twice the size of the surrounding buildings, and all Kira could think was that was definitely where she wanted to go.

"There," Kira told Tristan and pointed down the river.

"The London Eye? Of course." He nudged her. "Typical that in a city so drenched in history, you would pick the one modern attraction."

Kira rolled her eyes and tugged on his hand. "Just come on."

He followed her, and on the long walk over, Kira was grateful that Tristan had thought to rent a car and park it in a garage for the day. Expensive? Yes. Completely worth not having to lug their bags around for hours? Definitely!

Tristan relaxed as they neared the large structure. He slipped his fingers through hers, intertwining their hands, and softened his muscles when Kira leaned against his arm. *Just a couple taking an afternoon stroll*, Kira thought while glancing at all of the completely normal people around them who were doing the same thing. It was slightly overcast, but the sun peeked through the clouds every so often, casting diamonds along the choppy water. To Kira, it was perfect.

When they reached the London Eye, there was a bit of a line, but nothing too bad. After waiting for fifteen minutes, they slipped into one of the pods, which was essentially a glass globe large enough to hold ten or fifteen people. Before anyone else had the chance to follow them inside, Tristan pushed the door closed and the metal, automatically programmed to close in thirty more seconds, screeched in protest.

An employee rushed over and smacked the glass, trying to reopen the door. Tristan shrugged and shook his head in fake bewilderment, but the employee didn't look fooled. In fact, he looked downright suspicious.

Trying to hide her smirk, Kira stared in the opposite direction and put her hands against the window, searching for buildings she might recognize as the wheel turned to lift them higher into the air.

"What's that?" she asked Tristan, pointing through the glass at a huge white dome that stretched above the city's low buildings.

Tristan, who had lived in London during the nineteen sixties, put an arm over her shoulder and leaned over to follow the line of her finger. "That's St. Paul's Cathedral. Over to the right of it," he continued, taking Kira's hand in his and moving her pointer finger to a big blue and gray stone bridge, "that's the Tower of London and the Tower of London Bridge."

"Is it falling down?" Kira joked and felt the cool air of his exhale along her neck, making the little hairs along her soft skin rise. She glanced back, meeting his eyes for a second. They crinkled into a smile, but he looked back out at the horizon, moving her hand to a new spot.

"Do you see that circular straw roof? You can only just make it out, right along the corner of the river, almost across from the Tower of London."

Kira nodded.

"That's the Globe Theater, where—"

"Where all of Shakespeare's plays were performed,"

Kira interrupted and glanced back at his shocked features. "Hey, I paid attention in English class…sometimes."

"Really? I thought you spent most of English class distracting me with notes." Kira elbowed him in the ribs, but he of course didn't budge at all. *No fun*, Kira thought. She couldn't exactly push him around.

"Whoa, selective memory man, I think you were the one who distracted me with little portraits of my profile and my eyes—and my lips a few times, when you wanted me to know exactly what was on your mind." She raised her eyebrow at him in a challenge.

"You forgot whispering lines into your ear when our teacher wasn't looking," Tristan said softly, leaning closer to her body so they touched all the way from their legs to their shoulders. Kira leaned back, closing the distance, and Tristan wrapped his arms around her, holding her closer. She covered his arms with her own, hugging him back.

"So long as I can breathe or I can see," Tristan spoke lowly, in a deep sultry rumble, and Kira closed her eyes for a moment, "so long lives your love which gives life to me."

"What's that from?" Kira asked, still keeping her eyes closed.

"*Much Ado About Nothing*," he told her, "you'd like that one—it's a comedy."

"Good, because after a while *Hamlet* made me want to gouge my eyes out," Kira said with a laugh.

"You might like *King Lear*, then," Tristan said

sarcastically. Kira looked at him quizzically, her eyes furrowed in confusion. "There's a character who has his eyes pulled out..." Kira continued to stare at him blankly. "Never mind," he said with a sigh, which did make Kira smirk.

"You're too worldly for me," she teased.

"Let me put my years of knowledge to better use." He laughed and spun Kira around to point out London's landmarks—Hyde Park, Buckingham Palace, and more museums than Kira could count. He explained to her that since the city was built so long ago, many of the buildings were much lower than those in some American cities, like her beloved New York. In the distance, a ring of skyscrapers poked out of the skyline, looking unnatural against the beautiful and historic stone buildings of the old city.

Finally, they reached the peak of the Ferris wheel and turned around to gaze at the other side of London. Immediately, a gorgeous gothic-inspired building with pointed spires caught her attention. Against the blue river, and with the sun momentarily freed from the clouds, it seemed made of gold rather than stone. Parliament, Kira realized, remembering the photographs from her history textbook.

"I recognize that from *Peter Pan*." She pointed at Big Ben.

"You would," he said wryly before going into the history of the architecture. The building had apparently burned down multiple times and was at one time used as a royal palace. Kira listened politely, not really interested in the history but loving how excited Tristan was to talk about it. Get him started on history or art, and there was almost no way to make him stop. But Kira knew she was the same way with food, and she loved that he was so passionate about certain things.

His eyes lit up the more he spoke and Kira zoned out, blocking out his voice to instead study his features. His lips were asymmetrically curved, causing one of his dimples to emerge while the other stayed hidden in his cheek. Against pearly skin, his dark lashes perfectly framed his eyes, currently icy with his excitement. Higher up, his black hair was messy and fell slightly over his smooth forehead. Kira ached to reach her hand out and push the stray locks from his skin, but resisted.

Instead, she let her mind wander. Leaning against him in this foreign city felt so familiar, almost like home. The first time they met, he had been doing the same thing— showing her around Charleston, pointing out the famous spots and talking about the academic history. Still though, darker thoughts stirred behind his excited expression. Just like in Charleston, none of the history he mentioned was personal. Kira had opened him up so much, had freed him from his own guilt in so many ways, but still he was somewhat guarded around her—almost as if he worried that she would push him away if he told her everything.

"Kira?"

She blinked, finally realizing that he had stopped talking and was staring at her knowingly.

"I'm sorry!"

"I did it again. You are so bored right now." Tristan smirked, daring her to lie.

"Not bored, per se..." Kira trailed off, avoiding the question. "It's cute!"

"You used to say I was mysterious and sexy...now I get cute," he said with mock sadness.

"A very rugged and manly cute," Kira said, taking hold of his hand and pulling him closer.

"You can't distract me with a kiss. This is very serious."

Kira nodded in agreement, but slid her arms up his chest and around his neck before lifting on her tippytoes to bring her face almost eye level to his.

"I refuse to be seduced right now," Tristan said, looking away from her, "I'm supposed to be the one who does the seducing."

Kira continued to play with the little hairs at the base of his neck, moving her face slowly closer to his but waiting for him to make the final move.

He turned his face back to her, and Kira could see his resistance fading away. The moment hung between them and a stillness rested in the air. But an instant later, Kira's lips curved into a smile because Tristan gave in. His eyes clouded over and his face sank closer, until they were finally kissing.

A sudden whoosh of air made Kira pull away from Tristan, and she realized the pod had opened. They had reached the end of their half hour ride and the same suspicious employee from before was waving them toward the exit.

Kira ran to the bathroom, leaving Tristan alone to decide where their next stop should be. Had she been with Luke, Kira was almost certain they would be headed for Madame Tussauds, the famous wax figure museum. She could easily imagine an afternoon spent making funny faces next to celebrity figures and posing for pictures. Next, Luke would drag her to the famous Queen's Guards and he would tell jokes, swearing he could make one of them break face and laugh.

With Tristan, something slightly more mature would probably be involved. He would want to see some paintings for sure, maybe visit the palace. But he had seen all of the city before, so Kira wasn't totally sure what he would decide, which was why she was floored by his choice.

"You want to go to a park?" Kira asked when Tristan said he thought they should spend the rest of the slowly fading afternoon in Hyde Park, the biggest park in London and one of the biggest urban parks in the world.

"Just trust me," he said. Kira shrugged and followed Tristan back to the rental car. He drove through the streets, taking the scenic route to show her Buckingham Palace up close, before pulling over and parking street-side next to the park.

Tristan led her past lawns of crisp green grass, bright and healthy from London's frequent rains. Farther in the distance, Kira spotted a large, sparkling lake speckled with rowboats. For a moment, Kira thought that was their destination, but Tristan turned right instead of left, leaving the water behind them. They walked under a canopy of vines, a romantic enclave free of watching eyes, but Tristan didn't pause to steal a kiss like he normally would.

Eventually, his steps slowed as they neared a row of emerald hedges. *This is what he wanted to show me?* Kira asked herself, eyeing the small wooden gate Tristan had just opened for her. But his face read of anticipation—slightly wide eyes brimming with excitement and a knowing smile ready to spread even larger at her response.

Looking at him strangely, Kira stepped through the gate and gasped.

"Gorgeous, right?" Tristan whispered into her ear, but Kira was speechless.

For a moment, Kira thought she had left reality and had instead stepped into the pages of *The Secret Garden*. All she could see were roses. Everywhere she looked, there were fully-bloomed roses of every color she could imagine—red roses lining the path, yellow buds extending over them, pink floral twining high into the hedges and almost hiding the sky. And the smell, the smell was unbelievable. A sweet, almost vanilla scent filled her senses, enticing Kira farther and farther into the garden toward a cascading fountain in the center of the pathway.

"Tristan, this place is beautiful." Kira sighed, taking his hand and pulling him down to sit next to her on the edge of the stone fountain.

"I got something for you," he said while reaching into his pocket.

"When?"

"While you were in the bathroom." He smirked and she rolled her eyes. Kira had heard too many times before— from both Luke and Tristan—that she took forever in the bathroom.

He opened his palm to reveal a keychain with a cartoon drawing of the London Eye. Kira took it and flipped it over to reveal a photo of her and Tristan on the other side. The picture was of the two of them in the pod, heads close and eyes locked on one another, with Parliament in the background. Kira realized it must have been taken moments before they started kissing, but the timing of the photograph was perfect.

Kira shifted over on the rock so she could lie down and put her head on Tristan's lap. He ran his fingers through her hair, splashing it over his legs, and Kira looked up at the sky enjoying his touch. She lifted the keychain up to glance at it again, taking a moment to study the image.

Peter Pan, she thought silently to herself while noting the image of Big Ben in the background, *the boy who didn't want to grow up*. Was it better to not want to grow up or to not be able to grow up? For Tristan, immortality felt like a trap, keeping them apart and keeping him alone in the world. More than anything, he wanted to be human again and wanted to erase the many years he had struggled to cope with what he was.

For Kira, growing up seemed like the trap. She didn't want the responsibilities that came with it—learning to control her powers, being thrown into the conduit world against her will, and making life or death decisions no teenager should have to make.

Regardless of Tristan and Luke, there were decisions Kira needed to make about her future, decisions that seemed to haunt her as time slipped away. Could she give up life with the conduits like her adoptive mother had? She would be able to pursue her dreams of being a chef and she could have a somewhat normal life. But how did Luke fit into that plan? Giving up the conduits would mean giving him up as well.

But if she chose the conduit lifestyle of fighting vampires and wielding her powers, any semblance of normal in her life would vanish, and Tristan would probably vanish right along with it.

Kira was at a crossroads in her life—two paths both equally enchanting and equally foreboding in nature. But right now, there was only one path and that was the road to Aldrich's castle.

Kira sat up and Tristan nodded, thinking the same thing as her.

"Aldrich's?" Kira asked.

"Aldrich's," Tristan confirmed.

Kira gulped, unable to stop the growing sense that everything in her world was about to change.

Chapter Four

Really, no street lamps? Kira thought as Tristan continued driving along the dark, winding English road. They had been driving for just under two hours and the farther they got from London, the more deserted the streets had become. Large, well-lit roads were replaced with narrow, country lanes. Occasionally Kira saw the windows of a house gleaming through the fog, but it had been well over twenty minutes since she had seen any sign of life.

"Not to sound like a bored two-year-old, but are we there yet?" Kira asked while wrapping her arms tightly around herself. These silent streets were giving her the heebie-jeebies. Even Aldrich's castle seemed like an oasis compared to this dank landscape that lacked even the sparse light of the moon.

"About ten or fifteen minutes away I think," Tristan told her before turning from the road to focus his eyes on her. "Do you remember what I told you?"

Kira rolled her eyes. "Yes, Aldrich is not to be trusted. He's evil and will say or do anything to get what he wants." It was all he had been telling her for the entire car ride. As soon as the two of them stepped out of the rose garden, Tristan had been strictly business.

"Right," he said with a sturdy nod.

"Can I ask you a question?" Kira paused for a moment, not really waiting for his permission but waiting to gather her thoughts. "Do you think it's possible that he really might have my mother? That in twenty minutes I might actually meet her for the first time I can remember?" She gulped, trying to swallow her nerves. Even Kira couldn't believe the idea—it was too good to be true that her mother might just be waiting for her, living and breathing, even if she was doing it in the castle dungeon.

Tristan grabbed her hand. "I want to believe it."

"But you don't." Kira finished the thought for him. "Not really."

"I'm not trying to hurt your feelings, I just want you to be prepared. I know Aldrich—he is the cruelest man I've ever known. I just don't see why he would have kept her alive."

"For her blood?" Kira asked dubiously, thinking the answer completely obvious.

"Not for this long, not for almost eighteen years." Tristan shook his head, trying to reason it out internally.

"No one could survive being a blood donor for that long—it drains your body way too much."

"And if he wasn't using her for blood..." Kira said slowly, trying to understand.

"Why would she still be around?" Tristan filled the silence with the question Kira didn't want to think about.

"But it doesn't make sense," Kira said, running a hand through her messy hair in frustration. She could feel her body heating up, getting angry, losing control as always. The slight pain of breaking through the knots in her curls actually helped ground her to the car—the sting pricked her back into reality.

"What doesn't?" Tristan asked, looking at her warily. Kira realized he probably felt the burn of her powers heating her hands and hastily slid her fingers from his grasp. He held tight, not letting her slip away.

"Making us come to England doesn't make sense unless he has my mother. If he wanted me, he could have taken me from the ball. I was locked in a room with him—if he wanted to kill me or kidnap me, I wouldn't have been able to stop him."

Kira thought back to that night, easily recalling the fear that struck her senses when Aldrich sidestepped her powers, using his telekinesis to swat her arms and flames away. He could have knocked her out if he had wanted to. He could have made the ceiling fall on top of her and kill her if he had wanted to.

"And if Aldrich wanted to find you," Kira spoke up, thinking aloud so Tristan could follow her argument, "well, he did. And all he would have had to do was take me, and you would have followed him back here anyway. Why the ruse if my mother isn't really alive? Why did we need to come here of our own free will?"

"I don't know, but I don't trust him. He doesn't have an ounce of goodwill in his body."

"I know that, but I also know there is something in this house he wants us to see, and I just hope that it's my mother."

At that, almost as if on cue, Tristan turned down a straight driveway leading to a small square of light on the horizon. As they drifted closer, Kira realized the small square was really a menacing stone castle, half drenched in light and half drenched in shadow. Two giant columns joined together by a flat wall of stone lined with windows formed the front of the castle. In the middle, two glass lanterns hung on either side of the main door—a massive wooden slab that opened down the center. The windows around the door glimmered with light. As they drove even closer, Kira could see shadows dance across thin curtains. Distantly, she wondered if they were human.

To the left of the main house—the area that stole Kira's attention—were ruins. Stones crumbled into piles, old pillars of the original house stood tall but without floors or a ceiling to keep them stable. All the windows were empty holes and grass shrubs had invaded all of the cracks in the stones. Vines climbed up the steep walls, grasping at open crevices, reaching up the walls like arms clawing out of a grave. The deep opaque shadows that curled around the stones were so dense that Kira could see the skeleton of the remains but couldn't see what lurked behind the façade.

Kira gripped Tristan's hand a little tighter, hoping she would never have to venture into that area of the home. He squeezed, as if sensing her hesitation, and brought the car to a stop. Before either of them could move, the door opened and a brilliant ray of light pierced the driveway, sending the shadows away.

Aldrich.

Even though his features were silhouetted by the bright lights of the house, Kira knew it was him. His tall thin frame, short light-brown hair, and eyes of a deep midnight blue, so dark they were almost black—Kira could see it all in her mind even if the shadowed figure before her was a mystery.

"Ready?" Tristan asked. Kira sucked some air in before nodding. Slowly, she reached for the latch and let the door pop open. Unhooking her hand from Tristan's, Kira stood and faced Aldrich on her own.

"Kira," a man's voice called. It was slightly higher in octave than she remembered, but the pompous, highbrow lilt of the words was familiar. "I'm so glad you accepted my invitation. And Tristan…" He turned, shifting slightly so the side of his face was no longer shrouded in blackness. "Welcome home."

"This was never my home," Tristan responded coldly.

"Technicality," Aldrich replied with a shrug.

Tristan started to turn away, reaching back into the car for their things, but the door shut on its own, slamming firmly closed with a bang.

"My servants will take your things to your room. Come inside. Let me show you around." He swept his arm in a wide arc toward the door and disappeared into the house.

Without giving Tristan the time to even think about grabbing her and making a run for it, Kira followed Aldrich inside. Tristan appeared next to her in the door a second later, holding her protectively around the waist. They were in this together, for good or for bad.

The decor was completely different than Kira imagined. The floors were checkered with polished white tiles, the table in the foyer was a lacquered black that gleamed in the candlelight. In fact, the candles were the only things that seemed remotely old-fashioned about the space. Modern art graced the plain white walls of the hallway, and a giant iron chandelier hung from the ceiling.

Looking around, Kira spotted an open doorway leading to a large dining table surrounded by darkly stained wooden chairs. Whitewashed antlers hung on the wall, making Kira wonder if Aldrich had caught those with weapons or with his teeth. The thought made her shiver, and she shifted her gaze to where Aldrich stood at the base of a grand staircase. In the light, Kira really saw his features—opal eyes, pale white skin, a lean build even taller than Tristan's and light-brown hair that Kira would say was bleached by the sun if she didn't know any better.

He wore a finely tailored black suit that looked sleek, but it washed out his already light complexion. And his red tie was starkly bright against the monotone black, white and neutrals of the space.

"Welcome," he said, gesturing around the room. Kira remained silent.

Aldrich snapped his fingers and an Asian girl wearing a black sheath dress walked into the room holding a tray with three glasses—one glass filled with a clear liquid and two wine glasses filled with something red. The servant's skin looked smooth as porcelain, and Kira almost thought she was a vampire but for the two small holes piercing her neck. At the sight, Kira flinched, turning her head away from the thin girl. *Willing or forced?* Kira asked herself.

Tristan felt the small jerk of her body and gave her an apologetic stare. She noticed there was no surprise in his expression—the scene was exactly like he had imagined it would be.

The servant stretched her hand in Kira's direction, holding out a glass of what appeared to be ice water. Glancing at Tristan in her peripheral vision, she saw the small nod that let her know he couldn't detect anything wrong with the liquid. Kira accepted the cool glass gratefully and took a sip to refresh her parched throat.

A wine goblet was offered to Tristan but he declined, making Aldrich raise his eyebrow slowly. When the girl stepped closer to Aldrich, he accepted his cup and tipped it in Tristan's direction, taunting him. After a long sip, he lowered the cup and motioned up the stairs. Kira, however, didn't follow the line of his hand. Her vision was caught by the thick red liquid still gripping the sides of the cup—not wine, definitely not wine.

"Miko will show you to your room. I've had clothes laid out for the both of you, and I will be expecting you in the dining room in half an hour," Aldrich said very matter-of-factly.

At the sound of her name, the girl placed the tray down on a side table and started walking up the steps, not really waiting for Kira and Tristan to follow. Tristan moved first and Kira followed after him, but halted when Aldrich grabbed her arm.

"Your mother is very excited," he whispered.

Her heart dropped and lifted at the same time—soaring with hope that her mother was waiting somewhere in this house, and falling in fear that Aldrich spouted nothing but taunts and lies.

Tristan reached down to grab her hand, tugging her from Aldrich's hold with a hard look at the older man. His eyes turned an icy sky blue, threatening Aldrich, who just grinned and took a step back in surrender.

"I'll see you soon, for...dinner."

Kira couldn't bear the secret hiding behind the slight smirk gathering on Aldrich's face—he was up to something and Kira knew she wouldn't like it. So, she turned and followed the servant, Miko, down the sterile, museum-like hallways until the girl stopped outside of a door.

Without saying a word, she twisted the doorknob and stepped aside to let Kira and Tristan inside. When Kira walked past the girl, she looked into her vacant stare and glazed-over brown eyes. Was this girl drugged or just so brainwashed that she couldn't function anymore? The question left Kira feeling uneasy.

The door closed, leaving her and Tristan alone for what felt like the first time in ages, even though they had only left the car a few minutes ago.

"Are you all right?" Tristan asked while running his hands up and down her arms to get rid of the goose bumps that had sprouted against her skin. Kira closed her eyes and fell against his chest, taking comfort in his strength. Yes, she was a super powerful vampire hunter who could throw flames from her skin at a moment's notice. But, there was nothing wrong with having a big, strong man hold her and tell her everything would be okay.

Kira stayed silent against Tristan's chest for one more prolonged breath, letting the world stop for just a second, before pulling away to survey the room. Even though it was a bedroom, it was no cozier than the rest of the house. Still black and white, still very sparse, and still very modern. *Bleh*, Kira thought with disgust. How would she fall asleep in here? It seemed almost like a hospital room—completely devoid of character or any personal touches.

"We need to get dressed," Kira said with a sigh and pointed toward the suit and dress draped across the gigantic four-post bed behind Tristan. At least the pillows looked comfortable, she mused and walked over to see what outfit Aldrich had chosen for her.

Green—that was all she saw when she walked over. Layers and layers of bright seaweed and lime materials puffed up off of the mattress, leaking on top of Tristan's suit and cascading to the floor as well.

Kira sighed—*black-tie, really?* The last time she dressed up this much was for a school dance, and even that dress wasn't very expensive. Reaching over, Kira ran her hands over the smooth silk and scratchier chiffon. This dress definitely wasn't cheap.

"He's a little extravagant," Tristan said after leaning over Kira's shoulder to eye the outfits.

Kira rolled her eyes. "Obviously. A ball gown for dinner?"

"What can I say, the Victorian era always was his favorite time period to live in," Tristan told her wearily, as if he had experienced something like this before.

"What aren't you telling me?" Kira spun slowly, taking his expression in carefully. Sparks of pale blue spotted his otherwise navy eyes, and Kira new he was remembering something—something that made him angry. She may not have super senses like him, but vampires were sort of easy to read.

"Nothing." He shook his head, retreating from her to grab his suit. Kira clutched his hand, turning him back around and flashing him her angry eyes. His shoulders fell, and he looked away from her toward the window. "It's just...Aldrich used to make...well, he would give fancy dresses to..." Tristan trailed off, unable to finish the thought, but Kira could guess.

"To his food?"

Tristan nodded, and this time Kira turned away from him with a gulp and reached for the dress.

Now or never, she thought while looking for the zipper. If it meant getting even one step closer to her mother, it was worth it.

Across the bed, Tristan was unbuttoning his shirt with his back turned to her. Kira took a moment to watch the shirt fall from his shoulders, revealing smooth muscles underneath. He turned to pick up his dress shirt and caught her staring at his bicep. Grinning, he flexed his muscle as a joke and Kira immediately snapped out of it. He was right. This was so not the time for any of that. She gave him a "who, me?" look and turned around to get dressed.

Kira spread the dress on the ground, trying to create a hole through the top that she could step into. Finally successful, she dropped one leg through, then the other, and raised the dress to cover her exposed torso. One quick zip up the back and she was ready to go... she couldn't breathe, but she was ready to go.

"Holy crap this is tight," Kira said and spun around to search for a mirror.

"It looks..." Tristan took a moment to swallow. "It looks amazing."

Kira smiled to herself. It was nice to know she could make a one-hundred-and-fifty-year-old guy speechless.

Spotting the mirror, Kira started to walk across the room and realized after about one step that there was a slit in the floor-length dress—one that reached almost completely up her thigh. Behind her, she heard Tristan cough and compose himself.

Looking in the mirror, Kira finally understood his reaction. Green was definitely her color—of course, the skintight silk corset sucking her stomach in and pushing her boobs up didn't hurt.

Right below her waist, the corset loosened into a billowing skirt, which opened enough to completely expose her legs thanks to the sky-high slit. The entire dress was made of a beautiful emerald silk and the under layers of the skirt were composed of different, brighter hues that were revealed when she walked. In fact, if Kira didn't feel slightly like a high-class prostitute, she might have felt rather sexy. As it was…

"No way am I wearing this." Kira turned away from the mirror. "I'm meeting my mother!" Tristan was too busy staring at the dress to bother paying attention to her words. Looking down at the full-length of her left leg, Kira grabbed the fabric and closed the slit firmly shut, snapping Tristan to attention.

"Huh?" He looked up and finally took notice of her annoyed expression. "Hey." he shrugged. "You knew coming to Aldrich's would be difficult."

"Yeah, you're clearly suffering," Kira said under her breath and walked over to her bag, which had conveniently been resting in the corner when they originally walked into the room. Digging around, she pulled out a pair of Nike spandex shorts and quickly wriggled them on. She would wear the dress, but her way.

Looking at the four-inch heels resting at the base of the bed, Kira was tempted to pull out her sneakers in complete defiance. But she decided to give in. With her legs covered up a bit, she didn't feel quite so bad in the dress and if her mother really had been living here for ages, she would probably understand that Aldrich had picked the outfit.

"Okay, let's go," Kira said after clasping the strappy shoes in place. She pulled the chain with her father's wedding ring out from underneath the corset. Normally she liked to keep it hidden, for her private enjoyment, but for her mother, Kira would wear the ring proudly. Tucked below the ring was the small sun Luke had given her. For a moment, Kira thought about removing it just for the night. But the two went together perfectly, and as much as Tristan would hate it, Kira liked having a little reminder of Luke with her.

Aldrich was waiting for them at the bottom of the steps. Kira slipped her fingers into Tristan's as they approached and never let go of his hand as they sunk slowly down to meet Aldrich in the main hallway. When he saw her shorts, Aldrich wrinkled his nose in disgust. *Or maybe anger*, Kira thought as his eyes flashed white. He clearly wasn't used to people going against his orders, but Kira thought she was playing rather nicely at the moment. Her feet already ached because of the shoes, but was she complaining? No.

"You must be hungry," Aldrich said to Kira, or was that to Tristan? "Come."

They followed him into the dining room Kira had peeked into before. Walking in now, she saw the same large black table surrounded by darkly stained wooden chairs. The cushions were black silk, and a cast iron chandelier hung from the ceiling. But instead of electricity, there were candles with flickering flames. In this light, the antlers were more menacing—bleached white to blend into the wall. The candles cast dark, finger-like shadows that seemed to appear out of nowhere.

Kira noticed two doors against the far wall. The entire frame was made of polished white molding that reflected the light. Finally, Kira's eyes landed on a china cabinet. But it was filled with glasses—wine glasses, champagne flutes, goblets of all sizes—there were no plates or bowls in sight.

Two chairs pulled free of the table, distracting Kira as they scratched along the floor. "Sit," Aldrich said before walking to the head of the table, this time using his hand to move his chair.

"I hope the candles don't bother you," he said casually and leaned back in his seat. "I can't stand bright electric bulbs. Call me old-fashioned." He waved his hand absently through the air as if dismissing the thought.

"Where is my mother?" Kira asked. She was here for her mother and that was it. No more pretending that Aldrich was an old friend they hadn't seen in a while. It was time to get down to business.

"She'll be down in a moment, Kira. Patience," he chided her as if she was still a little girl.

But patience wasn't really her thing. The longer she sat, the more frustrated she became. And the more frustrated she became, the more Kira could feel her body heating up. Her blood began to boil. Fire stirred in her chest, sparking to life. Kira tried to breathe evenly and calm herself, but she was done with waiting. All she had been doing, ever since Diana had mentioned her mother to escape Kira's hold, was wait. Wait to wake up from a coma.

Wait because of Sonnyville. Wait to find Diana. Wait to visit Aldrich. She was done with that whole game.

"Why is it taking so long?" Kira said smoothly. Her voice was calm, but that was about the only part of her that was. Clenching her fists to keep her fire from jumping out of her body, Kira tried to sit still and remind herself that throwing a ball of flames at Aldrich's smug face wouldn't accomplish anything. Sure, she might laugh for a moment, but then he would be angry, and Kira didn't want to know how he would retaliate.

Tristan put his hand on her shoulder. His arm jerked slightly at the touch, and Kira knew her skin stung. But the cool note of his hand helped calm her flames, and she continued to focus on her breathing.

"She wants to look perfect for you, Kira," Aldrich said, still as relaxed as ever. Either he couldn't sense the storm brewing in Kira's chest or he wasn't afraid of it. For some reason, Kira couldn't shake the feeling that someone was up there shaking her mother out of a trance and forcing her into a pretty dress. Just like the Asian servant from before, Kira couldn't help but imagine her mother with vacant eyes, a lifeless walk, and bruises across her skin. She couldn't help but imagine two holes permanently poked through her neck from overuse and two lumps of scar tissue where a smooth nape should be.

"I told you I never harmed her," Aldrich said as if sensing Kira's thoughts. Kira spun to stare at him in anger, wondering if her own eyes were bright blue like Tristan's when he was mad.

"I'm sorry if that's a little hard to believe, seeing as we're mortal enemies and everything." Kira forced the words through her teeth.

"Mortal enemies? I'm sure Tristan is happy to hear that," Aldrich said with raised eyebrows.

"Don't twist my words around, you know what I mean."

Aldrich sighed. For a moment, Kira couldn't tell if it was heartfelt or more of an act. "Is it so hard to believe that I might have changed after a century?"

Kira snorted.

"Yes," Tristan said from the chair next to her. His eyes were narrowed, and his lips were curled almost into a snarl.

"Tristan," Aldrich chided, "you of all people should understand that all it takes is the right girl to change a man."

"Excuse me?" Kira asked in disbelief. "Are you trying to say my mother is, well, is like your girlfriend?"

"My wife, actually," Aldrich said calmly, "and here she comes."

Kira spun in her chair, eyes wide in disbelief. His wife? Seriously? What about her father, what about love will prevail, what about forever? They had given everything up to be together—friends, family, the only society they had ever known.

A woman appeared around the bend of the staircase, completely stopping Kira's train of thought. She was tall and thin with golden blonde hair piled into a smooth bun on the top of her head. Her dress was dark blue silk, cinched almost like a kimono with large sleeves and a sash that gathered at her waist. The skirt was narrow, but there were no curves on her mother's thin frame, so it looked classic.

As she came closer, Kira could make out the shape of her face. She had the same slightly wide eyes that Kira had, but they were downcast and looking at the floor. Her small nose was again similar to Kira's—there was no denying the resemblance. It was her mother. It had to be.

Finally, a slight smile gathered on the woman's lips, and Kira was sure. It was the same secretive look from the photograph in her locket. She had memorized that look, played it over and over again in her mind.

"Mom?" Kira said and reached her arm out as if she could pull her mother closer. Her heart was fluttering in her chest, beating wildly with nerves. Sweat rose on her palms and Kira started to feel lightheaded. It was really her. Kira had dreamed of this moment for months. No one else believed her. Luke and Tristan both thought she was crazy to believe her mother was still alive, stupid for even thinking it. But here she was, walking toward Kira through soft candlelight.

"Mom?" Kira said again, stepping toward the door to greet her. Would she hug her? Would she just keep staring, worried that if she reached out to touch her mother, the image would disappear?

The woman stopped in the doorway, until finally, in slow motion, she raised her eyelids from the floor to look Kira in the eyes.

Kira's heart stopped.

Blue.

Her mother's eyes were blue.

The secretive smile widened slightly, and two small teeth poked out from beneath her upper lip.

Kira's legs felt weak.

Her mother wasn't alive.

She was dead.

She was a vampire.

Chapter Five

Tristan caught Kira before she hit the ground, but she didn't notice. Kira was numb. Her mind was completely blank save one image—teeth. Two teeth—slim, dainty, sharp, and wrong. They weren't supposed to be there. They were ripping up her insides, shredding her nerves to useless strings, swallowing her thoughts like blood.

A face appeared above Kira. A hand, thin and unfamiliar, cupped her cheek. It was cool, like ice, and it stung her hot skin. Slowly the image came together. Blue eyes looking down at her, overly large just like hers. Two small pink lips were moving, speaking to her.

It felt like waking up from the coma all over again. Slowly her mind began to pull the pieces together. She was on the floor, resting in Tristan's lap. The woman above her was her mother. Her mother was alive and speaking to her, trying to say something.

Her mother was here. She was alive. Alive. She was all right.

"Kira, darling, are you okay?" Her voice was soft and warm. It was caring, like a mother's should be, and it lulled Kira awake. In all of her dreams, this was the moment Kira had imagined. The reunion.

"Mom?" Kira said, reaching her own hand to her mother's cheek. It was damp. "Mom," Kira said again, just to confirm the truth in the statement.

Kira's body lifted instinctively and her arms wrapped around her mother, gripping fiercely. "I thought you were dead," Kira cried softly into her mother's shoulder. "I never thought I would actually find you." Her mother shushed Kira and stroked her hand down Kira's curly hair, comforting her long lost daughter.

For a moment, Kira was blissfully happy. So happy she forgot herself, forgot her control, forgot where she was. It wasn't until her mother cried out in pain that Kira realized what she was doing and opened her eyes.

All three vampires stood on the other side of the room, crouched together against the flames bursting from Kira's palms. The wine goblets in the cabinet started to rattle as Kira met Aldrich's cold stare. He was ready to knock her out if need be. But it was an accident. She didn't mean to.

Kira quelled her powers, closing her fingers tightly around her palms, trapping the fire inside.

No one moved. The only things alive in the room were the flickering candle flames and the shadows that danced with them.

Kira looked away with shame. At first, the ugly feeling curdling in her stomach seemed self-directed. But peeking out of the corner of her eye, Kira realized the shame was not for her actions. The shame was for her mother, the blue dress cowering in the corner behind the sturdy bodies of Tristan and Aldrich. Kira couldn't look at her mother like that. Couldn't look at this woman, who in her dreams had understood Kira perfectly, who in her only memory had fought for Kira's life with fire.

Blinking away tears, Kira couldn't help but squirm with the wrongness of it all. She had been afraid her mother was really dead. She had been afraid that her mother was locked up somewhere, numb and bruised and weak. She had been afraid that her mother's mind had vanished from multiple feedings or beatings at the hand of Aldrich. But Kira wasn't prepared for this—for a mother who was afraid of her, for a mother who couldn't be healed by her flames, but could die from them.

Tristan was the first to break the stalemate. He approached Kira, took her by the hand, and forced her to look at him. He was worried, but Kira didn't miss the drop of hope in his irises. She looked away.

"Why don't we all take a moment to sit down," Aldrich's slick voice said.

With a hand on the small of her back, Tristan guided Kira to her seat then sat down beside her. On the other side of the table, Aldrich did the same with her mother. Six eyes stared at Kira, waiting for her to say something, but the words were stuck on her tongue. She didn't know what to say or where to look. So she focused on the soft glowing flames over her mother's shoulder, trying to draw comfort from the fire.

Again, Tristan broke the silence.

"How," he started but swallowed the words when he realized how laced with mirth they were. Kira's eyes were hollow, but his were happy and full of possibilities. Coughing, he spoke again, this time in a much more controlled manner. "How is this possible?"

"It's simple, really," Aldrich said, but paused when a new servant, one with the same vacant eyes, walked into the room holding a tray. Three goblets were placed on the table, one before each vampire, and a plate of food was set in front of Kira. Glancing down, Kira recognized chicken and smelled a hint of lemon in the sauce. For once, food did not interest her at all, and she shifted her gaze to Tristan.

"Simple?" he asked while leaning forward in his seat. His eyes were glued to Aldrich, turning lighter and lighter with each passing second as he let his excitement gather. Absently, he reached for the cup and took a sip. When he set the cup down, his lips were stained red.

"It's all about desire," Aldrich spoke, distracting Kira

with his own ruby lips. He smiled at her mother. The crevices between his teeth were crimson before he licked the excess liquid away. "Changing a conduit is really no different than changing a human, but the conduit has to want it." Two pearly white hands clasped closer together sharing a secret moment of love. Kira's heart flipped in her chest and the gripping fingers expanded to take up her entire line of vision, growing bigger and bigger, or maybe her focus was growing smaller and smaller.

"With a human, want doesn't matter. They can't fight the turning. Our bite consumes them. And when the blood exchange occurs, our blood overpowers them. But with a conduit it is different. Their blood boils and burns ours, cursing it from their system before the change can occur. But a willing conduit," he paused, took a moment to stroke her mother's palm with his thumb and bring her hand to his lips, "a willing conduit won't fight our blood. They will welcome it." Her mother smiled with pink-stained lips and Kira's eyes snapped up to those discolored teeth. The secretive smile she had dreamed of seeing in person was corrupted, stained like her mother's teeth, by blood. It was directed at the wrong man, a killer with brown hair instead of a father with red curls.

"How has this never been discovered before?" Tristan asked. Kira heard the words distantly in her mind.

"How many conduits have fallen in love with a vampire before?"

Tristan leaned back in his chair with thoughts circulating faster than even his quick brain could process. Kira, on the other hand, was slow and sluggish. Her gaze followed her mother's, honed in on Aldrich's open smile. She searched for some break in his calm demeanor, some evil flicker that would let her in on the secret and let her know the game was up. The love in her mother's eyes couldn't be real—she couldn't be looking at this murderer with affection. Kira thought of the holes in the servant's neck and her absent, haunting stare. How could her mom love a man who could do that? How could she forget about her father? About the man who sacrificed his life to save Kira, who jumped into a pile of vampires to try and save her, who gave up everything he had ever known for an unborn child. How could this woman in front of her have abandoned him for Aldrich?

"These Dawson women," Aldrich said with a smile before reaching for his glass again.

"She's not a Dawson," Kira whispered, surprising even herself. Aldrich's eyes snapped to her instantly.

"She speaks," he said mockingly, always acting superior. "What's that?" With his vampire senses, Kira doubted Aldrich had actually missed her words, but his haughty attitude goaded her and suddenly she was furious.

"I said, she's not a Dawson." Kira spoke through clenched lips and her hands began to burn. "My father was a Dawson. I am a Dawson. But she is not."

Kira crossed her arms and hugged her palms to her body to keep her fire from exploding. She didn't even realize she was shaking.

"That's no way to speak to your mother," Aldrich said. Her mother remained silent across the table and looked at Kira with cold blue eyes.

"Is she my mother?" Kira stood quickly, knocking her chair over. The slam of heavy wood against tile reverberated around the dining room, echoing in the silence of the accusation.

"Of course I am, sweetheart," her mother said and reached out her hand. Kira stepped back.

"The mother I remember fought with her life to protect me. I don't think she would have been content to wait eighteen years before seeing me again."

"There were reasons," she spoke softly, trying to break through Kira's fury.

"Like what?" Kira spat.

"Like I was a newly born vampire with no control over her senses, and you were a child with no idea of her powers," she replied, still calm and cajoling. Kira sat back down.

Behind her, Tristan pulled Aldrich from the room to give the two women privacy. The doors to the living room were sealed shut and in the small space, Kira had nowhere to look but at her mother, whose soothing voice did nothing but inflate her anger.

"I wanted to find you," her mother continued, "but I had to wait until the right moment. We both needed to have control over our bodies. But you have to know that for eighteen years, this moment is all I've dreamed of. I've wanted to be with you for so long, to hug you and never let you go. I just wanted everything to be perfect, can't you understand that?"

Her mother stopped talking and stared at Kira. But Kira wasn't really listening. She had always believed that people's eyes couldn't lie. They always gave the true emotions away. And her mother's eyes were blank and unfeeling. And it wasn't just the dark blue color and the fact that Kira had always pictured them differently. And they weren't vacant like someone possessed, just indifferent. And it made Kira retreat into her memories.

One day, months ago, after Kira had just discovered the truth about her aunt, Luke asked her why she wasn't angrier. They were lying next to each other on the grass, breathing heavily and exhausted from training, when he surprised her with the question. At first, she hadn't known what to say, but after taking a minute to think it over, she realized what it was—her aunt's eyes.

Kira had wanted to yell at her aunt. Part of her wanted to make her cry and make her hate herself for lying to Kira for so long. She was angry, so angry, that Luke had known more about her past than she did. After their initial talk, she had ignored her aunt mercilessly. She refused to speak to her or even look her in the eye. But after a few days of fuming, Kira was finally ready to talk again. She had thought about the right words over and over again, how she would scream at her aunt for lying and never stop yelling out her anger. So when her uncle and Chloe were gone, Kira cornered her aunt in the kitchen, ready to explode. But when her aunt turned around, Kira finally looked into her eyes and saw all of the pain and self-loathing she was looking for. Her aunt was killing herself with hurt over keeping this secret. And Kira's anger disappeared. Instead, she cried and her aunt rocked her back and forth as though she was a child, and they stayed like that for ages until they were both cried out.

But right now, looking into her birth mother's face, Kira felt nothing but anger. Unlike her aunt, her mother had chosen this life. Had chosen to abandon Kira—and for what? For an evil man? To become an evil thing?

Despite her mother's words, there was no remorse in those eyes. No pain or anguish. She was happy with her decision. And to Kira, that was unforgivable. Actually, it was downright suspicious.

"What's your name?" Kira asked. She righted her chair, sat back down, and crossed her hands on the table. Across the room, her mother rolled her eyes and did the same. Kira tried to ignore the attitude resemblance.

"Lana," the woman said quietly.

"Lana what?"

With a heavy breath, she replied, "Lana Peters."

"And what was my father's name?"

"Andrew Dawson."

Kira nodded, signaling she was correct and reached for her necklace for comfort. "Where did you grow up?"

"With all of the other Protectors in Sonnyville. Before you ask, it's a very small, secluded town in Florida that is completely off the grid."

"Nice sidestep," Kira said and leaned forward to gear up the intensity. "What Florida city is it next to?"

"Orlando," her mother said, still composed.

"What were my grandparent's names?"

"My father's name is Henry and my mother's name is my own." Lana lifted her lips at that, smiling to herself. Kira ignored the show.

"Tell me about my father. How did you meet?"

"Oh, Kira." Her mother sighed and finally leaned back in her chair. "You really are as stubborn as Aldrich said. Something you get from me I suppose..."

"Just answer the question," Kira said. She gripped her fingers tightly together, keeping her palms clamped inward. Her anger was rising and with it her heat, but she needed to stay strong.

"Fine," Lana said and leaned forward in her chair, boring her eyes into Kira. *Still blank*, Kira thought quietly to herself. "Your father and I were both twenty years old when we met. We fought like children, bickered all the time and debated politics until we had talked ourselves in so many circles that there was nothing left to do but shut up. We called each other once a week that first year, wrote soppy love letters to each other, and made ridiculous promises our parents would never allow us to keep.

"Gradually, young love matured and we couldn't stand to be apart. So we got married. Our honeymoon was in a log cabin deep in the forest where no conduit would ever go. It snowed for days, until the piles were so high we couldn't even climb out through the windows, so we fought the cold in other ways…" A small smile played on her lips again. Kira tried to read her face, but the woman before her was a mystery.

"We never thought of the future, and when I found out I was pregnant, we ran. We loved you, I loved you, more than anything in the world—"

"Then why did you leave me?" Kira asked, her voice cracking. It was getting harder and harder to doubt that this woman was her mother. Maybe the coldness of her eyes was just a side effect of the change? Kira continued the thought—Tristan had had more than a century to figure out how to bring warmth back into his icy blue irises, but her mother hadn't even had two decades.

"I didn't want to," Lana said, reaching her hands across the table to lay them over Kira's burning fingers. Her white palms stopped one inch short of actually touching her daughter.

"The only memory I have of you," Kira said softly while staring down at her lap, "is from the night that I lost you. We were playing one second and then the next you were gone, pulled away by vampires and killed."

"Hurt, but not killed. Aldrich saved me. Moments after you were pulled away by the conduits, Aldrich came and stopped the other vampires. I don't even remember it. I remember waking up in a cell, weak, in pain, and unable to think past my loss. At first, Aldrich kept me there, locked in a dungeon. He used me for my blood, but like with your father, I soon changed his mind."

"How can you love him?" Kira whispered. She didn't want to believe this story or listen to the earnest tone of her mother's voice.

"You don't choose who you love," her mother said while fiddling with the engagement ring on her finger. A bright diamond sparkled in Kira's eye, and she knew that one was from Aldrich, not her father. "If you could, my life would be much different." Lana stopped moving and dropped her hands back into her lap, retreating from Kira and from whatever memory was playing behind her calm features.

"But why didn't you come looking for me? Why did you turn into...into this?" Kira said, gesturing around the room and dropping off. She still couldn't finish the thought and say the words. Once they were out of her mind and in the air, Kira feared they would suffocate her—why did you choose Aldrich over me, choose being a vampire over finding me?

"Oh, Kira, this was for you," her mother said and stood up to cross the room. She walked slowly around the table, never once taking her eyes from Kira's face. Kira sat still, not moving to even breathe. Her mother knelt next to her, wrinkling the fine silk of her dress to place her knees on the ground, and rested her palms on Kira's thigh.

"I was dying. You see, I never truly recovered from the attack and with each passing day I grew weaker and weaker. My love for Aldrich helped sustain me, but I was content to die. And then..." She squeezed Kira's leg affectionately. "Then we heard reports of a mixed breed conduit girl, a mere defenseless baby, and I knew it was you. And I knew I had to live so I could find you. But I was dying and the only way for me to live was through Aldrich, through his blood."

Kira fell back into her chair, completely drained of energy, and reached up to grasp her father's ring again. She smoothed the pads of her fingers around the edges, feeling the slight scratches in the worn metal, and tried to understand this woman kneeling in front of her.

Logically, everything she said made sense. The story was pieced together very well. The emotions in her voice rang true. But still, deep down past Kira's lingering anger was a small ball of doubt curling around itself and settling in for the long haul.

"Your father's ring?" Lana asked, reaching through Kira's fingers to grab at it. "I haven't seen this in a long time." She poked her finger through the opening. It was far too big for her slim hands. "Mine was taken from me a long time ago, but I still remember the words. Love will prevail—and it always does," she said and dropped the ring to hold Kira's fingers instead. Kira tightened her muscles, clenching her fingers around her mother's hand. Like Tristan's they were cold, but that was not how she remembered them.

In her dreams, Kira remembered her parents. She remembered resting her tiny head on a warm bosom, tugging at strands of loose blonde hair, and poking at the freckles on her mother's face. Her mother's skin always felt hot and alive, always burned like Kira's did now. Her hands were always tan and sun-kissed, not pale and cold like the moon.

"What does it feel like?" Kira asked. "Being a vampire, I mean."

"Like perfection," her mother said. "I'm never tired. I'm never hurt. I never feel the ache of old age. There is no distance I can't run or length I can't swim. I can see past the horizon and hear the flutter of an insect caught in the wind. There is nothing I am afraid of. Nothing that can hurt me. Nothing that I fear."

"But how does it feel?" Kira asked, emphasizing the last word. She had asked Tristan this question once, and he had said that until Kira had come into his life and livened his senses, he had just felt empty and without purpose. He'd had all of the time in the world, but no one to share it with. He'd had all of the power in the world, but no good to do with it. He was surrounded by life, but felt dead all of the time.

"It feels," her mother began and took a deep breath. She closed her eyes and slowly released the air. As it left her lips they began to widen, pulling at the ends until her teeth were revealed. Two sharp incisors poked out, lengthening with the breath until they dented her lower lip. "It feels like bliss."

Kira looked away and brought her hand to her chest. One, two, three—she counted her heartbeat and felt the blood pump through her veins. It was warm and circulated heat to the rest of her body before crashing back into her heart to repeat the process.

Kira thought of that spot, deep in her heart, where the swirling blood cells came alive and turned to flame, of the boil that crawled along her skin with her power. The sun once stung her, once caused her pain, but now she welcomed it. Whenever she was afraid, whenever she was lost in the darkness of doubt or despair, she came crawling back to that spot in her heart where the sun filled her with life. In that connection, she knew there was nothing to fear and nothing that could hurt her.

Then Kira began to think of something else, of something ripping that warmth from her and replacing it with an icy chill that rippled through her limbs, a dead darkness that needed the lives of others to survive. Kira imagined pulling for the sun, attempting to gather her strength, and finding it gone—vanished.

Bliss, Kira thought with a shiver. Losing the sun was her worst nightmare.

Kira could understand fighting to survive. She could almost understand falling for Aldrich under the circumstances of her mother's life. Losing a husband and a child all in one day might make a woman seek out comfort in the most unlikely of places. Even turning into a vampire wasn't beyond Kira's comprehension.

But parting with her fire, losing the flames, rejecting the sun—and feeling bliss? That Kira would never understand and that Kira doubted any conduit would ever be able to truly feel. The absence should be a gaping hole in her chest, a pain that haunted her mother's immortality.

Kira broke her thoughts to stare at the woman kneeling by her feet, the woman still smiling with the happiness of her existence. Her ivory skin had no hint of the sun, not a single drawn out freckle. Her tightly pulled back hair was devoid of any wildness. Her smile held secrets, but none that Kira felt any connection to. And her eyes were as dark and monotone as the night sky at the end of the sunset, when all of the glorious colors had disappeared but the stars still didn't want to come out and play.

The woman flicked her pupils at Kira as if finally

remembering her daughter was there. Kira watched the candles flicker in the black of her eyes and watched as even the reflection of heat rejected her. Deep in the ebony pools of those unfeeling eyes, Kira finally found an emotion. Coiling at the base of that bottomless pit, Kira saw hatred and it snapped her back into her seat.

The woman blinked and it was gone, but it was enough. Despite her flawless appearance, carefully crafted story, and emotionally charged words, Kira knew with every fiber of her being that this woman was not her mother.

Now all she needed was proof.

Chapter Six

Slowly, Kira rose from the sturdy wooden chair and excused herself. Calmly, she walked to the door and looked back at the woman still crouching on the ground. She put as much love as she could into that look, hoping it was enough for that woman to believe Kira had been fooled by the show.

It took all of her strength to continue stepping at a normal pace up the stairs and down the hallway. Her muscles were tight, contracted. Her senses were alert, and she had to control her legs to stop them from stretching out in front of her and sprinting the rest of the way to her room.

Aldrich and that woman, who Kira couldn't even think of as her mother, had to believe Kira was happy— maybe tired and drained of energy, but happy deep down. In reality, all Kira felt was despair. All of this, every second she'd spent daydreaming of a future with her mother and planning a rescue mission, all of it was wasted. Her mother was gone. Kira knew it. And she suddenly realized just how stupid she had been to believe in the fantasy, how naïve she had been to actually risk all of their lives searching for a phantom dream.

But there was a nagging question in the back of Kira's mind—how? How had this woman faked her mother's appearance? How did she know so much about her mother's life? Was Kira just being stubborn again? Was she just screaming inside because she got exactly what she had wished for, but realized too late that it was a corrupted desire?

You can't bring the dead back to life, Kira thought but then corrected herself, *you can't bring the dead back to life and expect nothing to change*. After all, vampires were in so many ways the living dead, but none of them, not even Tristan, were the same as their living selves had been.

"Kira?"

Kira blinked. Tristan was standing in the doorway of their room, looking down at her with concern.

"Are you okay? You've been standing outside of the door for a few minutes, not moving, not really anything..." he trailed off. Kira blinked again then remembered the act.

"I'm great." She smiled, knowing Tristan would see it was insincere. But he didn't. He took both of her hands and led her inside. All the while, his eyes danced with an electric charge, a surging burst of energy that Kira just couldn't copy.

"Don't you see what this means?" Tristan asked.

That my mother is dead, Kira thought, *that I've been the biggest fool in the world?* But she didn't say the words out loud. Somehow, Kira didn't think it was the answer he was looking for.

Tristan didn't wait for her answer. Instead, he led her to the foot of the bed. Kira let him sit her down and he knelt at her feet, still holding her hands.

"Kira, we can be together. Forever." He kissed her fingers and held her hands against his heart, smiling from ear to ear. It was a full smile, showing all of his teeth. Something Kira was normally happy to see, but not now. Not when she wanted to die inside. Not when she wanted to confess that that woman downstairs was not her mother—that her real mother was probably dead. Not when she wanted to cry and release all of the pain piercing her insides.

Tristan shifted his gaze from one of her eyes to the other, shuffling back and forth, and tried to read her expression. He thought she was confused.

"Don't you see it? Your mother turned. You can turn."

Kira almost couldn't bear the excitement coloring his words. But she almost never saw him this open, so happy and relaxed...so full of hope. And that was the only thing that made Kira swallow her resounding no. Because even though Kira wanted to let it all out, she couldn't bear to fight with Tristan, not when she was already so close to breaking, not when he was the happiest she had ever seen.

But she couldn't open her mouth to speak. Instead, she let her body weight pull her down into his arms. Tristan caught her mid-fall and they were hugging. And he was lifting her into his arms, holding her like she weighed nothing at all and spinning her around in circles.

Kira held him close and let silent tears fall down her cheek. She buried her head in his shoulder to contain her shuddering breaths.

But Tristan didn't notice. His vampire senses were too hyped up on adrenaline for him to process how opposite their feelings were. Laughter bubbled out of his mouth, loud and uncontainable, joyful and disbelieving.

Kira drank it in and let it fill her up, pushing her sadness to the side. Suddenly visions were popping into Kira's mind, idle dreams she never really let herself believe because of how impossible they were. Or how impossible they used to be.

Traveling, that was what Kira had imagined the most. Seeing the African grasslands with nothing to fear and Tristan at her side. Staring down a lion while he watched on with laughter in his eyes. Or kissing under the Eiffel tower, visiting every ten years as an anniversary of sorts. Fifty years down the road they would come back to England, ride the London Eye again, and Tristan could bore her by describing every single way the city's skyline had changed.

But maybe they would come sooner and, back in that rose garden, Tristan might propose. He would slip a ring on her finger—something simple, a single shimmering diamond. They would laugh and kiss and he would twirl her around like he was doing now. They would be perfectly happy, there in that rose garden forever, breathing in the sweet smell of vanilla petals and eternity.

And they could get married. Kira saw it clearly, a small ceremony with her family present. Her father would walk her down the aisle, making sure not to step on her flowing chiffon gown—something relaxed, perfect for the beach. Maybe she would skip the shoes and instead let her toes dig into the sand as she gracefully stepped closer to Tristan. His eyes would be as clear and bright as the glistening water, and they would sparkle just the same. She would take his hand and promise him forever.

And forever was what they could have. When he ran, she would be at his side just as fast. They would be equals, on the exact same side for once, with nothing else to worry about. Nothing would be forbidden. Nothing would be judged. They would fight, of course. Kira was too stubborn to let him get away with anything. But then they would make up and that, Kira knew, would be magical. It would just be the two of them. The rest of the world would hardly exist except to make them happier for all of eternity.

So Tristan continued to spin her around and around, because time stopped mattering. They had too much time to worry about wasting it. And with his laughter ringing in her ear, Kira forgot everything about this night except for the sounds of his joy and the dreams playing like a movie in her head, the preview of a life suddenly possible.

By the time he collapsed on the bed with Kira draped over him, she was giggling with him, drunk on the endless possibilities before them.

Kira looked down at Tristan and cupped his cheek in her hand. His smooth skin felt like silk against her fingers and she let them drift into his dark hair, pushing it from his face so she could see him clearly. With her other hand she traced the line of his square jaw, ran her thumb over the contour of his cheekbone. His eyes, framed with thick black lashes, were turning lighter by the second, fueled by a growing hunger Kira couldn't dispute. Finally, she glanced at the two thin, pink lines of his lips and leaned down to cover them with her own.

Infused in that kiss was every ounce of love Kira had ever felt for Tristan—the flutter of their first meeting, the heart-stopping zing of their first kiss, the deeper warmth of shared memories, and the passion of bonded moments.

Kira felt the same from him and they were both lost in their feelings. The bed disappeared, the room disappeared, the entire world disappeared, until all Kira could sense was his skin on hers.

Much later, when Kira rested perfectly content in Tristan's arms, she wished only for sleep, not wanting to think about the day before or the hours to come. She didn't want to think about anything except how perfectly happy she felt in that moment.

But in sleep, her dreams did the thinking for her.

And as her sleep deepened, the colors dancing in the darkness of her closed eyelids transformed into an image. Pink blushes became rosy flowers. Blue swirls flattened into a rippling lake. Green beams sharpened into blades of grass. And the blackness receded, condensing into the shadows of the tree she and Tristan sat under.

The breeze against her skin felt like a ghostly kiss. The soft lapping of minute waves along the shore sounded like drums in her ears. She could hear cars driving miles away. Above her head, a bird stepped along the branches of a tree, crunching its little claws against the bark.

Tristan's hand over hers was firm, but not cold. For the first time, his fingers felt warm in hers and Kira looked down at their pale hands, intertwined and identical except for the difference in size.

Her hands looked white. Her gaze traveled up white limbs, down to white toes. Her skin looked like stone. She poked it with her finger. It was hard, like overworked unyielding muscles. Kira wiggled her toes, and Tristan laughed next to her.

He stood gracefully, moving his body like liquid, completely comfortable in his form. He offered his hand, ready to pull Kira to her feet, but she was already standing. She stuck her foot out for balance, not used to this lightning speed.

She smiled at Tristan, and he tilted his head, reading her expression even though Kira wasn't quite sure what her mind was thinking. His lips turned up into a smirk, his eyes challenged her and before Kira had time to think, he was gone.

But not gone, just in front of her, racing. Her legs pumped, chasing after him instinctively. Trees flew past her in a blur, leaves slapped against her face but they didn't hurt. Sticks crunched under her bare feet, breaking with the pressure.

Soon enough, she caught Tristan. She jumped onto his back, latching her arms around his shoulders and wrapping her legs around his torso, turning him into her pack mule. He continued racing forward until they reached a clearing. Mid-stride, he dropped to his knees causing them both to tumble to the ground and roll over in a pile of hands and feet.

But her giggles filled the silence, and she pushed his body off of hers as if it weighed nothing at all.

And then a gust of wind came, one strong enough to push the branches above Kira's head completely to the side, exposing her to the sun. Instantly her arms tingled with the sting, like sharp pin pricks stabbing her all over her body. It didn't hurt per se, but it wasn't pleasant. It was new though.

Curious, Kira stood up. She stepped forward, past the line of shadows and into the open grass. The sting strengthened. It felt almost like rain falling against her skin. But these raindrops were made of boiling water and they burst against her hands.

"Kira," Tristan called from the wood, "come back."

But Kira didn't look back. She continued to stare at her hand. She turned it over, moved her fingers around. She could almost feel the heat sinking into her skin, burning it in miniscule patches you would need a microscope to see. But she could see it. She focused her eyes, zooming her vision closer and closer to the surface of her hand, until cells came into view and she could see them shriveled up in the heat. One cell turned to ash, only to be instantly replaced by another and another. The black flecks were lost to the wind, but Kira saw them.

"Kira," Tristan said again. "Come back and eat."

At the word eat, Kira's nose picked up the scent of sugar and honey. But she wasn't in the mood for sweets, and responding to her demands, the scent changed to that of a fresh turkey club with a crisp pickle. Kira licked her lips. Lunch was exactly what she needed.

And when she turned, there was a girl next to Tristan. He cupped her wrist to his mouth and his eyes were closed. Following the smell, Kira walked closer and picked up the girls other wrist. She used her nail to cut a line in the girl's skin and fresh blood oozed from the wound. The smell dazzled her senses. It was any food she wanted it to be and no food at the same time. In a daze, Kira leaned down to lick the savory meal, but a voice stopped her.

"Wait!"

Kira jerked her head to the sound. A blond boy stood across the clearing. Freckles danced along his cheeks and his slightly off-kilter nose seemed oddly familiar to Kira.

She could smell the salt on his cheeks. She saw the wet lines that glistened in the sunlight.

Luke, *the name came unbidden to her mind. She rolled the* L *around her tongue, toying with the sound before agreeing that it seemed right.*

"Luke?" she asked.

"Kira," he said sadly and started walking across the clearing.

Kira stood up, food forgotten, and walked toward him.

They stopped two feet apart, and Kira couldn't help but feel sorry for the boy in front of her. He seemed so depressed. His eyes were curved downward, as were the corners of his lips.

"So you made your choice," he spoke softly but Kira heard every word.

"Choice?" she asked, wrinkling her nose in confusion. What choice had she made?

"You know, I was worried about you turning into a smurf on me, blue eyes and everything." He laughed quietly, almost like a sigh. "I didn't think I had to worry about this."

"About what?" Kira said. This boy, Luke, was very strange. He spoke in riddles.

"I wish I could help you," he said next, but Kira had given up on understanding him. "I wish I could." He reached his hand over her heart. "But she's not in there. My best friend is gone and this is the only thing I can do to save her."

And Kira was on fire. His hand scorched her skin, burning her to the core, melting her heart. She stumbled back on unsteady feet. What was happening?

Flames burst from his palm, following her as she fumbled backward, trying to escape. A shout reached her senses and Kira turned around blindly, just in time to see Tristan drenched in flames, circled by four men with red hair. He was trapped. Kira could see his skin melt. There was nothing she could do to save him. But she tried.

She ran to him, and another set of flames slammed into her from the side, sending her flying in the wrong direction.

When she looked up from the grassy patch that she had landed in, everyone was gone and she was alone in the clearing.

"Tristan!" Kira shrieked, but there was no answer. "Tristan!" she yelled again.

"He's dead," came the reply from behind her.

Kira stood and faced that sound. But it was a girl. A girl with curly red hair. No, curly blonde hair. No, both.

Her eyes were blue, bright light shards of cobalt with orange burns along the edges. They seemed to glow as they sunk into her skull, blinding Kira with their brightness. They seemed to burn, almost alive like fire.

But no, her hands were burning. Flames gathered on each palm, engulfing the entirety of her arms.

Kira turned to run, but before she could take a step, fire blasted into her back and she was thrown face first to the ground. She scrambled to stand, but the fire was unceasing. It sank into her skin, latching onto her bones. It coursed through her veins, bursting blood cells apart, traveling closer to her heart.

Her hands were like claws, sinking into the dirt, pulling for an escape. But her skin was melting away, turning to ash in the wind until she could see boils sprout along her forearms and bone stick out from the tips of her fingers.

The pain was unlike anything she had ever experienced. She was burning. She was boiling alive. Even her sweat was hot enough to sting. Her last ounce of strength was spent and she was falling, falling into a black abyss, a bottomless hole. And the flames chased after her, scorching her toes, raining down upon her as she continued to fall, and fall, and fall…

Kira jerked awake.

She bolted upright and her vision swam with the head rush, but she didn't care. She heaved, forcing air into her lungs. Her throat was dry. She couldn't breathe. The air was too thick and it scratched its way down into her burning lungs. Kira clutched at her chest, willing her heart to slow down before it burst apart.

"Kira?" Tristan's hand was on her back, trying to soothe her.

"Water," she croaked and he disappeared, only to return a minute later with a glass of cold water in his hands. Kira grabbed for it and greedily drank it down.

The chill brought her focus back. Kira blinked away the black spots in her vision, slowed down her breath, and collapsed against her pillow with wide eyes.

"Kira, what happened?" Tristan propped himself up on one elbow, looking down at her. Kira forced out a smile.

"It was just a bad dream, nothing to worry about," she told him. But deep down, Kira knew it was so much more than that. Already her mind was buzzing, trying to figure out what it all meant. She had killed herself. This wasn't just a simple, brush-it-off nightmare.

Tristan sighed happily and ran his fingers down the length of her arm. "I never thought the day would come that I could look at you and know it wasn't for the last time. There's no countdown anymore, Kira. We have all the time in the world now."

Kira wanted to mirror his excitement. She wanted to believe that forever was just within reach, but for some reason his words made her feel hollow inside.

"If we have all the time in the world, I think I'm going to use some of it for a nap," Kira said and rolled over. She nestled her head in the pillow and closed her eyes.

"We just woke up," Tristan laughed quietly.

"True, but that doesn't mean we can't go right back to sleep."

Tristan pushed her hair to the side and kissed her cheek. "I'm going down to speak with Aldrich. See you in a little while," he whispered into her ear before slipping off the bed.

Kira stayed curled up in a ball, listening to the soft shuffling of his feet on the rugs. She kept her breath even, only releasing a shuddering sigh after the door behind Tristan had clicked closed.

And then she felt alone. Completely and utterly alone in the world.

Kira clutched her necklace, felt the comfortable contours of her father's ring, but then dismissed that charm for the small little sun next to it. The edges were sharp, pointed, but still smooth. And most of all, it made her think of Luke.

For a moment, Kira could picture him right there beside her. First, he would look around the room—at the white tile floor, modern rugs, and porcelain mantle—and mutter something like, "Well, this doesn't scream ax-murderer at all." Kira would laugh while he continued on the rant. "Tile, in a bedroom? I guess it beats a coffin, but seriously." Maybe he would place one tanned hand against the white wall, and then his eyes would get that mischievous look Kira was so used to seeing.

"Luke," Kira would say sternly, chiding him for whatever idea was already running through his head.

"What?" He would pretend to be innocent, but then the truth would come out. "I was just thinking, wondering really, what Aldrich would do if we threw a bucket of bright orange paint on the wall. I've never seen a vampire temper tantrum." And Kira would giggle.

But then she realized she was giggling. Her vision of Luke evaporated, but her laughter remained for a second longer, until she remembered yesterday. Luke was pissed at her and for good reason. She had been horrible to him. She didn't deserve his jokes. She didn't even deserve the mirage of his voice. But she needed it.

Kira clutched the charm around her neck and thought about Luke. She gathered her power, let her hand turn to flame, and reached out with her mind to search for him. Blindly, Kira called his name with her head, hoping his subconscious would hear her plea.

But there was nothing. Luke was too far away for Kira to hear, and she felt as if she were suffocating again.

Kira ran from the bed and shoved the heavy black curtains to the side. In an instant, her entire room was shrouded in sunlight. The heat sank into her skin and Kira let it comfort and warm her.

She gathered two tiny flames on each of her palms, trying to heal herself, but even her fire wasn't strong enough to heal the wounds of a lonely heart.

She opened her eyes and looked up into the sun, not caring that the bright light stung her pupils. She needed the sun. It was the only thing she had left to comfort her. And with that thought, Kira finally understood why she had woken up feeling so hollow this morning.

She blinked away the sunspots in her eyes and looked at the landscape below her window. Her room overlooked the ruins of the old castle. While they had scared her the night before, Kira saw the stones clearly this morning.

They weren't scary, just sad. The old stones were once the pillars of a glorious castle, an undefeatable fortress that people might have feared in the middle ages. They could have been battered by cannons, pierced with arrows, sliced with swords, or bombarded with bullets. But none of those things brought these walls down. Time had brought them down as it did with everything. Some mortar had been loosened by the root of an ivy vine, and soon enough an entire wall came crumbling apart. No one bothered with repairs because by that time, castles were old and out of fashion. So the world continued turning, nature continued battering this old castle, bringing it down stone by stone. Heavy storms broke through the windows, winds toppled a column, and soon enough this glorious castle was nothing but a pile of rubble on the ground.

Looking at those ruins was like looking into her own heart. Time would never stop. The world would never disappear. And in the sobering morning light, Kira finally saw last night for what it had really been. Not her impossible dreams coming true. Not the beginning of perfect happiness. But an end—a desperate attempt to hold on to something that had already slipped through her fingers.

Time had already taken its toll. Time had already ruined what she and Tristan had, but it wouldn't ruin her.

Kira looked down on that castle with determination, not sadness. She was content. She loved Tristan, and part of her would always love him, but she had always known goodbye was inevitable. Even if she never wanted to admit it, the thought had always been there in the back of her mind.

Because she did love Tristan, but she loved herself more. And she couldn't do what he wanted. The cost of being together was too great. Standing there in the morning sunlight, Kira finally understood.

She was the sun.

She was the fire.

And she couldn't give up her power or her soul just to be with him.

Chapter Seven

Kira had thought that the lie she had told Luke would be the biggest in her life—that pretending to go to Sonnyville all the while planning a trip to a foreign country would be the hardest trick she would ever play. But Kira was wrong. This was far worse. Because until she uncovered what Aldrich was really up to, Kira would have to fool Tristan with the dream of forever. And that was truly unforgivable.

So as Kira walked down the grand staircase, in jeans and a T-shirt rather than the frilly dress Aldrich had left hanging in the closet, all she felt was guilt. It was a heavy, wet blanket cloaking her, weighing her down. And it took everything she had to shrug it off of her shoulders and put a smile on her face before turning the corner to the dining room.

If you want a show, Kira thought at Aldrich, *I'll give you a show.*

"Good morning, everyone," Kira chirped happily as she entered the room. She looked at the woman sitting at the table and deepened her smile. "Mom," Kira said warmly before taking her seat next to Tristan. Aldrich and her fake mother both sat with full glasses of blood, but Tristan wasn't sipping anything. Two cooked eggs, bacon, and toast were artfully laid out on the table in front of Kira's seat. *Still hot*, she thought gratefully and decided she may as well gather her strength with some food.

"Tristan seemed to think you were indisposed," Aldrich droned. "Glad to see he was wrong."

"I was just a little sleepy," Kira said and took a huge bite of food, wondering what sort of kitchen this house had. Surely the servants needed to be fed, and it seemed pretty stocked, but what sort of vampire kept such a nice kitchen in his house? Unless there were more humans here than she realized. "So what were you all talking about before I came in?"

"You," Aldrich replied. Tristan gave him a stern look.

"About how the talk with your mom went last night," he said and rested his hand on her thigh reassuringly.

"How did it go?" Kira asked, trying to keep the ice from her voice.

"I thought quite well," the woman said. "But there is so much more that I want to tell you."

"Well that works out perfectly, because there is a lot more I want to hear." *Like what you did with my real mother and how you learned so much about her life*, Kira wanted to scream. Instead, she took a long sip of orange juice and swallowed the words back down. *Be cool*, she chided herself.

"So…" Kira said, wondering how to make idle chit chat with a man who probably wanted to kill her and a woman impersonating her mother who also probably wanted to kill her. "Nice day out," Kira finally said. Weather was almost always a safe topic, unless of course you were talking to vampires who hated the sun, she realized a second too late.

"There's a beautiful garden outside," the woman said, her face still plastered with a smile. "Feel free to walk around. Aldrich has a marvelous sculpture collection."

"Do you still have that Augustus Saint-Gaudens we stole?" Tristan asked with a smirk.

Aldrich copied his expression before replying, "Of course."

Since when did Tristan treat Aldrich like an old friend? Kira thought. *Yesterday he was offering up endless warnings about trusting this man and now he's reminiscing about days gone by?*

"That's a funny story. You should tell Kira," the woman said, and Kira noticed that though her eyes were on Tristan, her hand held Aldrich's.

"What year was it? 1892?" Tristan asked and Aldrich nodded. Kira couldn't quite decipher the look in his eye. It seemed almost like satisfaction, like all the pieces of his plan were falling into place.

Kira looked away and tuned into Tristan's story, which was already half-done.

"So we snuck into his studio, curious about this second Diana statue he was putting together. And we found a third copy that nobody knew about—an even smaller version—and we took it. Saint-Gaudens must have realized, but he never told the papers or the police. Not like we could have been caught anyway." Tristan finished with a laugh. His eyes were glazed over thinking of the memory.

Kira couldn't stand it, the camaraderie with Aldrich. It was too much. Without realizing it, she was standing and all three of them were looking at her.

"I, uh," Kira fumbled for an excuse. "I need some fresh air. Might as well go see this infamous sculpture for myself."

With that, Kira walked out of the room, right out the front door and into the daylight. At the edge of the circular driveway, Kira saw a stone path and decided to follow it.

The walkway took her around the side of the house to the gardens in the backyard, and Aldrich wasn't lying, they were impressive. Box-like hedges cut geometric patterns through paths of stone and within the triangles of crisscrossing lines were mounds of colorful flowers. Jutting out from the flowers were sculptures, maybe a dozen of them. Most of them were classical figures cut from white marble, but a few were aged bronze. On the far side, Kira saw the sculpture of a woman balanced on one foot hoisting an arrow, and she realized that must be the Diana they were talking about. Kira looked away. She didn't really want to relive that story time.

Like the inside of Aldrich's home, the garden seemed gaudy and too perfect to be really beautiful. Kira preferred wildness, like the rose garden in London—gorgeous chaos. She looked back at the castle behind her. It was masculine, demanding. The stones were rough, some of the lines were uneven, and the design wasn't quite symmetrical. The garden, with its pristine and controlled grace, didn't fit the building behind it.

Kira found a bronze bench hidden in the hedges and sat down. She pulled her phone from her pocket and did the only thing she could think of doing in that moment.

Luke? She sent the text message to his phone. She couldn't call him—not with Tristan so close that he could hear every word they said. It didn't matter anyway. There was no reply.

I'm sorry. She sent the message before remembering he had smashed his phone yesterday and probably didn't have a new one yet.

I miss you. She sent that last one more for herself.

"Kira?"

She turned at the sound of Tristan's voice and made room for him to sit next to her.

"Kira, what's wrong?" he asked and when she opened her mouth to dismiss the notion, he beat her to the punch with an, "and don't say *nothing*."

Kira sighed. Maybe this total and complete lie wasn't worth it. Maybe she could let a few of her doubts show. Surely Aldrich was expecting some resistance.

"I just don't understand," Kira started but then changed her tactics. "I mean, yesterday you were 'Mr. I Hate Aldrich, Aldrich Is Not To Be Trusted'. And now you're the president of his fan club. At breakfast you were like two frat brothers talking about the good old days. It doesn't make sense, Tristan." Kira curled her knees into her chest and hugged her body close.

"He's changed, Kira. I don't know how, but he has."

"How can you be so sure?" Kira asked. Tristan's hands were in his lap and he rested on his forearms. His eyes stared straight ahead, past the garden to the rolling green hills in the distance.

"Yesterday, when you were talking with your mom, Aldrich and I went to his study to talk. You want to know the first thing he said to me? I'm sorry!" Tristan shook his head in disbelief. "He actually apologized for all of the vile things he made me do when he turned me. He said they were wrong. He said he doesn't do it anymore."

Kira opened her mouth to speak, but Tristan kept talking. "I didn't believe him either, not at first, but I searched the house. I reached out with my senses, listening for the moan of a girl in pain or the sound of a cell locking shut. I couldn't hear anything, anywhere."

"What about the girls we saw last night?" Kira asked, thinking of their empty stares and scarred necks.

"Contractual. They give him blood for a period of five years and then he turns them."

"Still," Kira said, looking at him with wide eyes, "you saw their faces."

"I agree it's not ideal," Tristan said, "but it's not like it was before. And who knows? With time, maybe he'll stop using live donors completely. Maybe we can help him."

"Tristan, do you even hear yourself right now? This man made you torture people, he made you hate yourself for decades." Kira stood and started to pace. "All he ever did was use you for his own pleasure. He never cared about you or what you wanted. He's a killer!" Kira shouted the last part and ran her hands through her hair, practically ripping it out. She needed to calm down. This wasn't going anywhere, and Aldrich could definitely hear everything she was saying.

"I've killed people," Tristan said softly.

"Not the same way, Tristan. Not without remorse."

"People can change," he whispered. Kira looked into his wounded eyes and wondered for a moment if he was speaking about Aldrich or himself.

"They can only change if they were something they never wanted to be in the first place," Kira told him and sat back down, taking his hand.

"But what about your mom?" Tristan asked. "If she

found a way to love him, can't you believe there must be something redeemable in him?"

"Maybe," Kira said, mostly because she didn't feel like fighting anymore. Tristan squeezed her hand.

"He wants to help us, Kira. That's what he told me last night. The only reason he invited us here was to atone for his sins by helping us be together, forever. He can give us a future."

Kira turned to look at him, ready to chide him for being so easily fooled, but the look in his eyes stopped her. It was yearning—pure, unadulterated yearning. He wanted so badly to believe in the dream Aldrich presented—the idea that even the most evil person can change, that in Aldrich all of their prayers were answered and they could stay together. And because he wanted so badly for that impossible future to be true, he couldn't see any of the flaws in his logic. He couldn't see past the dream. So Kira decided to keep lying, to let him dream for a little while longer, before breaking that hope into a million pieces.

"I know, Tristan," she said and wrapped his arms around her, so she leaned against his chest. "I want it too." She dropped her head on his shoulder. "I just need a little more proof."

He tightened his arms around her, hugging her closer to his chest, and they sat like that for a while. Not talking, just enjoying one another's presence. Kira was grateful for the silence because she honestly didn't know what to say.

Which of them was right? Was she just being stubborn because she didn't want her mother to be a vampire? Or maybe it was something else.

Part of the reason Kira loved Tristan was because he made her feel so normal, so human. Whenever they were together, they spoke of everything but the supernatural. He let her live in a fantasy world where conduits and vampires didn't exist, and they were just two people.

But if Aldrich was telling the truth, and her mother had turned into a vampire, then everything was different. Suddenly the dreams Tristan spoke of weren't just a fantasy—they were real. They were achievable.

And that scared Kira, because the instant a future with Tristan became a reality, she realized she didn't want it. Being a conduit was not only what she was, but who she was. But did that mean everything she'd ever had with Tristan was a lie, a fantasy she let herself believe because she wasn't ready to face her destiny as a conduit?

Yet out here in the garden, his arms felt so right as they hugged her close. It couldn't all be imagined—it just couldn't.

"You two look precious." Kira recognized the overly sugared sweetness of her fake mother's voice. "Tristan, would you come with me? I want to talk to you about something."

He nodded and Kira eased out of his arms, feeling cold in their absence. The bench seemed too big for one, so

Kira stood to wander around the garden. A walk was just the thing she needed to clear her head, so she chose a path and continued following it until she reached a statue.

It was a discus thrower carved in marble and stuck forever in a grimace. His arm reached back, pulled painfully taut in the moment right before he could finally release the throw. Kira looked at his face. Somehow, even though his eyes were made of stone, Kira could tell they held determination and also a slight fear. Fear of losing? Fear of not being the best?

Kira kept walking, stepping around the statue and taking the next left to another flower patch. This statue was of a dancing woman with her clothes half-falling off. *Typical,* she thought, *the boy is playing sports and the girl is frilling around without even noticing that her dress is basically on the floor.* Kira distantly wondered if this was the Roman equivalent to thinking that all girls did during sleepovers was have lingerie pillow fights.

The next statue was different. A man was twisting to look over his shoulder. His hand stretched close to the ground, grasping for empty space. His eyes stared down into the hedges by his feet. In them, Kira saw the look of a man who could see his future disappearing right before his eyes. His features were mid-fall, a strange mix between utter joy and utter despair. His eyebrows were raised, yet poised to turn down. His mouth was open and smiling, but the corners were slanted as if he had just cried out.

Even his body was fighting against itself. His stance was that of someone ready to pull something close, ready to help a girl stand to her feet. But his outstretched arm pushed the other way, reaching into a void, grasping for something that had disappeared.

Without realizing it, Kira reached out her own hand. Her fingers inched forward for his open palm, somehow hoping to soothe this miserable creature trapped in rock.

"I wouldn't do that," a voice stopped her an inch from the sculpture. Kira dropped her hand and spun around to face Aldrich.

"Why not?" she asked and tried to calm her rapid pulse. He had scared her, but that was the last thing Kira wanted him to know.

"It's bad luck," he replied, stepping closer to the statue and to Kira. He reached out his hand, stopping in the same place Kira's had been the moment before.

"Why?" she asked, watching him carefully.

"You don't know the story?" Aldrich asked. He turned to face her and let his hand drop to his side again. Kira shook her head.

"Orpheus," Aldrich began, "was the son of a muse. His voice was bewitching and powerful, and no one could deny the beauty of it. When he played his lyre, no one could resist the gentle lull of his music and no one could resist him. Especially not Eurydice, a local maiden, a beautiful woman, but also an ordinary woman." Kira heard the slight disgust in his voice at the word *ordinary*, as if the idea itself insulted him.

"On their wedding day," he continued, "Eurydice was so happy that she and her bridesmaids celebrated by dancing to his songs in the meadows beside the ceremony. But happiness is not what this story is about," Aldrich said. He leaned down and let his hand disappear in the flower around the base. "Hiding in the grasses was a viper, and with one bite," Aldrich pulled a flower from the ground, ripping it from its roots, "with one bite she was dead." Aldrich offered Kira the flower, but she didn't want to touch it. So instead, he closed his palm, crushing the petals. A second later, the crumbled remains were lost to the wind.

"Orpheus was overcome with grief, and he vowed he would not lose his love. So using his music as his weapon, he went into the underworld and convinced the Lord of the Dead to give him back his bride. His music was so sweet, so irresistible, that even death could not deny him. So Eurydice was returned to him, but on one condition. He could not look at her or touch her until they both reached the surface. Orpheus was patient, and he walked through the darkness until it started to turn gray, until eventually the sun shined down on him and birds chirped in his ear. He had reached the top. He was free. He turned to reach for his bride, to make sure she was still there. He needed to see her, to pull her close to him, but she was still shrouded in the mists of the underworld. In that instant, he realized his mistake, but it was too late. Orpheus grabbed for Eurydice, but she was already gone, a ghost disappearing into the ground."

Kira looked at the sculpture, understanding it now. This man was the definition of lost hope, and the artist had perfectly captured the moment that someone's life completely turned on itself.

"It's so sad," Kira mumbled, shaking her head.

"Is that what you really think?" Aldrich asked. Kira met his eyes and watched him studying her.

"It's tragic," Kira said and stopped herself from continuing. Aldrich narrowed his eyes.

"And…" He let the thought linger, suspecting Kira had more to say.

"It's just, he was an idiot. A complete moron." Kira sighed, getting frustrated. Aldrich's eyes lit up, like this was the reaction he had expected. "Who is so stupid? You have your entire future hanging on one idea—do not turn around—and you can't stop yourself? It's just, it makes me angry. He not only ditched his happily ever after, he let Eurydice down. He basically killed her." Kira stopped. She was getting way too impassioned by the story.

Aldrich laughed and smiled at Kira, as if she had passed one of his tests. "Ah, Kira, you are such a delight."

"Why?" Kira eyed him wearily, not sure she really wanted an answer.

"Because you are the first person I've told that story to who has had the same reaction as me," he said and placed a hand on her shoulder. Kira tried to hide her revulsion, at his touch and his words.

"I doubt that." She shrugged free of his hold.

"It's true. We are far more similar than you'd like to think."

Kira retreated from the statue and started down another pathway. Aldrich followed closely behind.

"We're both logical, we don't let our emotions control us."

"That's not true," Kira retorted. She couldn't even count how many times she felt overwhelmed by her feelings, how many times they seemed to stifle her.

"Isn't it? In the past few months, your entire world has turned upside down. Yet here you are, fighting. A lesser person would have given up, would have let the heartbreak overwhelm them."

"That's not because I'm 'logical,' it's because I'm too stubborn to lose," Kira said, glaring at Aldrich over her shoulder.

"To lose what?"

"Anything I care about," Kira replied.

"But I see you, Kira," Aldrich said and reached for her hand. He stopped her and forced her to turn around and look at him. "I see the wheels in your head spinning. I see the doubt circling. Dreamers would have already surrendered, would have been satisfied with the idea that all of their hopes could actually come true. But not you. You're realistic and you need proof. You need the logic."

"Tristan—" Kira started.

"Tristan is a dreamer. He's always been ruled by his emotions. It's why he is easy to predict, but you're different."

"What's your point, Aldrich?" Kira asked. She was tired of talking in riddles.

"My point is that you don't believe me yet. You don't believe that I've changed. You don't believe my motives are pure, that all I want to do is reunite two star-crossed lovers and make up for the sins of my past. My point is that you are Orpheus. The story is not about a man turning around out of joy, the story is about a man turning around because he couldn't believe that all of his dreams were about to come true. He needed proof that Eurydice was following him, he needed her touch to confirm she was real. And Kira..." Aldrich looked down at her, his almost black eyes even seemed to warm for a second. "Sometimes the dreamers have it right. Sometimes, you can't have proof. Sometimes, you just need to believe."

Aldrich turned on his heel, walking away from her and out of the garden. Kira watched him leave. His movements were confident. Even in the maze of his garden, nothing slipped his control. He thought he had her. He thought he was starting to tame her, to trim her down like the hedges in his perfect garden. And as Kira watched his lean body and sandy brown hair retreat around the bend,

Kira couldn't help but feel defiant. Ever stubborn, Kira couldn't help but doubt him.

That little story had done nothing but make Kira more confident that he was hiding something. Tristan was a dreamer and it was one of the reasons Kira loved him. But he had fallen into Aldrich's trap without even thinking, without even pausing to breathe. His dreams and his love had become a drug that clouded his judgment. And even if it made her cold, Kira couldn't be the same way. She couldn't just believe in something when all of the signs were telling her it was a lie.

Aldrich had it wrong. Kira wasn't Orpheus—she wasn't giving all of her dreams up in the search of reality. She already had her proof. The look of hatred in that woman's eyes was all she needed to see in order to know it wasn't her mother. Aldrich might not have realized it yet, but his plan had already cracked, and Kira had already seen flashes of the truth.

What she needed now was not proof, but answers. What did Aldrich want? Why was he trying so hard to convince her that turning into a vampire was not only possible, but also the right choice?

Kira looked at the mansion. All the answers she needed were hidden in there somewhere. She just needed to find the right crack, the one would bring Aldrich's carefully constructed façade crumbling down.

Chapter Eight

It turned out that getting answers was hard—a lot harder than Kira initially realized. Almost a week had passed and Kira was no closer to finding out Aldrich's real motives. Instead, the four of them had fallen into a strange sort of routine.

In the morning, Kira would call her parents and tell them fake stories about Florida. Thank goodness her smart phone had service, because she was basically living off of her weather application. A huge storm had blown through Orlando last week and her father wouldn't stop asking about all of the gory details, so Kira had had to search for photos of downed trees to send him. Luckily, her mother was less nosy and instead asked only about Luke, something that was much easier for Kira to lie about. Maybe because she was already sort of lying to herself about it.

Luke was definitely still mad. At least, that was how it

seemed to Kira. He finally bought a new phone, and she had tried calling him a few times during the half an hour she had before breakfast, but he never answered. Occasionally Luke texted her, to make sure she was still alive or to update her on his location, but nothing personal. So Kira was left to her own daydreams and imaginings. She'd gone over their reunion one hundred times in her head—exactly what she would say to apologize and make him understand. She envisioned all of his possible responses to ready herself, but it was starting to drive her crazy.

After Kira exhausted all of her phone calls and pointless fantasies, she would make her way downstairs for breakfast. She had gotten the timing down perfectly, so that when she entered the dining room, her food was still hot but all of the blood-filled glasses had already been emptied and taken out of the room. While Kira ate, an hour of pointless small talk would begin.

Then Tristan would disappear with Aldrich, who was helping him channel his mental abilities to make them stronger. Kira would go off with her "mother" to talk more about the process of changing into a vampire, and sometimes Kira would grill her for details about her father. After a few hours, when Kira knew her fake smile was no longer believable, she would leave her mother to wander around the castle.

In the past week, Kira had pulled on every book, looked behind every painting, and twisted any knob within reach, but still she hadn't found anything that looked remotely like a dungeon or trapdoor. Kira was sure Aldrich was hiding something, and she was determined to scope it out, but she had come up completely empty.

Eventually, when Kira felt ready to put her happy façade back on, she would go find Tristan. Being with him tore her in two. One half relished his presence and let him soothe her into a peaceful happiness. The other half couldn't fight the knot in her stomach, the one so tightly roped around her lies that they seemed to choke her. Kira wasn't sure how much longer she could go without telling him the truth, without telling him that she would never turn into a vampire and would never give up her conduit powers.

So after a week of this strange balance, Kira woke up ready for things to change, ready for something to happen, because she wasn't sure she could keep up the show much longer.

And then something did change. On the nightstand, a foot from her head, Kira's cell phone was ringing. She reached for the device, ready to answer all of her parents' questions for an eighth time, when she saw the caller ID. It was Luke.

Kira fumbled for the phone. She knew Tristan would be able to hear, and Aldrich too, but she didn't care.

"Hello?" she answered and sat upright on the bed.

"Hey," Luke said. Kira melted into the sound of his voice. It had been so long since she had heard the subtly deep but always warm lilt to his words.

"Hi," she said lamely.

"So…"

"Yeah?" Kira asked, wanting to shake herself. Seriously? One-syllable sentences—was that really the best she could do?

"I'm just calling because I thought I should let you know that I'm at the airport and should be landing in England later tonight."

"Really?" Kira asked. Clearly actual sentences were off the table for her right now.

"Yeah, I'll be in London, staying with some conduits."

"Where?" This was becoming ridiculous.

"I'll text you the address."

"Great," Kira said. There was a slight silence on the line, and Kira knew it was up to her to break it. "Luke, I—"

"Don't Kira," he said, cutting off her apology. His tone wasn't angry or mean, like Kira might have expected. It was oddly excited, like he was ready to hear what she had to say and wanted to hear it. So then why had he cut her off?

"Luke," she tried again.

"Can you meet me in London?" he asked, cutting her off again. "I think we really need to figure some things out, talk in person."

Would Aldrich let her leave? Did she need his permission?

"I'll be there tomorrow," Kira said. After all, there was a car parked out front with her name on it. And if Aldrich tried to stop her, well, she hadn't used her powers in a while, and there was a lot of pent up energy inside of her that she would happily throw in his direction.

"Good," he said, and Kira heard the electric buzz in his voice. He was definitely excited to see her, which left Kira happy but also ridiculously confused. In all of her make-believe scenarios, he was angry or furious or ambivalent, but never excited.

And with the knowledge that he wasn't furious with her, Kira found she was grinning. And she wasn't sure how she knew it, but something told her Luke was grinning too.

They were silent for a few seconds, stuck in a comfortable stillness neither one of them wanted to break. But in the background, Kira heard an airport gate agent call for boarding.

"That's me," Luke said.

"See you tomorrow."

"See you tomorrow."

And he hung up, leaving Kira with a blank screen.

She slid off the bed to get dressed and face the three vampires waiting for her downstairs. Every one of them had probably heard the entire conversation, and she was sure she had more than a few questions waiting for her at breakfast.

Sure enough, when she turned the corner to sit down

at the dining table, six eyes were staring at her.

"Good morning," Kira said before sliding into her seat. When she looked down, she noticed something else had changed. There was no breakfast for her. Not a big deal really, but odd that after such a static week, another thing would be different. Without food as a distraction, Kira decided to just face the firing squad.

But the twilight zone kept on coming, because when she met Tristan's gaze he wasn't angry at all. Kira reached for his hand and slipped her fingers in between his.

"Was that Luke?" he asked, but his voice was perfectly friendly. Kira raised an eyebrow slightly. Tristan always got freakishly possessive when she talked to or about Luke. What had changed?

"Yeah, he's coming to England. He'll be here later tonight and," Kira took a breath, determined to stick her ground, "I want the car to go see him."

"Of course," Aldrich said. "You're not in jail, Kira. You are perfectly free to do as you please."

"Okay," she said. Something wasn't quite right about this situation. Everything was a little too easy. Aldrich was being a little too polite. But her stomach was rumbling and she was too hungry to deal with it. Instead, Kira asked, "Where's my food?"

"Miko dropped it on her way up from the kitchen," her fake mother said. "She'll be bringing you another plate shortly."

"That's okay." Kira stood. This was the perfect opportunity to check out the kitchen she had been so curious about. Cooking would also be a welcome distraction. "I can go make it myself. Will you point me in the right direction?"

"I'll take you," Tristan said. Kira followed him out of the room and around a few bends before they reached an oversized black door. When she opened it, Kira almost wanted to laugh.

The kitchen, unlike every other part of the house, was old. There were no white tiles in here, the one place where white tiles would actually be acceptable. The floor was made of slate slabs, and the counters were constructed from scratchy granite that had definitely seen better days. Wooden cabinets hung from old stone walls that were clean, but not polished or flattened. The equipment was older than anything Kira had cooked with before, but definitely still useable. The only thing strange was the amount of food—there was a lot of it, but no one around to eat it. In her quick sweep of the room, Kira noticed two refrigerators, a freestanding freezer, and a pantry wall stuffed to the brim with spices and dried foods.

The only other person in the room was Miko, who practically ran out the door as soon as Tristan and Kira walked in. Kira avoided her blank stare and tried not to look at the tired girl who seemed so willing to be a vampire's plaything. It was sad really.

But she and Tristan were finally alone, and as Kira searched the cabinets for eggs and bread, she asked the question that had been on her mind since they left the dining room.

"So why aren't you mad?" Kira questioned, still perusing the cabinets for a pan and vegetable oil.

"About what?"

"About Luke." Wasn't that part of the question obvious?

Tristan slid up behind Kira and gripped her hips, surprising her. He placed a soft kiss on the nape of her neck.

"Why would I be mad?" he asked innocently.

Kira spun in the circle of his embrace, leaving her supplies on the counter behind her.

"Oh, I don't know." She gave him a coy smile. "Maybe because the last five thousand times I've talked to Luke or even mentioned his name, you've been pissed off by it."

He grinned down at her. "I think that's a bit of an exaggeration."

Kira stared at him in disbelief.

"Okay, okay, Luke's not my favorite person in the world." Kira rolled her eyes and reached for the pan on the counter behind her. "But that's all in the past," Tristan concluded.

"Has your old age finally enlightened you?" Kira asked with a smirk and turned on the stove.

"I thought we made an agreement about old man jokes," Tristan deadpanned. Kira barked out a laugh.

"You're right, I'm sorry. Continue—it's all in the past because...?"

"Because he's almost out of the picture. You're going to see him to say goodbye, right?"

"I guess," Kira said, feeling her stomach drop to the floor and her cheery mood completely deflate. Needing to look somewhere besides Tristan, Kira spun to reach for the carton of eggs she had pulled from the fridge.

Everything made sense now. Tristan's mood and Aldrich's obliging attitude—they thought she was going to see Luke to make her final farewell. It made perfect sense in a strange way. Kira had made all of them believe she wanted to turn and wanted to become a vampire, so why wouldn't she say goodbye to Luke. He was a conduit. If she turned, Luke would become her enemy.

"Do you want me to come with you?" Tristan asked. His voice was earnest and concerned. "I know it won't be easy for you."

"No," Kira whispered. She took a deep breath, hardening her nerves to turn around and look at Tristan. His face was open, caring. His eyes were slightly down-turned with worry about her. The last thing Kira wanted to do in this moment was lie to him, but she had no choice. "I need to talk to Luke on my own. He needs to know it's my choice and mine alone."

Tristan nodded and reached across the counter to hold her hand. "I love you," he said.

"I love you, too," Kira told him, holding off the catch in her throat. Those words weren't a lie, but she wasn't sure how much longer she could go on saying them when the countdown had already started. "Can I have some time alone? Just to clear my head and think about what I'm going to tell him?"

"Of course." Tristan squeezed her hand and kissed the top of her head before stepping out the door. Kira let a single teardrop fall from her left eye. She needed to find out about Aldrich's plan. She needed answers, because she couldn't do this much longer.

Her stomach growled, reminding Kira that even with the turmoil stirring in her head, her body needed sustenance. But even after eating two eggs with a side of toast, Kira was still hungry. It was one of those times when her taste buds yearned for a specific flavor, but her brain hadn't yet figured out what that craving was.

She opened the refrigerator, perusing the shelves. Orange juice? No, tangy wasn't really what she was feeling. Salad? Definitely not. Yogurt? No.

Kira closed the door, frustrated. She clicked her tongue against the roof of her mouth, trying to figure it out, and decided to search the freezer. She could use some ice cream. But there was only one carton and it was vanilla.

Gross, Kira thought with a grimace, *who doesn't have*

chocolate ice cream? Vampires, that's who.

Now completely positive that ice cream was definitely what she wanted to eat, Kira crossed the room to search the freestanding freezer for more flavors. Ice cream would help her figure out this whole situation. It was amazing what a little sugar—and by a little, Kira meant an entire tub of *Ben & Jerry's*—could do to clarify the mind.

She reached for the handle and pulled, but the door didn't open. She furrowed her brows and yanked again, but the door still wouldn't budge. *The vacuum seal must be too tight*, Kira thought and reached around to dig her finger into the plastic securing the door, trying to get some air in to break the seal. But the material was solid and not squishy. Curious, Kira inched a foot to the side to look at the door. From the front, this had seemed like a freezer, but looking at it from the side, Kira wasn't so sure. It looked fake in an odd way.

Kira careened her head to search the wall for a plug, but there were no wires. Instead, the entire back of the fridge extended and molded into the wall.

What the heck? Kira thought. She tugged on the handle again, yanking until her arm was sore. And then she saw it— a tiny, miniscule little button barely the size of a pea was on the side of the handle, in an awkward spot just out of reach of her thumb. Kira pressed it, and the door swung open without making a sound. She couldn't see very far, but it looked like some sort of passage. Of course—where better to hide the entrance to a secret tunnel than in the kitchen?

No vampires would ever notice it. Good thing Kira was a foodie and was way more curious than was healthy.

She stepped inside and the door sealed shut behind her, trapping Kira in the dark. Luckily, she was a human light bulb.

Kira brought a flame to her palm and watched as the fire danced around the reflective surface of the tunnel. With her free hand, Kira rubbed the wall. At first, it had looked like stone, normal in a castle. But now Kira realized it was glass. Extremely thick glass had been fixed to the stone. Looking down at her feet, Kira saw glass there too. For a second, she felt like a fish in an aquarium. But rather than harp on it, Kira stepped farther into the tunnel.

She squeezed down the narrow walkway, wandering aimlessly until finally something like light appeared around the bend. Kira walked closer, stepping hesitantly, until she saw Tristan. The glass remained unbroken, but there was a hole in the stone and through it, Kira could see Tristan sitting on a sofa reading a book. Kira waved in big, exaggerated motions, but Tristan didn't notice her.

"Tristan," Kira whispered. He still didn't move. "Tristan," she said a little louder, but nothing. Finally, in her normal voice, Kira called out his name. Nada.

Kira tried to think of the design of the room. Surely she would have noticed a big gaping hole in the wall that led to a glass tunnel. What could possibly keep Tristan from seeing her? And then Kira remembered. A mirror. There was a medium sized mirror hanging over the mantel in that living room—it must be a one-way mirror.

And the glass, Kira suddenly realized, it must be completely soundproof—so soundproof, that even visiting vampires wouldn't be able to hear Aldrich walking around.

That asshole! Kira wanted to yell. Then she realized she was in a soundproof tunnel and she did let out a shriek. Tristan, very cute sitting and reading his book, didn't even bat an eyelash at the noise.

Kira, feeling nauseous all of a sudden, remembered that there was a mirror in the bedroom she and Tristan were staying in. It hung on the wall right over their pillows.

"Oh my god," Kira said and covered her open mouth with her hand. What a pervert! She had gotten undressed and changed and everything in that room, and Aldrich could have been watching the entire time. It was disgusting!

Kira turned and ran down the hallway. She needed to get out of there. Suddenly the glass was suffocating her. She couldn't breathe. But she had no idea where she was going. Every time she rounded a corner, Kira expected to find some clue as to where she was, but the passage didn't quite follow the line of the house—either that, or Kira had already forgotten where the kitchen was in comparison to the rest of the house.

She passed by more spying windows, saw more rooms that she had sat in or searched without realizing Aldrich may have been watching her the entire time. Was he at all suspicious that Kira was tricking them? Did he already know her secret—that there was no way she would ever turn into a vampire? Or had Kira managed to avoid detection?

For some reason, Kira thought she was still undiscovered. If Aldrich had known that she was playing them all and telling half-truths to Tristan, there was no way he would let her go see Luke. It was a small comfort, but it was enough to make Kira slow down for a minute and calm her nerves. Aldrich didn't know she had found out his secret, so why not use it against him. Maybe she could find him and do a little spying of her own. As they say, payback's a bit—

Kira stopped walking. Somehow, despite being completely and utterly lost within the actual walls of the castle, she had stumbled onto Aldrich. There he was, with her imposter mother, sitting and sipping blood in a room Kira had never seen before.

Why would he have a spy-hole into his private room? Or maybe it was that woman's room, which meant she didn't know about Aldrich's little set of hidden passageways. Interesting.

Kira pressed against the glass to peer as far into the room as possible. To the far left, just barely within view, was a bed. Her breath caught. A pale foot fell over the side, immobile. Traveling up the unmoving leg, Kira's eyes found Miko's face. She was expressionless, lying still with wide open lids. Blood dripped from her neck, staining the satin sheets below her body. But she blinked and Kira realized she wasn't dead, just too weak to move. Who would willingly let people do that to them, just to become a vampire? And Kira knew it was willing, because Tristan would have heard it if they were hurting her or forcing her to do anything. Something that would have made him question Aldrich, Kira knew it in her heart.

Unless they were sitting in a soundproof room as well.

Looking away from the bed, Kira examined the walls. They weren't made of glass like the tunnel, but Kira doubted Aldrich would be casually talking where Tristan could overhear him.

She flipped her attention to the two seats by the window where Aldrich and the woman sat. Heavy drapes kept the sunlight out, but the room was very well lit with candles. Kira wasn't quite sure what Aldrich's deal with electricity was, but it seemed strange for a vampire to willingly light fires all around himself. They couldn't hurt him, but still, didn't they remind Aldrich of the one thing that could kill him—conduits?

Not what she was here to think about—Kira focused on Aldrich again. He was saying something, but she couldn't quite read his lips behind the wine glass. Move it just a little bit, Kira silently urged, wishing she were the telekinetic one. But then he stopped, and it was the woman's turn to speak.

Her back was to Kira, so all Kira could rely on was Aldrich's reaction, which luckily was a big one.

Above the glass, his eyes hardened. The normal ebony-blue was rapidly transforming into a glacial steel, and he placed the goblet back on the table. He grabbed her fake mother's hand, pressing his nails into her skin until blood sprouted, staining her pale flesh. His lips opened to talk, and Kira concentrated on reading his words.

"I don't care. Make her believe."

A blonde head shook back and forth as the woman tried to reason with Aldrich, but after a moment, his hand slapped her face making her head whip around so far that Kira could see the tear stains on her cheek.

"We have been planning this for years, and I will not let you ruin it. You are a three-hundred-year-old vampire and she is a teenage girl. Figure it out!" He let her go and licked the blood from his fingertips.

The woman slid from her chair to kneel at his feet, placing her hands on his knee to beg for something—his forgiveness? Her life?

Aldrich eased back into his seat and ran his fingers over her cheek. His eyes lost their glow and returned to the umber Kira was used to. His expression softened.

"I'm sorry. You know how angry you make me sometimes."

The woman nodded and sat up a little higher. He brought her hand to his lips. The blood lingering there left a mark on her skin, like a tattoo, as though he had branded her.

"When she gets back from visiting Lucas, we'll know. She has one day, one day to come willingly or we'll have no choice but to kill her. And if you do your job, neither one of you will have to die."

He reached for his glass on the nightstand and took a sip of blood, staining his lips a deep red again. Over the brim of the glass, Kira met his eyes. For a moment, she thought he could see her standing there, watching him. But Kira blinked and the sensation was gone. She was safe, safe in the biggest gift Aldrich could have given her—a free way to spy on him.

Kira eased away from the glass, thinking about what she had just heard, when a moan broke through the absolute silence of the tunnel. Kira's head snapped to the sound— was someone else in here with her?

Chapter Nine

Kira took one last look at Aldrich, who was sipping calmly and staring at his own reflection, before following the noise.

As the darkness deepened, Kira let the flames surrounding her palm grow, partially to see and partially to prepare herself for whatever was in there with her. She strained her ears, reaching out for a sound, but Kira couldn't hear anything. Stepping slowly, carefully, Kira kept walking. No bend had broken the hallway, so there was nowhere to go but straight ahead. If the noise was real, it was definitely coming from this direction.

After a while, the path started sloping downward. At first, the angle was subtle, almost impossible for Kira to notice, but the farther she traveled, the steeper the walk became. And colder. Small goose bumps rose on her arms because despite the summer heat, the air nipped at her skin.

Okay, Kira thought, *enough of this.*

She put more energy into her power, making the flames surge higher to illuminate the entire path. She couldn't see anything in front of her but a hallway that slowly faded to black. Kira was about to turn around when she heard the sound again, a strained and muffled scream—of pain or frustration, Kira couldn't say.

Tired of the slow approach, Kira started to sprint. Her feet pounded against the glass, thundering in the silence of the tunnel—only challenged by the crackle of her fire.

Finally, after two minutes at full speed, Kira saw something ahead—an open door. *No, wait*, Kira stepped closer. There was no door, just an opening. Beyond it, there seemed to be an open chamber flickering with candlelight.

Kira slowed her pace again. As she neared the opening, her heart stopped.

Kira knew what this was.

It was Aldrich's dungeon. New. Modern. Clean. But a dungeon nonetheless.

Through the opening, all Kira could see was one rail-thin body curled into a ball on the ground. Kira rushed into the room and the scene became even more gruesome. Five bodies, six glass cells, and not a single ounce of movement from anyone.

"Hello?" Kira asked, hoping someone would give a sign of life. The only reply she received was another moan, quieter this time, from a shape huddled in the corner of the cell on the far left.

Kira rushed over and placed her hand against the glass. A man leaned against the wall of his cell, naked except for a pair of tattered pants. He looked no older than thirty. His red hair was matted with sweat and run through with knots. It was long enough to frame his face and cover his shoulders. His skin was bloodied; bite wounds punctured his chest, his arms, his neck. A shudder ran through Kira.

He moved his eyes, slowly glancing up at her with all of the remaining strength left in his body. A jerk shook his limbs when he saw her face. He pushed his feet, trying to back away from her, but he was already at the farthest corner his square glass cage would allow. But Kira wasn't paying attention to that—she was distracted by his eyes. They were green in the center, fanning out to an orangey-red flaming hue she was familiar with.

"Are you a Punisher?" Kira asked, placing her other hand against the glass, anticipating his answer.

He nodded, eying her with fear. Her eyes, Kira remembered. They were blue. He must think she was a vampire. Kira searched the glass for a hole or a door, surely there needed to be an entrance somewhere. And then she found a crack in the glass, a small indent that must be the handle to a sliding door. Kira pulled, but the door wouldn't budge. It was either too heavy or locked in some way she couldn't detect. But there was a smaller sliding door along the floor, maybe for food. Kira crouched down on her knees, and slid her hand through the opening. She put her palm up and let a small flame hover over her fingers.

The man's eyes widened slightly. He moved his own hand, but no fire appeared. He winced in pain, and Kira realized he must be too weak to channel his power. Somehow she had to heal him.

"Can you move? Can you come closer?" Kira asked.

"No," he replied with a raspy voice that came out barely louder than a whisper.

"Stay calm," Kira said and let her power grow brighter. Kira pushed her flames toward him until the entire cell seemed on fire. When the first tendril touched his skin, Kira felt the blow in her own stomach. He was so weak, so close to death. She couldn't give him food or water, but as Kira felt along his body with her fire, she realized the obvious problem. His blood was seriously depleted. Concentrating, Kira focused on replenishing his dried veins.

Her fingers tingled with heat as she channeled more power, happy that so far underground, her connection to the sun was still strong, still comforting. And after a few minutes, when the wounds on his chest had sealed without a scar, Kira had done everything she could, so she called her power back into her body. The flames retreated, sinking into her skin, and Kira looked at the stranger again.

He was still thin, still tired and hungry, but color flushed his cheeks and he had regained enough strength to come closer to her. He walked slowly and collapsed into a heap on the floor a few inches from her outstretched hand.

"Thank you," he said. The words were full of intensity despite his meek and airy voice.

"I'm sorry I don't have water or food," Kira told him.

"Who...what are you?" he asked and his eyes found hers. They were slightly widened, as if straining to stay open. He was looking at her almost as though Kira were a vision, something he thought might disappear if he blinked.

She crouched lower down so she could reach further into his cell and cover his hand with her own. It was dirty and still covered in dried blood, but it was solid. More importantly, he knew Kira was solid and not going anywhere.

"I'm a friend, a conduit like you."

"But you, you healed me. And your eyes...they were glowing blue."

Kira looked away.

"I'm," Kira started but she wasn't sure what to say. "I'm not your normal conduit."

"For a moment, I thought you were an angel, an ancient warrior called back to save me. An original, from the time of God and Satan and the heavenly battles."

Kira blinked. *What?*

"Uh, okay," she said and patted his hand. Must be some sort of Punisher mumbo-jumbo. "What happened to you?"

"A year ago," he said, breaking to cough against the scratch in his throat. "A year ago, I was captured. During a raid, I was hit with something. I blacked out and woke up in this cell, weakened with barely any blood in my body. I couldn't move. I couldn't call my power. I've been stuck here ever since."

Kira nodded, absorbing the story. He had been down in this cell for an entire year. A year without the sun, without a human touch, without family, without hope.

"Look, I'm going to help everyone else, and then I need to talk to you again. We need to figure out a way to get you all out of here."

He nodded, still looked at her with an awestruck expression. Kira shook her head and stood up to walk to the next cell. A redheaded woman was lying in this one, not moving, with closed eyes. A coarse cotton gown covered her features. Kira reached out with her power and healed her as best she could.

Kira flexed her fingers. She had hardly used her powers for two weeks, and it felt good to stretch her fire, to finally let it out. Her skin was flushed with the warmth of her own flames, but it was a comforting burn and Kira sighed happily. Almost like an odd sense of déjà vu, Kira got this feeling like she was exactly where she was supposed to be, doing exactly what she was supposed to be doing.

She called her flames back, and the redheaded woman, who seemed to be the same age as the man in the cell next door, blinked with confusion. Kira spoke to her softly, telling her the same things she had told the man before moving on to the next person.

This girl was blonde and looked slightly older, making Kira's heart catch. But on closer examination of her profile, Kira saw that it was not her mother. Her nose was too pointed, her cheekbones too pronounced, and her shape was just wrong. But instead of fighting another punch of sadness, Kira felt oddly relieved. She was happier her mother was dead. Better that than trapped in this hole, living a fate far worse than even nightmares could produce.

Kira healed the Protector and moved into the next cell, which was occupied by a brunette girl who screamed when she woke encircled by flames. Even before that, Kira could feel she was human. Her fire didn't sink into this girl's skin like it did with a conduit. Kira had to force her power into the wounds to seal them shut. The process wasn't quite natural, but still easy enough to pull off.

In fact, it was a lot more difficult to calm her down than it was to heal her. She was bruised, broken-limbed, but not injured in the same way as the conduits. Her blood was almost all there. Kira realized this girl was probably a plaything to Aldrich, not food. Her dress spoke of the same conclusion. Unlike the dirty brown rags adorning the conduits, this girl was dressed in fine orange silk that cinched around her small waist. Her wrists were circled in gold cuffs—a cross between jewelry and jailing that made Kira cringe. She was Aldrich's Barbie. He had dressed her up just to break her down, just like Tristan had told Kira.

The conduits had to be kept injured and weak so they couldn't fight back. But this girl had been for fun. Kira swallowed the vomit in her throat back down. She had one more person to heal.

The last cell held another girl—clearly, Aldrich had a preference for the female sex. She was stretched out on her side, facing the wall. Full, wavy black hair piled around her head and her grimy dress was too big, covering everything but her white and bony feet. She looked human, but her clothes were just as worn as those of the conduits.

Kira reached out with her fire, slipping it through the hole in the door of the cell in the same way as with the other prisoners. When the flames enshrouded the girl's body, Kira tried to heal, but she was blocked. The fire wouldn't sink through her skin, wouldn't bend between the breaks in her cells, instead it tried to burn through it. Confused, Kira pushed stronger.

Suddenly, the girl's head spun around and she hissed at Kira. Sharp teeth protruded from her lips and her eyes were white.

Kira stumbled back, falling on the ground with shock. Her flames followed, snapping back into her body like a broken rubber band, stinging her skin slightly.

As soon as her fire vanished from the cell, the girl slumped down lifeless again. Slowly, she sat up, leaning her tired head against the back of her cell. She opened her eyes, now gray-blue like the ocean during a storm—dirty somehow—and examined Kira.

"You shouldn't have healed them," she said. Her voice was weak, but still audible and much louder than those of everyone else in these cells. Kira realized that she had been acting, partially, to silently observe Kira. Her skin was ashen and pale, sickly compared to the pristine pearl of every other vampire Kira had ever met. But she had strength, despite the fact that Kira couldn't heal her.

"Why not?" Kira asked. She crossed her legs, trying to get comfortable. Who knew how long this vampire had been here? She had to have some information that might help Kira.

"Aldrich will know someone has been here," the vampire said matter-of-factly.

Shoot, Kira thought. How had she not thought of that? But, Kira realized, she would have healed them regardless. She would not have been able to simply walk away from conduits and humans walking such a fine line between life and death.

"When will he be back?" Kira asked. She couldn't fix the situation, but maybe she could avoid it.

The vampire shrugged. It was such a human gesture that Kira paused and took a second look at the girl. Her features seemed exotic, even without their natural coloring. Something about the arch of her eyes and fullness of her lips reminded Kira of a gypsy. But more so, something about her seemed human, in the same way that something about Tristan had always seemed human. Maybe it was the spark in her eyes, the sense that she would fight for her survival. Regardless, Kira couldn't fight the feeling that this girl wasn't her enemy. That maybe she could even be an ally.

As if sensing the flip inside of Kira, the girl narrowed her eyes. "He hasn't been here for a few weeks, not since he drained a few of those conduits over there for some party. But his servants come in daily to pass around a few meager scraps of food. Not like those duds would notice anything." She paused, shifting her eyes to scan the faces of the other prisoners. "No, you might be okay. He usually waits for them to heal a little bit more before he comes back. But he'll notice their scars are gone when he does."

"I'm hoping he'll be dead by then," Kira said.

It was a slight risk to let this vampire in on her plan, but if she was trapped in one of Aldrich's cages, Kira doubted the girl would tattle. If she felt included, she might be more willing to give up information. Like Kira expected, the vampire raised her eyebrows.

"Do tell," she said. Her head slid forward slightly, an unconscious movement revealing her interest in Kira's words.

"Tell me what happened to you first," Kira said. "Why are you trapped down here? What did you do to him?"

The girl laughed. It was a shallow, bitter sound. "The question isn't what I did to him, but what I didn't do."

Kira waited for the girl to continue.

After a few seconds, the girl sighed and relaxed against the wall. "What do you know about vampires?"

"A good amount," Kira said, keeping thoughts of Tristan from leaving her lips.

"So you know about our powers? Well, some of our powers?"

Kira nodded.

"I happen to have a very valuable one. I pull people's memories into my own head. I can't just go in at any time and sift through someone's mind. But if I'm touching them, I can draw the images out like a movie and then play them in someone else's mind."

"Show me," Kira said.

"What's in it for me?" she asked. "I don't exactly have tons of energy to just go wasting on you." Her body slackened to prove the point.

Hesitant, Kira held up her wrist. "Blood."

The girl responded by licking her lips and sitting up a little taller. The eyes of the other conduits were on Kira questioningly, accusing her. She had a feeling she was breaking a cardinal rule—never willingly give a vampire blood. But information was more important than following the rules.

Kira pushed her fingernail deep into her wrist, biting her lip at the pain. After a few seconds, her skin gave way and a bright pool gathered around her finger. She reached her arm through the hole at the bottom of the cell, letting her blood drop onto the floor.

The vampire started forward but Kira jerked her hand back. "Wait," she said. Giving up blood was one thing, letting somebody bite her was totally different and not happening anytime soon.

After a minute, Kira lit an internal flame, bringing the fire to her blood long enough to close the wound. She sat back down, waiting as the girl slid across the floor to drink.

The ashen gray retreated from the vampire's features and a luminescent glow sprouted on her cheeks. The smoke left her eyes, leaving a glossy royal blue hue behind. The curls in her hair tightened into coils and a flush colored her lips.

She reached her hand back, beckoning Kira. "I won't bite," she said with a smirk. Kira tentatively stretched her fingers out until she was holding the girls hand.

Suddenly, her mind was taken over by darkness. Rich swirling hues buzzed in front of her eyelids, covering the glass cells, until they merged into an image—a fire.

A large, sparking fire surrounded by people in bright clothes and linen-covered wagons. Drums were beating in her ears, and the crowd was swaying in unison to the sound. They started clapping, softly at first, until the noise became as loud as thunder. People were calling out, laughing and yelping, until a hush spread around the fire and a dancing figure jumped into the middle of the circle. Her red pants were wide and billowing in the slight breeze. Her shirt sparkled with gold medallions and a sliver of her stomach was revealed underneath the loose top. She paused, brought her hands up over her head, clanking two small symbols together and surveying the crowd, waiting for their voices to rise again and goad her into a dance. Her eyes met Kira's, and though a bright piercing emerald, Kira recognized them as belonging to the vampire girl.

Kira looked away from the stare, and at the other end of the fire was a man with jet-black hair, who, for a split second, reminded her of Tristan.

"My, my, you are a bit of a rebel aren't you," the female vampire said. Kira snapped her hand back and let the vision disappear.

"What do you mean?"

"Who's the guy?" She raised her eyebrows, challenging Kira.

"No one."

"You seemed pretty hot and heavy—"

"You were just supposed to show me your power!"

The girl shrugged. "No harm done and now that memory, that steamy little gem, is all in here," she said and tapped her skull. "Pretty handy, at least that's what Aldrich thinks."

"How long have you been in here?" Kira asked, sinking back in her seat to keep as far away from the cell as possible. No way was that girl touching her again.

"Maybe twenty-five years. Such a drag after a couple hundred years of absolute freedom. But Aldrich knows I'd run if he ever let me out." She blew a curl from her forehead.

"So why not do what he says?"

"I'd rather be prisoner than a slave," the girl said quietly. Kira saw her fists clench. After a second, her fingers relaxed and she turned to Kira. "Your turn to share. Why are you here? Last time I checked, Aldrich didn't really keep conduits as houseguests. But you're special, aren't you?"

"I'm a half breed conduit," Kira said. She didn't look around at the shocked faces of the Punishers and the Protector in the cells around her. The vampire looked unimpressed.

"Tell me something I don't know," she said and rolled her eyes. "One look at your hair, your eyes, and your healing, and that was obvious. I want to know what that means. What is so damn special about that, other than the dual immunity, which you can clearly see Aldrich doesn't need."

"That's what I'm trying to find out," Kira muttered, annoyed.

"I might have an idea," a scratchy voice said from behind her. Both Kira and the vampire girl turned to look at the Punisher man who Kira had first helped when she walked into the dungeon. He was leaning against the front of his cell carefully watching both of them.

"No one really knows how vampires and conduits came to be," he said. His voice grew quieter and quieter the more he spoke. The lack of water and energy was clearly affecting him. "Protectors will tell you it was nothing more than a virus, a scientific abnormality—not that they can prove it. But Punishers, we believe something different. Something a little more divine." He coughed, cutting off his story. Kira stepped over to his cell and let her hand warm his, infusing his body with a little more energy.

"What do you believe?" Kira asked, intrigued on multiple levels. Luke never shared Punisher beliefs with her. He thought they were nothing better than legend. But wasn't history like that sometimes?

"We believe vampires and conduits were once brothers in heaven, sacred creatures who worked alongside God as angels. When Satan fell, he became the first true vampire—an angel so twisted by evil that he needed the blood of humans to survive. But this blood, this pure elixir of life, gave him strength and powers that rivaled even God, so he turned more corrupted angels to his side and they rained down from the heavens, falling to the earth like comets from the sky. The pure angels, unaffected by Satan, saw what his rule was doing to the earth. He was turning the very essence of man darker with his presence. So they begged God to be released from the heavens, to use their powers of goodness and light to chase their fallen comrades from the earth.

"God agreed, and the angels came. Channeling the source of God's power, the sun and the light, they tried to bring their brothers back to the heavens. But the fire burned the corrupted angels' skin. You see, once an angel falls, he can never return to heaven, and eventually the pure angels realized that the gift of mercy was not possible. Death was the only alternative, because the souls of their former friends were the only parts with enough good to return to the heavens.

"After being hunted down, the dangerous fallen angels became extinct. But their children, the humans turned vampires, remained on earth. And the angels, to prevent unstoppable angelic vampires from ever gracing the earth once more, divided. And with that division, their strength was cut in half—they were no longer divine angels. There was no danger of falling from grace, because now they were just conduits. More controlled and less dangerous, but also less divine."

The man gripped Kira's hand, using what strength he had left to pull her closer to his cell. Her nose was touching the cool glass and she fought the urge to release his hand and retreat. His eyes were wide and searching hers, examining her blue irises. He was waiting for her to speak, to say something about his story.

"Don't you see?" he asked Kira, desperation covering his words. His eyes continued to search hers for some spark of understanding.

Kira shook her head, not completely sure she wanted the answer.

"You, an entity filled with Protector and Punisher strength, have become more angel than conduit," he said and brought his hand to rest on the glass by Kira's face. His pointer finger moved slowly, zoning in on her eyes. "But the darkness has started calling you. You are falling and you need to stop yourself before it is too late, before the evil consumes you."

Kira stood up and backed away from the finger still pointing in her direction. She met the eyes of the other two conduit women and read betrayal in their expressions, as if they could see the cloud of evil surrounding her. The man didn't move his hand. He hardly blinked. Only half an hour before he had looked on her with gratitude, but that expression had already darkened, had already turned suspicious.

I healed you, Kira wanted to yell, *I helped all of you when I could have just walked away.*

But their stares were melting her skin, burning her in a way that fire never would, and the words stalled on her lips. Instead, she backed away, closer to the door and further from their judgment.

As she passed the vampire's cell, Kira couldn't help but turn her gaze to the girl who was watching her with a smile. She let her fangs poke beneath her upper lip and winked at Kira wickedly.

Kira ran. She left the room and never looked back. Not even as the girl screamed, "Bring some blood next time, and I'll show you some memories I know you'll want to see!"

Kira lit her fire, used it as a guide through the dark tunnels, and tried to keep the vision of bloodthirsty fallen angels crashing to the earth at bay. Would there be a day when the fire stung her? When her actions would become too evil, no matter how well intended? Would she wake up with not only blue eyes, but pale skin and a taste for blood too?

Kira forced the thoughts from her head and focused on one thing—Luke. There was a reason he had never told her what Punishers thought, something he maybe never wanted to admit even to himself.

Kira reached the end of the tunnel and finally saw a door before her. She quietly eased it open and stepped back into the old, slightly dusty kitchen of Aldrich's manor.

As she let the opening swing silently shut, Kira could only think of one thing. The lies needed to stop. She needed to tell Tristan the truth. She needed the truth from Luke. They all needed a plan.

And there was only one way for all of that to happen.

She was going to London.

Immediately.

Chapter Ten

Kira walked out of the kitchen and calmly made her way toward the front staircase, peeking into every room she passed for a sign of Tristan.

Nothing.

When she reached the front of the house, Kira reached for the door, hoping to catch him outside. But when she touched the handle, the unmistakable sound of footsteps clunked in the hallway behind her. Kira's entire body stopped. She held her breath, waiting for Aldrich's voice in her ear, waiting for him to somehow know where she had been.

"Kira—"

"Tristan!" Kira practically screamed and turned around to jump into his arms. Her heart pounded inside her chest. They needed to leave now, before Aldrich could stop them.

"Where have you been? I've been looking everywhere for you!" he said quietly into her ear.

Kira stepped back and shook her head. She couldn't tell him anything while Aldrich was around. He might still be in his soundproof chamber with that horrible woman pretending to be her mother, but Kira didn't want to take that chance.

Tristan tilted his head, looking at her questioningly. Kira bit her lip and sighed, before realizing she had the perfect solution. Kira pulled out her phone and let her hands slide along the keyboard.

"We need to talk, where Aldrich can't hear us. We need to leave right now." She typed and handed the phone over to Tristan, whose eyes widened at the words. He nodded and a few stray strands of black hair fell over his eyes, hiding them from Kira. She reached her hand up to brush them from his face, staring at his chiseled features for one prolonged moment, relishing the love ever present in his expression. Soon, that look would be gone.

Kira shuddered at the thought, not wanting to think about the next hour of her life. Living it one time would be enough, so she retreated from his strong figure to twist the doorknob.

She opened the large wooden door, turning to make her way outside, when it slammed shut in her face. Kira tugged on the door, but it wouldn't budge. And then she heard footsteps on the stairs, solid thumps that echoed in her chest sending a chill down her spine. With one deep breath, Kira turned around to face Aldrich.

"Leaving so soon? We were just coming down to join you for a mid-afternoon snack," Aldrich drawled. His black suit was stark against the white marble steps. The only color on his body was the flush in his lips, letting Kira know his former snack had only recently ended. Kira hoped Miko was still breathing somewhere in the castle.

Behind Aldrich, the blonde vampire started her descent. Kira noticed she had changed into a deep purple gown with a corset that cinched into her small waist. The folds of this dress were smooth, not wrinkled from begging for her life at Aldrich's feet. The crescent-shaped cuts from Aldrich's nails had disappeared from her hand, and her expression was warm and loving, as any mother's should be.

Thinking quickly, Kira grabbed her phone from Tristan's hand, holding it up like a trophy for Aldrich to inspect.

"I just got a text from Luke. He's landed in London, so Tristan and I were going to leave early," Kira said and turned to try the door again. The handle didn't even budge. Aldrich was suspicious.

"I thought you were leaving tomorrow morning, alone. Surely, the trip can wait until then." Kira racked her brain for some excuse, something Aldrich would let her get away with. Before, she had overheard him say that Kira needed to make her choice. That if she didn't agree to turn in the next day, he would kill her. Maybe that was all she needed to do, to finally give him her official decision.

Kira reached to the side and slid her fingers into Tristan's, pulling him over next to her. Tristan, with a gesture that felt more natural to him than breathing, put his arm around her shoulder and pulled her close, never letting go of her hand. Kira silently thanked him for the unconscious gesture, because it made it seem like Kira had already clued him in on the plan. They were the happy couple, united and sharing happy news.

"Well, you see, Aldrich, I've made my final choice." Kira leaned her head on Tristan's shoulder, finishing off the picturesque pose. She squeezed the hand Tristan had resting on her arm. Kira looked up at him through her lashes and smiled. He was already looking down at her with a grin, but Kira could see in his eyes that it was fake. His irises were dark and cloudy, like a coming storm, and they read only of suspicion. A coldness settled in the pit of Kira's stomach, almost like she could feel the warmth of Tristan's love retreating from her, seeping out of her.

Kira turned back to Aldrich, trying to keep her voice light.

"I want to become a vampire, but I need to tell Luke first. Tristan and I want to leave right away, so we can be back to perform the turning tonight."

Aldrich clapped happily and reached out to pull Kira into his arms, hugging her close. Kira tried to loosen her stiff pose, and it took all of her strength to hug Aldrich back. His tall thin frame felt like bones beneath her arms, and she hated how close his fangs were to her neck. But he pulled back, looking Kira in the face, and Kira saw the sparkle in his black eyes. He believed her. Too sure in his own power, Aldrich never truly believed Kira would disappoint him.

He dropped her arms and turned to Tristan for a hug. He patted Tristan loudly on the back, congratulating him.

Kira's fake mother walked over with tears glistening in her eyes.

"We'll finally be together again, like a real family," she said breathily, as though her voice were too overcome with happiness to speak properly. *And maybe it is*, Kira thought. After all, Aldrich had no reason to kill her now. In fact, if the lie was supposed to hold, she had just ensured herself eternity.

"I love you, Mom," Kira whispered into her ear, focusing on the blonde locks filling her vision, wishing her real mother were there with open arms.

Behind her, the door shot open. Kira heard the crunch of gravel as Aldrich used his mind to move the car in front of the front door, acting as an imaginary chauffeur.

Tristan grabbed her hand and tugged Kira outside. As they neared the car, the passenger side door opened and Kira ducked inside. The door shut loudly behind her. Tristan slid in next and revved the engine to life. They both waved behind them as they zoomed out of the driveway, but only Tristan looked back at the retreating figures of Aldrich and the woman in the doorway.

The farther from the castle they sped, the better Kira thought she would feel. But as the silence settled in around her and Tristan, Kira felt suffocated. She opened the window, hoping the gusty breeze hitting her face would make her feel better, but nothing did.

Tristan's pale hands gripped the wheel firmly, and he shot down the empty roads far faster than any speed limit would allow. Time after time, Kira turned with an open mouth, just to stop and look back out the window, completely lost for words.

He wouldn't look at her, and as the better part of an hour flew by, Kira knew it wasn't just the fear of Aldrich overhearing that kept Tristan silent. He knew she had been lying. Kira only wished she could read his mind to see how much he had already guessed. Or maybe he just knew that Kira was about to tell him something that would change everything. Maybe he didn't know what it was. Maybe all he knew was that he didn't want to hear it.

Half an hour later, Kira's phone buzzed. She looked down at the lit up screen and read the message plastered across it.

"In London! I'm sending you the address to the conduit headquarters. See you soon." A moment later, the phone buzzed again and an alert popped up that said she had two unread messages. Kira was too afraid of Tristan's reaction to even touch her phone. Luke's address would just have to wait.

She stared straight ahead, out the window toward a sign that said London was only thirty-seven kilometers away, whatever that meant.

Then, for the first time since entering the car, Tristan's gaze landed on her. She flicked her eyes to the rearview mirror, meeting his, and something unspoken passed between them. It was finally time to talk.

"Tristan," Kira started, not knowing where her words were actually going.

"Let me find a place to pull over." Tristan sighed.

He turned off the highway, taking the first exit they came across. It led them down a winding road speckled with old stone houses that eventually led to a bustling town square. The sunny day had brought tons of people out of their homes, and Tristan continued driving past the crowd. After a few more minutes, a small duck pond came into view. The area was deserted and there was a spot in the shade, right by the lapping lake that seemed to have their names written on it.

Tristan pulled over, easing the car to a stop and stepped out. Kira followed him across the grass and to a seat underneath a white willow tree whose leaves seemed to droop with Kira's mood, stopping mere inches from the surface of the water. Tristan held a branch aside, letting Kira inside the privacy the tree offered until the two of them finally seemed completely alone and distanced from the world.

"What's going on?" Tristan asked. Kira leaned against the trunk of the tree. Tristan was across from her with one leg outstretched and one knee bent with an elbow resting atop it.

She had only had an entire car ride of silence to think of what to say and how to begin, but still Kira was drawing a blank. "I," she started and then stopped to stare down at her interlaced hands. They were gripped tightly in her lap and Kira eased her palms apart, stretching her sore fingers. She needed to relax. Otherwise, she might lose Tristan before she really had the chance to explain herself.

"Aldrich has a dungeon," Kira said. It was as good a place to start as any.

"Kira, I told you I couldn't hear anything. Do you think I would have lied about something like that?" he asked, hurt by her distrust.

"Of course not," she said quickly, aching to reach out and comfort him. But Kira tried to stay focused. "I saw it, with my own eyes, but there was no way you could have heard anything."

Kira started the story and continued to tell Tristan everything she had discovered that morning—the hidden passage, the spy holes around the entire castle, the use of soundproof glass—until Kira got to the part about the prisoners. She told him that she healed the three conduits and the human, and then began to talk about the vampire she had also found locked up.

"Pavia," he interjected when Kira mentioned her powers. Tristan looked up, slightly shocked. The words seemed to surprise him as much as they surprised Kira after so much silence. "Her name is Pavia. Aldrich was looking for her even when I was with him," he said, finishing the thought. And then Tristan fell silent again, without a word about anything that mattered, so Kira kept talking.

But she hesitated when she reached the part about the male Punisher's words, about his accusation that she was falling into evil, that she was already turning. Kira couldn't bring herself to say any of it out loud, so instead, Kira said that she had gotten afraid Aldrich would find her and decided to run away to find Tristan, to tell him everything.

And then Kira too became silent, listening to the rustle of leaves and waiting for Tristan's reaction.

"I was an idiot," he said softly, his words almost lost to the wind. "A complete idiot to think that Aldrich could have changed so much." He looked up at Kira with a pleading expression. "But you have to understand, Kira, he has this way about him. I don't know what it is, but it makes you want to forget all the bad things he's done. My life with him was horrible, but there were some good things and that was what he made me remember." A shudder passed through his body, visible even to Kira. "I don't know how I could have forgotten all the horrible things he made me do." Tristan stared down at his hands, frightened of the memories they held.

Kira hated herself at that moment. Tristan's features were quickly clouding over with the same self-loathing that darkened his face the first time they had met. He was retreating into that horrible place Kira had pulled him out of, and she couldn't let him go back. After all, Kira was the one who, in a way, urged him into believing Aldrich. She was the one who lied, who let him believe that she wanted to become a vampire, that Aldrich could be their salvation. If she had only told him her doubts from the beginning, Tristan never would have fallen into Aldrich's trap.

"Tristan," Kira croaked, her voice tight with shame.

"No, Kira," he said, looking up at her with a small spark of hope in his eyes. "We'll just use Aldrich and then let him go. After he turns you, we can just leave. We'll take your mother and run away. He'll never catch us, not with three-to-one odds." Tristan finished, excitement bubbling with the idea that not everything was lost.

"She's not my mother," Kira said hastily. The time for lying had passed. She should have mentioned that fact from the beginning, but it had slipped her mind when she started talking about the dungeon.

Confusion brought Tristan's brows together, and he shook his head, running his hand through his hair. "Kira, how can you even say that?"

"I'm sorry, Tristan," Kira said and reached for his hand. "I'm so stupid. I should have started with that. My real mother is dead—I'm sure of it. That woman is just a vampire that looks a heck of a lot like her."

"Kira," Tristan said sternly, "I know it might not be what you wanted, but she is your mother. I mean, I saw that photograph in your locket. She looks exactly like her."

"I know," Kira said gently, understanding his confusion. Kira had felt the same way at first, until she saw hatred stirring behind that woman's eyes. "But I read Aldrich's lips in that room, he said she was three hundred years old. She can't be my mother."

"I think you misunderstood what he was saying. It's not that easy to read lips," Tristan said, trying to comfort her. But Kira's patience was wearing thin. She knew Tristan wouldn't want to hear what she had to say, but he needed to understand.

"I didn't misunderstand, Tristan. She is not my mother."

"Then how does she know everything about you? How does she look exactly like your mom?" he asked, challenging her.

"I'm not sure," Kira said truthfully, "but you need to trust me when I say that that woman is not and never was my mother." Kira was breathing heavily when she finished talking. She hadn't realized that her voice had molded to stone—harsh, rigid, and demanding.

Tristan wasn't moving. He was watching her. His eyes were staring straight into her own, unmoving and unblinking. Kira looked away, focusing on his hand tightly clenching his knee and the muscles in his arms that were taut, stuck in a flex. His hair moved in the breeze, catching Kira's glance and drawing it back up to his face, which had become even paler than usual. His lips were drawn in a tight line, barely visible. A fleeting thought entered Kira's mind. She might never kiss those lips again. And the fear that that thought might be true made her meet his stare, which had gone from hardened and angry to hurt and betrayed.

"It was all a lie," he whispered, waiting for her to deny it.

But she couldn't. Kira couldn't even move. She felt paralyzed.

"You never believed she was your mother. You never thought that a conduit could turn. You never..." he trailed off into silence, unable to finish the thought. His gaze flitted over her features, jumped from her hands to her lips, from her hair to her feet, but never back to her eyes. His mind was catapulting ahead of his senses, taking him right to the truth and Kira sat rigid, unable to provide the solace he was looking for. His eyes were becoming frantic, moving faster than Kira could process, fast enough to make them water, until they stopped, right in line with her heart.

It was absolutely silent. The branches on the tree stopped moving, the wind stopped churning, the ducks in the pond stopped quacking, the water stopped rippling and even Kira's heart stopped beating.

Time ceased, as if it too understood that there would be no going back after this moment.

"You never wanted to turn," Tristan said, squinting as if he couldn't even believe what was coming out of his mouth, "you never wanted to stay with me."

And the bubble around them burst.

But no, Kira realized, the world had never stopped, just her heart, which was at that moment breaking apart like shattered glass, cutting her insides as it fell.

"I can explain," she said weakly. Tristan stood up to leave and Kira scrambled to her feet. She jerked on his hand, stopping him.

"I love you, Tristan—"

"Clearly not enough," he said, unable to turn around and meet her eyes.

"It's not about that, Tristan. I just, it's me, what I am. I can't give it up," Kira mumbled, hoping he understood the confused and partial sentences coming out of her mouth.

"It's not you, it's me. Really?" he said, angrily turning around to meet her pleading stare. "I get it. You don't want to become a monster, like me." He looked down at his hands and savagely said, "A killer. A predator."

"No," Kira cried, clutching his face to keep him from looking away. He knocked her hands off and stepped back. She tugged on his shirt, needing to hold some part of him so she knew he wouldn't disappear. "It's nothing to do with not wanting to be a vampire. I'm a conduit. I can't give up my powers, my fire. It's who I am, and I can't let it go. If I turned, Tristan, it wouldn't be me turning. It would be someone else, someone dead inside. You wouldn't love me like that and you know it."

"But I would have," he said sadly, the anger gone from his voice. He stopped pulling against her grip and looked down at her, holding her gaze to let his words sink in. "And ten minutes ago I would have said there was nothing you could ever do to make me feel differently, but I would have been wrong."

Kira shrank from him, not wanting to hear the words tumbling from his lips. But now it was Tristan who was holding her, preventing her escape.

"If you had told me the truth, we could have figured something out. We could have worked together. I would have never let you walk away from me. But you lied. You dangled our future, all of my hopes and dreams, right in front of my eyes like some toy for me to helplessly chase, all so you could fool Aldrich. All so you could learn his plan. But what about me? Did you ever, for one second, stop and think about me?"

You were all I thought about, Kira wanted to say. But instead, deflated, she just whispered, "Tristan."

Kira couldn't deny the truth. She had known she was being mean and cruel to him, but she had done it anyway.

Everything he was saying was true. Kira had known this was the inevitable end to her lie—that he would never forgive her. And even now that all the pieces had come crumbling apart, Kira wouldn't change her actions.

She didn't want to be a vampire. She needed to know Aldrich's plan. And she needed Tristan's help. Something in her gut told her that this was bigger than their relationship. It was bigger than their future.

"I know that no sorry could ever make up for what I've done, but I'll say it anyway. I'm sorry, so, so sorry, that I've hurt you. That was never what I wanted, but there was no other way to fool Aldrich, to stop him from killing both of us the second he thought we wanted to leave." Tristan's expression softened for a moment, as though he understood she was telling him the truth. But it passed and his features hardened against her again.

Kira stepped closer to Tristan and he didn't move. She brushed his hair back with her hand, unable to fight the pain in her gut that it might be the last time she ran her fingers through his silky black locks. Her other hand came up to rest on his cheek while her thumb ran slowly over his bottom lip. Reaching on her tippytoes, Kira gave him one last soft kiss.

"I do love you, Tristan," she said and this time he didn't look away. "And I'm sorry that it may not be enough to keep us together when the whole world wants us apart. But this thing with Aldrich isn't about that. There is a reason he wants to turn me. There is something he is planning that is bigger than you and me, and we need to figure out what that is. I need you. I can't do it on my own."

Tristan closed his eyes and let his face relax into her hand while he breathed deeply. He knew she was right, that Aldrich had something dangerous planned. And if Kira knew Tristan, no matter how hurt he was, he wouldn't be able to walk away from doing the right thing.

A few excruciatingly silent seconds passed. Both of them cupped the other's face, but neither moved, too afraid to break the momentary peace, the momentary reprieve from their breaking hearts, the momentary trip back to a time when three little words were bigger than everything else. They were holding on to the fleeting belief that maybe this wasn't the end...

"Come on," Tristan said finally, "we'll figure out a plan on the way back." He stepped away and paused before reaching for her hand.

"Tristan," Kira sighed. His fingers stopped in midair, inches from Kira. He looked at her, with an expression mixed between daring and disbelief.

"Tristan, we need to go to London first," Kira said hesitantly. "We need the conduits to help us take Aldrich down."

"We need Luke, you mean," he said bitterly, jerking his arm back to his side. Kira hated the snarl gathering on his lips.

"No, we need help. We need a plan," Kira urged.

"Don't bother denying it," Tristan said and laughed darkly. "You know, I thought we might be able to get through this without talking about Luke, without mentioning him. But now I'm the idiot." His voice was rising with his anger. "I heard him tell you he loved you outside of the ball. I've listened to your heart flutter every time he's walked into a room after that, heard your breath catch every time you've met his eyes, heard—"

"There's nothing going on between Luke and me," Kira interrupted, reaching for Tristan. He moved away.

"Keep telling yourself that," he spat, then turned and started walking away from Kira, swatting the leaves of the willow tree out of his way.

"Tristan!" Kira yelled and ran after him, but it was no use against his speed. His black hair had almost disappeared behind the trees on the road by the time Kira stepped free of the willow. He paused for a moment before turning around to look at Kira one more time. He reached his hand up to his mouth, cupping the air around his lips.

"Do me a favor," he yelled across the pond. Kira nodded. She would do anything to make things better between them.

"Please just..." The shadow of sadness flickered across his face before a hard exterior returned. "Just don't tell him we broke up."

And with that, Tristan was gone.

Chapter Eleven

Broke up.

The phrase kept spinning through Kira's mind as she continued the drive to London on her own. She mindlessly followed the directions on the GPS, barely registering the computerized voice as it navigated her through the twisting English countryside.

Broke up.

A honk screamed at her and Kira focused her eyes on the road again, blinking away the bleary film blocking her vision.

Broke up.

Kira loosened her hands on the wheel, feeling blisters start to rise on her palm. She tried to control her heaving breaths, tried to breathe in and out to the count of four.

Broke up.

Ahead, a sign told Kira she was less than ten

kilometers from London—from Luke. But was she driving toward someone or away from someone else?

Broke up.

Kira readjusted in her seat.

"We broke up," Kira whispered to herself. Finally saying it out loud made it feel real, made her insides coil a little tighter, and made the pain in her heart ache a little harder.

She was in shock, yet she had seen it coming. As soon as Kira had started the lie, had chosen being a conduit over being with Tristan, she had known that the end of their relationship was coming, that there was no escaping this moment. But still, those two words sounded wrong.

Kira was a conduit. Tristan a vampire. People had been telling them for months that they couldn't be together, that they were wrong for each other.

But they weren't, Kira thought sadly. For the past few months, they had been exactly right for each other. Until Kira decided to change the rules. Until she, without realizing it, bumped Tristan down to number two on her list of priorities. Because, if Kira was being honest, as soon as she had stepped foot in Sonnyville, her mind had started shifting. Being a conduit started to become more and more important. Her powers not only strengthened, but wove themselves tightly around her heart. And only when she was faced with the possibility of losing them did Kira fully understand how much being a conduit meant to her.

Kira took one hand off the wheel and placed it over her chest, letting a string of light warm her heart. The heat was comforting. It felt like the very essence of life was pumping into her veins, strengthening and calming her. And even though the flames couldn't heal her pain at having lost Tristan, they reminded Kira why she had done it in the first place. She loved him. She really, truly did love him. And part of her would probably always ache for him. But another part of her was okay with what had happened, okay with the loss.

"You have arrived at your destination."

Kira looked at the GPS. The green arrow representing her car was blinking over a red and white target, announcing her arrival at Luke's address.

Her heart seemed to stop and speed up at the same time.

What would she do when she saw him? Touching him, even just to hug him, seemed like a betrayal. Tristan's last words echoed in her brain. She couldn't blame him for the nasty tone and snide remark. He was hurt and angry, and was it possible he had been right?

Looking away from the small map, Kira parked the car and turned it off. Without the air conditioning on, the vehicle started to heat up, but she didn't feel like moving.

Luke hadn't seemed angry on the phone. Kira thought he might have even sounded excited. But what if he was lying? What if he was still angry with her about the airport? Kira didn't know if she could handle another fight right now.

But Aldrich's beady black eyes invaded her vision, and she opened the car door, stepping into the somewhat clean London air. This was all about finding out what Aldrich was up to—and after so much heartache, Kira almost wished Aldrich had an apocalyptic plan in the works. At least then, her actions would be justified. At least then, it wouldn't all have been in vain.

And with that thought pushing her along, Kira punched the access code to the building and walked through the front door. Looking around, she realized it was an apartment building. She took the elevator to the top floor, walked down one long, perfectly straight hallway before stopping outside of apartment ten.

She heard muffled voices through the wooden door. Laughter. A deep response that didn't sound like Luke. Unable to fight the urge, Kira reached out with her mind, searching for Luke's. After a few seconds, Kira felt it, felt him. Light, bubbly, and unconcerned despite the nature of his visit to London. There was no anger, no hint of bitterness. It was pure Luke. Kira let his confidence roll over her, hoping his ease would sink into her brain, before releasing the hold. It wasn't really fair to spy on him when he had no idea she was there.

No longer nervous, Kira raised her hand, poised to knock, when the door swung open, catching her in the act.

A boy, blond but not Luke, was looking at her with a confused squint. Kira opened her mouth to speak, but her eyes slid over his shoulder and the sound caught in her throat.

Luke.

His hair was disheveled and longer than Kira remembered—a mix of gold and honey that now stuck over his ears a bit. His tanned skin was spotted with freckles, from his cheeks down along his arms. He was too tall for the old English apartment. Kira saw him duck through a doorframe, bending his long torso to squeeze underneath. A smile played on his lips, teasing with a hint of laughter as though left over from a joke Kira had just missed. It made her smile, turning her lips without her realizing it.

"Who's ther—" Luke started to say, but froze when his eyes met Kira's. Kira caught the emerald sparkle even from this distance and saw his features lighten just a shade, but it was enough. Enough to know that he really wasn't angry, that maybe she was even forgiven.

"Kira!" He grinned.

As if under a spell, Kira found herself pushing past the boy in the doorway to run for Luke.

"Oi!" the boy said with a distinctly English accent, but Kira was already catapulting off the ground and into Luke's arms. She flung her hands around his neck, burying her face in the crook of his shoulder, relieved when he caught her in a tight embrace. Tears sprang into her eyes as the stress of the past couple of days caught up with her, but she was also laughing against his chest. The rumble of his body let Kira know Luke was laughing as well.

"'Suppose they know each other, then?" the other boy said.

"Looks like," another British accent responded, but this one was higher pitched and female.

Self-consciously, Kira unbent her legs, searching for the ground with her feet. Luke set her down, but kept an arm around her waist. She didn't have the will to push it off, but turned her head toward the voices she had heard.

A boy and girl, a little older than Luke, were standing together in the entryway, looking at Kira with mild amusement. Realizing how crazy she must look, Kira wiped at the water just below her lashes.

"Hi," she said with a wave. "I'm—"

"Kira," the boy supplied. "We know. Luke's only been here for an hour and already he won't shut up about you." Luke's fingers tightened on her waist affectionately.

"We thought he was a bit of a nutter, really," the girl chimed in. "He never told us you were dating."

Kira stepped away from Luke as Tristan's face flashed into her head. "Uh, well, we're not," she said awkwardly. Two pairs of eyebrows raised.

"Anyway," Luke coughed. "Kira this is Jack and that's Mary Beth, the two London based conduits who agreed to host me."

"Nice to meet you," Kira said, fighting the heat rising on her cheeks.

"We'll just be in here." Luke shrugged toward the door behind him and pulled Kira through the opening...into a bedroom.

Picking the corner farthest from the door, Kira sat down on the mattress and tucked her feet beneath her.

Before Luke had time to close the door, Kira blurted out, "I'm sorry." He opened his mouth to speak, but Kira charged on.

"No, wait, let me finish. It was torture, and I mean absolute torture, to think that something I had done made you hate me. And as soon as I sat on that plane, I knew I had made a mistake. I tried to call you, but then we took off and it was too late. And that plane ride was the worst in my life. I could barely even function, thinking I had lost you as a friend. I just—I felt lost and alone, and I hope that you can forgive me some day."

Kira paused, looking up from her hands, which were clenched in the folds of her T-shirt. To her surprise, Luke was grinning. Barely five minutes together and he was already annoying her.

"What?" Kira asked. "Do you think my total anguish is funny?"

"A little, yeah," he said and flopped down next to her on the bed.

"Well, it was all your fault. You're the one who said

you were done and wouldn't call me back!" Kira crossed her arms.

"Whoa, no way." Luke shook his head. "No way are you turning this around on me. It was your brilliant plan to completely ditch me in the airport with no warning or explanation." Kira could hear the slight tightness in his voice. He wasn't totally over it yet.

"So yell at me," Kira said. It was what she had been expecting anyway.

"Nah." Luke shrugged and laughed at Kira's exasperated expression. She, in turn, could feel her stubborn side coming out full force. Kira raised her eyebrows and stared him down, waiting for some explanation for his bizarre attitude.

"Well, what do you want to do then?"

"Nothing." He folded an arm behind his head and fell back against the bed. "I'm just going to lie here and enjoy being in charge for once."

Kira slapped his leg. "Seriously?"

"Seriously." He nodded and kept his eyes on her. Kira didn't like the mischievous gleam gathering there.

"I haven't always been in charge," Kira said slowly, getting a snort from Luke.

"Come on." He sat up quickly. "First, I was the one who kept being a conduit from you. So when you found out, you totally guilt-tripped me. Then you saved my life and landed yourself in a coma, putting me in your debt for life.

Now, you can go inside my head whenever you want and know exactly how I'm feeling. Following Diana to Baltimore was completely your idea, and do I even need to mention this little European adventure?"

"Okay, okay," Kira said, not liking the slightly smug look on his face. "Well, what do I have to do to make things even again?"

"I think I'm charging you…" He looked around the room, pretending to be deep in thought. His eyes landed on her, sending a slight jolt down her spine. Kira put all of her concentration into keeping Luke's mind separate from her own. She could feel excitement and heat coming from the other side of the barrier, making a slight flush rise to her cheeks.

"You owe me one kiss," Luke said. The lighthearted grin was gone. Kira hesitated before breaking contact.

"Luke, be serious," she said and attempted an easy laugh, trying to play it off as a joke.

"I am," he said, and something in his tone made Kira pay attention. "You see, I realized something. Well, actually, my sister helped me out with this one. But I finally realized that you are totally into me, you just won't admit it."

"How'd you get there?" Kira said, letting mirth flow into her words in an attempt to keep the mood light.

"I admit it. I was mad at you—I mean really furious—after you left me in that airport. I didn't want to think about you or even look at you after that happened.

When I finally got home, everyone kept asking where you were and why you didn't come back with me. I told the council that our plans had changed, made them think I was in on it, but I was really seething." He clenched his fists with the memory.

The slight movement made Kira wince. She didn't want to remember how badly she'd hurt him or the coldness she'd heard in his voice little more than a week before.

"As you can see…" He put his arms out wide. "That all changed. My sister knew something else was up. She's got this like freakish sixth sense. Anyway, she pulled me aside and made me tell her what happened. I thought she would hate you—I mean, you two weren't on the best terms during your last visit—but instead, she was happy when I finished telling her what happened. And that's what she helped me realize. If we had just been friends, if you really didn't feel anything for me, you would have told me what you were up to. You would have explained that it was for my own safety, you would have given me some sort of heads up, and maybe still sneaked off, but it wouldn't have been a complete and utter lie. No, you weren't afraid that telling me would make me want to follow you and come along. You were afraid that if you told me the plan, you wouldn't be able to leave me behind. You sort of love me, and if you had told me the plan, you might not have been able to go somewhere alone with Tristan. You might have wanted me to come along instead."

"That's a great theory," Kira whispered. Her ears were drowned out by the thumping of her heart.

"That's what I thought too," he said happily, turning to Kira in his normal teasing manner. "And, not to sound too self-confident, but one kiss ought to show you I'm right."

"So when does this kiss need to happen?" Kira asked, looking at the wall behind Luke rather than at his face.

He looked down at his empty wrist. "I've got some time right now..."

Kira wanted to throw a pillow at him. But getting a pillow would mean she had to reach over his stretched out body, and she wasn't sure if she could deal with the proximity. Something in Luke's words rang uncannily true to Kira, but she couldn't get Tristan out of her head. The cold, accusing chill to his words when she mentioned Luke's name still stung. She owed it to everything she and Tristan had had to turn the conversation back to Aldrich, back to what she had actually come here to discuss.

"We have more important things to talk about right now," Kira said softly, letting a foreboding deepness lace through the words.

"What? Did Tristan lose a fang?" He threw a playful pout in Kira's direction.

"No," Kira paused and took a deep breath. "But I might gain some."

"What?" The grin was gone from his face, and he

reached a hand out to touch Kira's arm. His lips were drawn in a tight line.

"Aldrich said he can turn me into a vampi—"

"You can't be serious!" Luke interjected, tightening his grip on her bicep. "Kira, it's not—that's crazy. What are you even saying?"

She rolled her eyes.

"Would you let me finish?" Kira said with a shaky laugh. "Aldrich said he can turn me into a vampire, but I obviously don't want to become one." Luke leaned back a little, loosening his hold. "That's not exactly what I told Aldrich though," Kira continued and began telling Luke everything that had happened since she had landed in London.

Kira started with his castle, with Aldrich's bizarre sense of style, which got an expected grimace and "creepy" from Luke. Without stopping, Kira moved onto meeting her mother—the shock of believing she was a vampire and Aldrich's notion that the ability to resist was the only reason conduits were never turned. Kira had to stop Luke from interrupting. He kept shaking his head and trying to explain how it was not possible for conduits to turn, how some had tried before and failed, that they had run extensive experiments with conduit and vampire blood. Eventually, Kira slapped her hand over his mouth to stop him.

"I know," she said firmly, going on to describe the look in her mother's eyes that had told her she was a fake.

Kira skipped over the night with Tristan, wanting to keep it private and to herself. Luke didn't need to hear about his shattered dreams or Kira's brief belief that being a vampire wouldn't be as horrible as it sounded. Better for Luke to think that Kira never swayed, never faltered in her desire to keep her powers.

Kira rushed past the next few days of sitting with her mother discussing the transformation and talking with Aldrich about his past.

Eventually, she reached that morning, reached the glass tunnel system within the house. Luke nodded when Kira confirmed that the woman was not her mother, but was an old vampire only pretending to be Lana. She described the dungeon she'd found, telling Luke that finding out Aldrich's plan wasn't the only thing they needed to figure out. A rescue mission was also in order. She told Luke about the female vampire Pavia, and how she thought the girl knew a lot more than she was letting on.

But then Kira hesitated. Thinking back to the flaming redhaired man and his accusation that Kira was already falling, had already taken one step toward turning into a vampire.

"What?" Luke asked, sensing that Kira was holding back.

Did she really want to hear what Luke had to say? Kira remembered the way Luke had looked at her when her eyes had first turned blue, the way he'd stepped back, shocked and like a stranger. It had only lasted a second, but fear tainted his expression in those few moments after Diana's death. What if he couldn't deny the Punisher beliefs? What if all he did was make the possibility that Kira's soul was blackening seem all the more real?

"Nothing," Kira finally said. Luke put his hand on her knee reassuringly.

"You can tell me," he said. Kira looked at him and smiled weakly.

"I'm just a little scared, you know? I don't know what to do." She shrugged.

"Why don't you just leave? We can treat this as a normal rescue mission and send the trained conduits in. I promise they won't come shooting through the windows this time."

"I can't. Part of me knows that Tristan and I should have both left that castle the minute I realized it wasn't really my mother waiting for me, but a bigger part of me knows I needed to stay. I can't fight this feeling that whatever Aldrich is planning is huge, and definitely involves me. We just need a mode of attack." Kira started chewing on her lip, lost in thought about how they could corner Aldrich and get the information out of him. How do you trap someone who can move any object in the world just by thinking about it? He would bring the house down on any conduits who tried to trap him. He could easily knock Kira out, kill Tristan, and escape without straining a muscle.

"This is really important to you? Important enough to not run away?" Luke asked. Kira nodded affirmation. "Then the only thing to do is let him try to turn you."

"What?" Kira blinked. Those were probably the last words she ever expected Luke to say.

"Delay him for one night, make some excuse, and tomorrow let him go through with whatever ceremony he has planned. When you've learned what he is up to and why trying to turn you is so important, you and Tristan can attack. Aldrich will be vulnerable. He won't be expecting it and I'll bring a team of conduits, so we can enter the house while he's distracted. Half of us will go save the prisoners and the other half will help you destroy Aldrich. It's risky, but I don't see any other option."

"But," Kira started. It was a solid idea, and the only solution to finding out what Aldrich wanted. Tristan would be fine, Kira knew, Aldrich would never hurt him. He viewed Tristan as more of a son than an enemy. And when all of the conduits arrived and his plan was thwarted, Aldrich would probably do the smart thing and run. But there was a knot in Kira's throat preventing her from agreeing to Luke's idea.

Realizing what her real hesitation was, Kira quietly asked, "But what if I do turn?"

"Kira, it's not possible. I—"

"But what if it is?" Kira interjected. "What if I heard somewhere that mixed breed conduits can turn?" She still didn't want to go into the depths of the Punisher beliefs, but if she was offering herself to Aldrich, Kira needed to be prepared.

Luke took both of her hands, forcing her to look him in the eyes. "Do you really think that I would ever suggest this plan if there were the slightest chance that you would turn? Conduits cannot become vampires. It is just not possible. I believe it with every fiber of my being."

What if I'm more than a conduit, Kira thought quietly, *what if I really am some sort of angel?* But the word sounded ridiculous to her, silly even. An angel? Who was she kidding?

Kira took a deep breath and clenched Luke's fingers, which were sturdy and warm. "Okay then, let's do it."

"Excellent," Luke said, then turned toward the door to shout, "Jack! Mary Beth!"

"Yeah, mate?" An intermix between male and female voices shouted back at them through the door.

"Get in here."

The door opened a moment later and Mary Beth's blonde head peered nervously around the bend. When she saw Kira and Luke sitting a comfortable distance apart, her features brightened and they walked in.

Kira looked toward Luke and could practically see the wheels spinning in his head as he started formulating a plan with Jack and Mary Beth. Paper and pens were soon supplied to all four of them, and Kira drew plans of

Aldrich's home, describing each room and remembering the secret tunnel system as best she could. To slightly shocked gazes, Kira asked them to let the vampire Pavia go free when they reached the prisoners. Vampires caught by conduits were usually bound and questioned, but Pavia had already been imprisoned for too long. And Kira had a feeling that Pavia would happily join the fight if given the chance.

Before long, conversation switched to conduit tactics, and Kira lost track in the jumble of names and strategies she had never gotten the chance to study. They started talking about the part of the fight Kira wouldn't be involved in, and she turned away to look out the window at the gray London sky. Her mind began to wander, and eventually she found herself glassy-eyed and thinking of Tristan.

His presence was vital to the plan. Aldrich had to think everything was going his way, that Kira wanted to turn. But she couldn't bring herself to tell Luke what happened, that Tristan had run away. She didn't want to face the fact that he might not be coming back. The minute doubt in him was there—heck, had Kira and Tristan switched places, Kira probably would have run away and never looked back.

But Tristan knew that if he didn't return to Aldrich's with her, it would probably cost Kira her life. She tried to picture his muscular frame, walking slowly down the side of a country road, mind lost in thought and body immune to the damp air. He was out there. He had to be waiting for her somewhere.

"Uh, Kira?" Luke asked. His open, honest eyes looked at her with concern.

"I have to go," she said and stood abruptly, ruffling the papers by her legs. She needed to leave. No one needed her here any longer, and she had to find Tristan. Things would be better, somehow.

Remembering her manners, Kira turned to Jack and Mary Beth, saying how pleased she was to meet them. Kira told Luke to text her tomorrow, updating her on his progress. And then she was following her feet as they led her to the hallway, out the door, and over toward the rickety elevator. Kira pressed the down button and waited while ascending numbers lit up above the door.

"Kira!" Luke careened out of the apartment and walked determinedly toward her. Kira turned and waited for him to keep talking. He stopped a foot away from her and looked down at his feet, jumping on his toes a little bit.

"So I was thinking, I don't really like being in charge." He grinned.

"Really? You seemed to have it all under control in there," Kira said, eying him warily.

"Still," he said, letting the word drag out as he stepped closer. Kira could feel the heat gathering in the small space between their bodies. "I think it's high time I do something really stupid."

"Luke," Kira said and turned away from him. He grabbed her hand. An electric charge zipped up her arm at his touch. She tried to ignore the buzz spreading throughout her body, flushing her cheeks and setting her nerves on end. Luke gently pulled her around so she faced him and slipped his free hand up to her face. Gently, he rubbed his thumb along her cheek, tilting her head up ever so slightly, forcing Kira to meet his eyes. They burned her skin.

"Luke," Kira said. It came out as a whisper and not in the stern, commanding way Kira had meant it to.

"You can yell at me after," he said softly and kissed her.

Chapter Twelve

As soon as Luke's lips touched Kira's, a torrent of emotions rushed through her body. The barrier she had spent so much time building crashed, letting Luke's thoughts flood into her like a tidal wave. Her mind was consumed with his excitement, his happiness, his fulfillment. It was Luke's pulse rapidly beating through her veins, his heart bursting with the perfection of the moment, his limbs that tingled with each touch of her hands as they trailed up his chest.

But his feelings were Kira's. They were one, completely matched in the moment. One of his hands found its way to her back, burning a path along her skin. He pulled her closer, or was it Kira who pulled him closer? Her fingers stretched into his hair, playing with the short, soft strands at the base of his neck. He matched her movement, running his hand up into her curls, bringing her lips even firmer against his.

And then, a feeling settled in her heart, matched by Luke's surging in her head. She felt light, as though she were floating on a cloud, and Luke's body was the only thing keeping her grounded. Pure gold seemed to pump through her veins, making every touch richer, every emotion fuller. Every outside distraction disappeared, and a rush of fire pulsed down her body.

They kept kissing until there was no air left in their lungs and an innate will to live forced them apart to catch a breath. Kira rested her forehead against Luke's, breathing heavily, and she slowly opened her eyes to find his. The yellows and oranges in his irises seemed to dance they were so bright, reminding her of flickering flames. Kira knew her eyes must be burning a stark blue, but Luke never flinched, never looked away.

A smile tugged at her lips, but from the corner of her eyes, Kira saw real flames swirling, burning and sinking into Luke's skin.

Shocked, Kira pulled away from him, clenching her fists down by her side.

"I'm sorry, Luke. I didn't even realize." Kira looked away, cursing her lack of control. Luke captured her small hands in his, covering the flames and letting them sink into him.

"You can't hurt me, Kira."

But the cool air she was sucking in through her lips had cleared Kira's head.

"I have to go," Kira said as Tristan's wounded face glimmered to life in her mind. How could she have lost control like this?

"Kira." Luke tugged on her hand, not letting her leave. The elevator dinged, opening behind her, and Kira wrenched free of his hold.

"I have to go," she pleaded. "I'll see you tomorrow." The door slid closed and Luke's confused face disappeared behind a wall of metal. Kira wished it would be so easy to get Tristan out of her mind. But his features settled in like stone, determined to haunt her.

He had only asked one thing of her, one little thing, to not fall right into Luke's arms. And though they were open and waiting, Kira still didn't think she would fly into them so willingly or so quickly. Luke was her best friend, there weren't supposed to be feelings there. He was her guardian, her protector. But that kiss was seared into her memory—was he right? Was one kiss all it would take? Kira had mistaken his words for typical Luke cockiness, but as her body stirred at the mere thought of what just happened…but no, she pushed the memory from her head.

She needed to find Tristan. She needed to apologize, even if he didn't know what she was apologizing for. Because Tristan could never know what just happened. It would kill him, hurt him more than her powers ever could.

They had broken up, broken apart. But that didn't mean Kira wanted to lose him forever.

When the elevator slid open again, Kira ran to the car and revved the engine to life. The sky started to darken as the sun disappeared behind London's buildings, sinking into the earth, signaling the night.

She found her way back to the small pond, hoping Tristan was waiting for her to return. Pushing aside the swaying branches of the willow tree, Kira discovered an empty space filled only with sleeping ducks.

As she continued down country roads, her headlights fought with the misty air. Every shadow caught her attention. Every shape in the distance looked like Tristan, looked like a lone walking figure, until she drove close enough to recognize them as a tree or a gateway or an animal. Her breath caught in her throat as her eyes played tricks on her. Every moment of anticipation made her heart race, and disappointment darkened her thoughts the longer she went without finding him.

Kira's eyes flashed to the GPS. Aldrich's house was moving closer and closer to her tiny car, or maybe it was the other way around. But Kira felt like it was Aldrich who was creeping up on her, suffocating her and pulling her toward him.

And then, close to the ground, Kira saw something pristinely white through the fog—a T-shirt connected to a still body. She slowed the car, stuttering to a stop. Kira knew it was Tristan. He sat next to the road with his knees bent, head sunk in between them with hands gripping his neck.

His shirt was damp from the misty night, and it clung to his strong shoulders.

After what seemed like an hour, he slowly lifted his head up. His normally bright eyes were dark, matching the scene around him, barely shining against the flood of the headlights. They looked bloodshot, if that was even possible for a vampire.

Kira turned the car off. She stepped out, hesitantly. He watched her, never taking his sight from her as she approached.

"Tristan?" Kira leaned against the hood of the car, afraid to get any closer.

"Did you find him?" Tristan asked. His deep voice broke through the silence in the air. Kira knew what he was really asking.

"Nothing happened," she said. The lie burned her tongue. "I didn't tell him anything." Tristan's muscles relaxed and he let out a prolonged breath.

"Did you figure out a plan?"

"Yeah." Kira nodded.

"Fill me in during the ride back to the castle," he said and stood up. Even in misery he was graceful. His movements were fluid, like a panther in the night. But Kira forced her gaze away. Tristan wasn't hers to admire anymore.

"Tristan," Kira said when they were both settled in the car.

"Don't," he said, "let's just get through the next day."

"Okay."

Kira started the car and pulled back onto the road. For the first few minutes, no one said anything. Tristan stared out the window. Every time her gaze flicked toward him, Kira was greeted with dark hair and the back of his neck.

"So what did you and..." He swallowed. "What did you guys decide?" Kira filled him in—tactical discussions were safe territory. They would go through with the ceremony, trapping Aldrich at his weakest moment. The conduits would come and help with the fight. And Aldrich would run away or Kira would kill him. Those were the only two endings she saw.

"When will we make our move?" Tristan asked, speaking for the first time since Kira started talking. He had been nodding silently along with her words, agreeing to everything she said.

Kira thought about his question. When would be the perfect time to attack? Aldrich and her mother had told her most of the process to becoming a vampire. Aldrich would need to bite her, drink some of her blood. Her neck was the best spot—close to her heart and a major artery—but Kira wouldn't be offering anything more than her wrist. Then everyone would wait a few seconds for her blood to pass through his heart and circulate through his veins, mixing with the already vampiric blood, blending into his system until it started turning. It was the blood, they said, that turned and gained qualities of a vampire. Blood always had to change first.

And when Aldrich felt Kira's foreign blood transform to match his, he would cut his own hand and press it against the open wound in her wrist, forcing his blood into her body. Then, like a virus, the vampirism would enter and begin to turn her normal blood. When all her blood had changed, the rest of her body would start to follow.

Kira shivered at the thought, but knew what she had to do.

"When he starts to flood his blood into mine, that's when you need to attack him. Go for the kill right away," Kira said. "He'll expect me to struggle, but not you. Aldrich will be caught completely off guard."

"You sure you want to risk that? Letting him go so far in the process?" Tristan asked, trying hard to keep any bitterness from his voice.

Thinking of Luke's steadfast denial that conduits could turn, Kira nodded. "I can fight the change, I know it," she said softly, trying not to hurt Tristan any more than she had to.

"Then there's nothing else to talk about."

"I do have one more thing," Kira said quickly, before he had time to shut her out again. "Pavia. I need to talk to her again. She's hiding something, something that might help us."

"What do you mean?" Tristan asked. His cloudy mood cleared a bit as genuine interest colored his words. He was curious.

"I think," Kira started talking, not really knowing what she meant. But then the realization hit. "I think Pavia must have stolen my mother's memories. When I met her, she showed me her power, just the flash of an old memory. But it makes perfect sense. If Aldrich ever did have my mother, Pavia could have taken her memories and given them to this other vampire woman, the one who looks like my mother. That must be how she knows so much, so many personal details."

"Yeah." Tristan tapped his fingers against his knee, thinking. "Yeah, that makes sense. But I still don't understand how she looks so much like her."

"Me neither," Kira said and shook her head. One more mystery for her to solve. "But maybe Pavia does. You need to distract Aldrich tomorrow, distract him long enough for me to sneak back into those tunnels."

"Right after breakfast, I'll pull him away and tell him we need to talk in private. I'll make sure to give you as much time as I can, but I can't promise more than an hour or he may realize we're up to something."

Kira nodded, opening her mouth to discuss their plan a little bit more.

"We're about a minute away from Aldrich's hearing distance," Tristan interrupted.

Knowing time had run out to really make things better, Kira reached her hand across the car, latching onto Tristan's. "I'm so sorry. You know that, right? I wish things could be different, that we could be together."

Tristan kept hold of her hand but didn't respond. Kira turned her attention back to the road and tried not to listen to the seconds tick by in her head. They seemed long and drawn out, passing too quickly but also not fast enough.

And then suddenly, Tristan looked at her and said, "Kira, I know that Luke is upset, but does he have to call you every five minutes? What is his problem? He lost. He's got to let it go."

They had passed the line of Aldrich's hearing. The show had begun.

"I know, Tristan," Kira said, looking at the hurt in his eyes even though his voice sounded like that of a champion. "I told him I'm changing, that I wouldn't be able to see him again. It'll just take some time for that to sink in, I think."

"Well, he has a day to get it together if he ever wants to apologize for the way he screamed at you."

"A day?" Kira asked, following the plan she and Tristan had thought up. Aldrich was expecting the change to happen tonight, but they had decided that that was too fast to put the entire plan into action. The conduits needed a day to regroup, and Kira needed a day to get her feelings under control. They wanted Aldrich to believe the delay was completely organic, not a rallying day.

"Yeah, I think we need to push it off for a few hours," Tristan said, rubbing his thumb over the back of her hand. "I don't want our new life together to start while I'm angry at Luke. I don't want anything in my head but love." His words sounded sincere, but Kira saw the slight glisten to his lashes.

"Me neither," Kira said, trying to keep the sadness from her voice. "Why don't you relax for a little while, we're almost back to the castle."

Tristan nodded, turning on the music in the car to drown out the silence. They had planned to talk more, to explain more in the car for Aldrich to overhear. But it was too much too soon. Both of their feelings were too raw, and Tristan leaned back in his seat to close his eyes.

Kira hummed along with the songs she recognized and kept going over the plan in her head. Much too soon, the now familiar driveway appeared around the bend. Kira turned in, and Tristan pretended to wake to the sound of crunching gravel as Kira approached the castle.

It was eerie how similar the trip was to the first time Kira pulled in, so similar and yet so different. The ruins to the side of the castle, with their twisting and turning shadows, still frightened Kira. The castle loomed over them, still menacing. The thought of Aldrich still pierced just a little. Kira couldn't quite cut the fear that he was onto them, that any minute he would walk out enraged and ready to fight.

The only difference was that Kira felt alone in her fight. Tristan was beside her, helping her, but they weren't a team—not anymore. And Luke, Kira didn't know what to think about it. Last time she drove to this castle, she was afraid Luke would never speak to her again. Now Kira was frightened because speaking to him, just talking, might not be enough.

And like the first time, Aldrich had heard them. As soon as the car stopped, both doors popped open on their own. The front door swerved open, revealing a silhouetted figure in a dark suit.

"How was the trip?" Aldrich cheerfully called to them.

"Difficult," Kira said, not needing to lie at all. Aldrich would know if she were lying. The next day would be all about hard to discern half-truths. "But I did what I needed to do."

Tristan circled around the car and put an arm around Kira, kissing her on top of her head as he did it.

"And how did Lucas take everything?" Aldrich asked.

"As well as could be expected," Kira said with her thoughts focused on Tristan. "I think it came as quite a shock."

Aldrich laughed. Kira fought the urge to kick him for finding even the pretend idea of Luke in pain funny. "As long as he doesn't come around with a false sense of chivalry, trying to save his fair maiden." Aldrich's eyes flicked to Kira with a hard look, a warning Kira thought. But maybe she was seeing things.

"Luke definitely doesn't have any false ideas," Tristan said with a grin. But he squeezed Kira's arm at the word "false" and she knew what he was really accusing.

"Yeah, he's totally out of the picture." Kira returned the squeeze. Two could play at that game. She may have technically done the breaking up, and she may have technically done the one thing Tristan had asked her not to, but that didn't mean she was okay with biting remarks. They had twenty-four hours more of the charade, and it was way too soon for bickering innuendos.

Aldrich stepped inside, looking over his shoulder at Kira. "And how are you, Kira?"

She thought about the next day, the battle that was about to begin. "I'm ready," she said and meant it. Kira was ready for answers, ready for the fight, and ready to take Aldrich down.

"As am I," Aldrich responded. Flashes of icy blue pierced his nearly black eyes, giving away his excitement. "As am I," he repeated, this time with a note of finality, just a hint of victory. He blinked and the expression was gone, almost as though it never happened.

"I'm afraid we'll have to wait a day though," Aldrich continued speaking. Tristan and Kira were hoping for this. Aldrich had overheard them and was pretending that he wanted to delay things. As Kira assumed, Aldrich was being very accommodating. He didn't want to scare her off.

"Why's that?" Tristan asked, pulling Kira up against his body, trying to let Aldrich see he didn't necessarily want to wait.

"My dear wife…" It took everything Kira had not to flinch at that word. "Has gone to bed. Her excitement got the better of her."

More likely, Aldrich threw a fit when he first realized Kira wanted to wait to perform the ceremony tomorrow. Judging by the intimate scene Kira had witnessed before, Aldrich would have had no problems taking his frustrations out on the other vampire. But better that than the prisoners.

"Well, I guess we'll just be going to bed too then," Kira said casually, probably overly so.

"Actually," Aldrich said as Kira felt an invisible tug on her shirt, holding her back from the step she had begun, "I was hoping I could speak with you for a moment."

"Of course," Kira said smoothly. "We're about to become family after all." She turned to Tristan, wrapping her hand around his arm and leaning in for a quick kiss. "I'll see you up there," she said, ignoring how tense his muscles were. Tristan slipped free of her hold and stepped slowly up the stairs. He wouldn't meet her gaze, but just kept on walking. Kira listened all the way, until the quiet thud of his steps disappeared to her human ears.

Aldrich led Kira into the living room down the hall, and she sat down on the sofa across from him.

"Things seem tense with Tristan," Aldrich said. It was a statement, not a question, which meant Kira wasn't playing her role well enough.

"Just because of Luke." She sighed. "He didn't take it well," Kira continued, hoping Aldrich believed she was talking about Luke, when really the image of Tristan retreating around the bend and leaving her was playing on repeat in her mind. "He felt so hurt and abandoned."

"I hope that hasn't swayed you at all."

"No," Kira said sternly, catching the menacing tone in Aldrich's seemingly kind words. His hand on her knee tightened involuntarily. A minute movement for a vampire, but the ounce of pain in her leg revealed his threat.

"Good, because even a sliver of doubt might stop the turning tomorrow." He leaned toward her, eyes narrowing as he searched her face for any sign of hesitancy, "and turning into a vampire is not a pleasant process."

Kira didn't back down. The icicles in his eyes were probably mirrored by the fire in Kira's as she responded, "I'm not afraid." *Of you*, Kira added silently to herself.

He leaned back, satisfied. "No, I did not think you would be. Unsure maybe, doubtful even, but not afraid."

"I think Tristan is more nervous than I am," Kira said, hoping Aldrich would take the bait.

"Ah yes, worried about your safety no doubt. I'll speak with him tomorrow." *Hook, line, and sinker*—Kira thought and kept the grin off of her face. The plan was progressing perfectly.

"I should probably go talk to him a little bit now," Kira said and stood up. She could only handle Aldrich in small bursts before his superior attitude made him completely unbearable.

"Have a good last night, Kira." His wink curled her insides.

Kira nodded, keeping her face controlled, and turned away from him, but not before a slow smile spread across his lips. He folded his hands, palms together, and brought both pointer fingers to his lips. His eyes glazed over, lightening with every second, and Kira decided to go as quickly as possible.

When Kira reached the bedroom she shared with Tristan, the curtains were open and a sliver of moonlight dipped between them, creating a perfect pathway to the bed. Tristan lay there, facing away from Kira. She wondered if he was actually asleep or if his eyes were staring out the open window, wide and watery.

Quietly, Kira inched around the room and changed into her pajamas. She stepped closer to her side of the large bed, wondering why the space there had never seemed as large as it did in that moment.

Trying not to disturb Tristan, Kira pulled the covers back and slipped underneath. At first, she rolled to her side, looking at the silvery lines of the moon glistening against his dark hair.

"Tristan?" Kira whispered, aching to reach across the bed and turn him toward her. His wide shoulders cast a shadow across the mattress that barely touched her outstretched arm, but it might be the only touch she would get from him that night.

"Tristan?" Kira whispered again. Maybe he really was asleep. His body lifted and fell with heavy breaths.

A dull throb started deep in her chest, pressing down on her heart until it felt like a weight was actually resting atop her body. The more Kira stared a foot across from her at the back of Tristan's head, the wider the distance became. He stretched further away from her, shrinking back from the hand reaching out to touch him. A centimeter from the taut muscles in his back, Kira paused.

If he needed peace, a reprieve from the ache in his own heart, it was the least she could give him.

Reluctantly, Kira flipped over to her other side and fluffed her pillow. It wasn't nearly as comfortable as the crook of Tristan's arm, but for the night she could make do. What was really odd, Kira thought as she hugged the blanket closer, was how cold she was without Tristan's body close to her. Despite the frost of his skin, Kira missed it. That chill was welcome. It cooled down the heat of her own body. But the chill she felt this night was bone deep, and Kira didn't even think her fire would get rid of it.

But just as a shiver reverberated up her spine, the swish of skin on cotton warmed her heart. A cool arm encircled her waist, pulling her a foot across the bed and into the hard body that had always felt so soft to her. A tiny kiss, almost from a ghost, landed on her shoulder.

Kira fought the urge to turn around and break the spell. One last night in each other's arms wasn't too much to ask, and the time for words had passed.

Chapter Thirteen

When Kira woke up the next morning, Tristan was already gone. She brought a hand to her shoulder, trying to trap the feel of the soft kiss she had fallen asleep to. But like everything else in her life, it was too late, and with a sigh she rolled off the bed, landing silently on her feet.

Dressing quickly, Kira made her way downstairs to the dining room where all three of the vampires awaited her. In her rush, she missed the timing and there were still three goblets nearly emptied of blood on the table.

Kira couldn't help but notice the red tint to Tristan's lips, the slight flush on his cheeks. Controlling her reaction, she sat down next to him, kissed his cheek, and brought his hand into her lap.

"Good morning, everyone," Kira said after a moment.

"Did you sleep well?" the woman asked.

"It was the perfect last night," Kira said, squeezing Tristan's hand while she spoke and hoping he caught the real meaning of her words.

"And morning," Aldrich droned, "it's past noon already."

"Really?" Kira asked, and her stomach rumbled loudly. She laughed under her breath. Finally, some perfect timing. "Seeing as I'm still human, I need some grub."

"I thought you might like to make it yourself," Tristan told her. The idea sounded sweet, but the gesture was pre-planned—she needed a reason to be digging around the kitchen.

Kira turned to Aldrich, raising her eyebrows as if asking for permission.

"My house is your house," Aldrich said. "Besides, Tristan and I have things to discuss. Lana, my dear, why don't you start preparing for the ceremony in the meantime."

The woman nodded, and Kira caught the worshiping look in her eyes. She was a slave and didn't even realize it. The idea made Kira's toes curl in her socks.

But then Kira's stomach growled loudly again, breaking the silence.

"I'll take that as my cue to go." Kira jumped up from her seat. She kissed Tristan on the cheek, trying her best to maintain their soul mate status and ignore his rigid posture, before disappearing around the bend.

Now the work really begins, Kira thought. She walked into the kitchen and used her phone to turn some music on. Then she lit the fire on the stovetop, ran some water, and started pretending to ruffle the shelves, looking for ingredients. In the refrigerator, Kira found a secret stash of medical blood and stole two pints. Perfect for bribing Pavia.

She quickly fried some eggs, put potatoes in the oven, and started a pot of fresh oatmeal. Just in case any vampires were listening, it would sound like Kira was really in there cooking one heck of a last breakfast.

In reality, she was taking one last deep breath and standing in front of the freezer. Steeling her nerves for whatever Pavia had to show her, Kira pressed the small button on the side of the handle, and the door to the tunnels cracked silently open.

Tristan said he could guarantee her an hour of alone time, and fifteen minutes of that had already passed. When Kira found herself completely shrouded in darkness, she lit a flame and hit the tunnels at a run. Along the way, she spotted the female vampire in her room, laying out a deep red dress. But there was no sign of Tristan or Aldrich, and Kira just hoped they were in a soundproof room, oblivious to what she was doing.

Five minutes later, Kira found herself panting at the entrance of the dungeon with five curious pairs of eyes pointed in her direction.

"Didn't think we'd see you back here again after that

oh-so-dramatic exit yesterday," the female vampire, Pavia, drawled in a voice laced with sarcasm.

Still breathing heavy, Kira panted, "I came to," she stopped to breathe again, taking this as a reminder to exercise more often. "You're all going to be free in a couple hours' time." *Why not just get to the chase?* Kira thought.

"I'm starting to enjoy these little visits," Pavia said with a smirk, while the male Punisher sat up and asked, "How can this be?"

Kira chose to ignore Pavia, and she faced the other prisoners instead. "Conduits are coming to save you all. They'll be here in a few hours. I won't be with them, but I promise that you can trust everyone and that they'll keep you safe."

One of the Protector females started to speak, but Kira reached her hand out to stop her.

"I'm sorry, I can't explain anything else. I don't have time," she said, rushing her words and not caring that they lacked finesse. Then Kira turned to Pavia. "Yesterday, you said something about showing me some memories you knew I'd want to see. You know who my mother was, don't you? You know something about Aldrich's plan?"

Pavia shrugged. Her face was inscrutable. "Did you bring anything with you?" She sniffed the air, letting a smirk lighten her features. *No use hiding it*, Kira thought and retrieved two bags of blood from the grocery bag she brought with her.

"I'll give you one now, and you'll get the other one if you give me information that I can use."

"Deal," Pavia agreed and then moved languidly toward the opening of her cell. Kira dropped the bag to the ground. Lightning fast, it was cracked open and at Pavia's mouth. Before Kira could blink, the blood vanished and the bag was drip dry. Pavia smacked her lips, satisfied, before turning to Kira with an open expression. "What do you want to see?"

"Let's start with your memories. You have met her, haven't you?" Kira asked, trying not to let her voice sound too hopeful. Pavia nodded and stretched her hand out of her cell, waiting for Kira's touch. For a second, Kira met her blue eyes, and they almost seemed friendly, maybe even concerned or sorry.

But then their fingers were touching and Kira was falling, her vision was receding, her senses disappearing, her mind swirling into mush…

Kira opened her eyes, struggling against the cavity of pain in her stomach. She was hungry, so hungry. Her hands stretched forward, touching glass. She couldn't get out. But then voices were echoing down the hall, getting closer. A sweet smell startled her—sugar and wine and strawberries—floating closer and closer. Only one thing could smell so sweet, so delectable, and then a blonde woman—bleeding, hurt, barely conscious but oh so lovely—was thrown into the room.

"I want to know everything in her tiny little head," a voice snapped. Kira's attention was pulled from the woman, and she focused

on the hard black eyes of Aldrich. An instant hatred rose in her chest, a challenge. He rolled his eyes. "You are so predictable, Pavia. Must it be a fight every time?"

She didn't move.

Aldrich leaned against the glass, fingers clenched to hold in his anger. His voice was tight and commanding. "You know I always win, so quit the games and maybe I'll reward you with a taste." She tried to keep her senses closed off, but the smell of fresh blood leaking from fresh wounds was too much to ignore. The scent, now buttery and baked, filled her mind, making her inch closer to the door of her tiny cell against her will. She was so hungry.

And then her hand was reaching out, and memories flooded her body in quick flashes she couldn't even process properly. A house with a white-picket fence. A smiling woman and stern man. Blonde children running around. A bright green square. A circle of older men talking to a crowd. A dark city. An attacking vampire. A redheaded man. Fire—consuming her, lighting her up. The man again, older, love written across his features. And then concern. And then a sense of fear. A small child with blonde and red curls dusting the top of her head. Flames sprouting from pudgy hands. A house in the middle of the woods. Secrets and fear. Finally a walk through a forest. A sudden attack. Teeth sinking into her skin. A baby's cry, a man's grunt of pain, and then silence.

Kira fell back against the floor, her mind buzzing with the images, her nose buzzing with the scent.

Deep ebony black eyes stared at her, breaking through the confusion.

"Pavia, what did you see?" Aldrich asked, urgently.

"A baby..." she said slowly. Trying to gain control over the memories flashing fast-forward in her head.

"What baby?" His eyes were starting to lighten, turning from night to day in an instant. Speckles of blue that were almost white spotted the irises like falling snow. Uncontrolled excitement was evident on Aldrich's face as he reached his hand under the barricade. "Show me," he demanded, grabbing her hand.

Before she had time to register it, the memories were flooding into Aldrich's skin, sinking deeply into the crevices of his mind. She wanted to fight, wanted to deny him the thing he so clearly wanted to know, but his fingers dug like claws into her hand, and she was so hungry, she couldn't fight it.

Maniacal laughter pierced her senses, and the door of her cell was flung open. "Your reward, Pavia," Aldrich hissed and threw the blonde woman into her cell. The body landed a foot away from her, so tantalizingly close that she forgot escape was just a foot away if she could move fast enough.

But she hesitated, looking at the glistening red blood dripping on the floor next to her.

And with a hiss, her moment was gone and the door was shut once more. Kira looked down at the sallow, sunken face of the woman before her. But she didn't see a person. She saw a meal and her fangs ached for the feel of flesh. The body never even stirred as she sucked the last seconds of life from it...

The blackness took over Kira's real vision again.

"I only have one more memory of your mother,"

Pavia's voice distantly said. But before Kira could respond, swirls of colors flashed past her eyes like a spinning vortex, and she was falling once more. She blinked rapidly, trying to clear her vision, trying to bring the dancing hues together into an image…

Kira felt metal wrap tightly around her neck and felt the gaping hole in the pit of her stomach, the pain far worse than it had been before. Her vision was blurry, just barely broken out into separate colors.

Moving her finger, feeling the scratch of dry veins, was excruciating, but still she tugged at the collar around her throat. A hand struck her cheek, whipping her head to the side and making her almost steady vision go haywire again.

"Show her," a harsh voice said, savage desire evident in the words. If her mouth weren't sandpaper, she would have spit at the polished shoes she now saw below her.

Another slap, another swimming sense of vision, another unfulfilled urge to dishonor the man standing before her. Finally, the image pulled together and she recognized Aldrich looming above her. His fangs poked out and he hissed in her direction, angry. Despite the pain infiltrating her senses, a slight sense of happiness pulled through at the sight of his distress.

"Let me," a hesitant but soothing voice spoke from behind Aldrich. He shifted to the side, revealing a brown-haired woman with pearly skin and classic English features.

Aldrich growled, and the woman bent to her knees before Kira, taking his noise as a sign of ascent.

"Pavia," she cooed, bringing her hands to Kira's cheeks. Her thumbs wiped away tears that Kira didn't realize were there. "Pavia, it is almost over. All you need to do is show me, and I will let your hunger end. They don't matter to you, they are not important, not as important as your life. Don't you want to eat, don't you want the taste of fresh blood on your tongue again?" The more the woman continued in her soft monotone voice, the more Kira fell under her spell. Dizzy with hunger and delirious with the dream of warm blood, the memories poured from her.

As the images left her hands and met the woman's skin, her features began to change. Her dark brown hair lightened, at first a shade or two, and then quickly the roots turned blonde, stretching out to the tips in a wave of yellow. Her nose shrank, the button tip elongated slightly and the crown narrowed, forcing two large eyes further apart from one another. Her cheekbones rose, turning a round face into a more angular one, until all of a sudden, Kira was staring into the face of her own mother. Except for the eyes—the eyes were still blue and untouched.

"It is done?" Aldrich asked. The woman nodded, and Kira felt a kick break her spine as she cried out and fell to the floor...

But suddenly it was the real dungeon floor that smacked against Kira's cheek, and it was her own scream being ripped from her throat as reality came crashing back, wracking her body wave after wave after wave.

"You killed her," Kira said. Her cheek was still pressed against the cold stone floor. Her eyes weren't moving, but from the peripheral she saw Pavia sink back from the front of her cell into a seated position.

"Aldrich killed your mother, I just finished the job," she said. Her tone was serious and quiet.

"But you did it, you sucked the last breaths from her body," Kira said. Her voice was scratchy and soft.

"I did, and I can't say it was just the hunger, even to ease your pain. I'm a vampire. It's what we do," Pavia said. Her voice held no remorse. The words were matter-of-fact.

"And the woman?" Kira asked. She hadn't moved. Her body was contorted on the ground in the same way that she had fallen out of Pavia's memories. In an odd way, she probably looked like her mother, minutes before death.

"A weak vampire with the unique power to change her features—otherwise known as Aldrich's plaything." Disgust rang heavy in Pavia's voice.

"Why didn't you show me yesterday?" Kira asked, finally pushing her heavy body from the floor to sit up. Her head pounded as though stepped on.

Pavia shrugged. "Yesterday, you had nothing to offer me. Today you have food and freedom—everything an imprisoned girl dreams of." She smirked. "And you grew on me, what can I say?"

"I wish the feeling were mutual," Kira snorted, waiting for her headache to subside.

"Eh, I can tell that you don't really blame me for what happened. You know just as well as I do who the real culprit is."

After a second of thought, Kira tossed the other bag of blood through the opening of the cell and ignored the stares of the conduits and the human behind her. She ignored their protesting voices too. Pavia had earned her payment.

"Do you still have my mother's memories?" Kira asked. Pavia looked away, toward the two emptied bags of blood at her feet. Kira had nothing else to offer her.

"Do you still have time?" Now Kira looked away, down at her watch. Ever elusive, time was yet again slipping away from her. But she was so close to her mother, so close to knowing what kind of woman she was.

"Can't you just transfer them to me? Like you were doing with Aldrich?"

"It doesn't work that way with humans," Pavia said, and this time Kira knew she sensed a bit of regret in her words. "You have to live the memories, experience them in real time. Your bodies aren't strong enough."

Kira looked at her watch again. A few minutes and her hour would be up. But if she didn't do this now, who knew if she would ever find Pavia again?

Kira reached her hand under the cell and put all of her faith in Tristan's ability to hold Aldrich at bay just a while longer. "Show me one memory," Kira whispered, "the happiest one you can think of."

Pavia nodded and gently brushed her fingers over Kira's hand.

Maybe because Kira knew she was going somewhere she was welcome, but the process didn't feel like falling this time. As soon as Pavia's skin touched Kira's, her vision disappeared, and Kira felt as though she were flying. Her direction was clear. The colors swooshing by were comforting and not scary. When she sank into her mother's conscience, a warmth settled over her mind. This person was familiar—her mind worked like Kira's and accepted Kira instantly. Kira fell softly into her mother's memories...

When Kira opened her eyes, she was looking into a roaring fire. Natural flames burned in a hearth, dispersing a comforting smoky smell throughout a small living room. She was rocking back and forth, pushing her feet melodically against the ground to keep the baby girl asleep in her arms from waking up.

She looked down at her daughter, at the mass of hair already sprouting wildly from her tiny head. Definitely from her father. But those big eyes, now shut in slumber, though normally wide and curious, were all hers.

The baby shifted in Kira's arms, and her pudgy lips opened with a yawn before easing contentedly shut again. Her fingers, barely the size of a doll's, were wrapped around a strand of Kira's blonde hair, tugging it gently. But she didn't mind the dull pain—it reminded her that the bundle in her arms was real and not just a dream.

A door behind her opened, letting a rush of cool air in as heavy boots stomped against the floor.

"Shh!" Kira sighed with an amused shake of her head. Her husband, Andrew, was many things, but quiet was not one of them.

"Is the baby asleep?" he asked, peeking into the peripheral of her vision.

"For now," she whispered and watched him shrug off his heavy winter jacket to reveal a strong frame, one she knew would always keep their family safe. In the soft orange light of the fire, the grooves etched into his forehead seemed deeper. Barely in his mid-twenties and her husband already showed the stress of age. She ached to run her fingers over those lines, smoothing them out, ridding his face of worry just for one night.

As if sensing her thoughts, the baby stirred, reaching toward her father even in sleep. A barely visible string of light shot from her outstretched palm, hitting his chest. Even though her powers were weak, his features softened.

"Looks like Kira wants her daddy," she whispered.

"Like mother like daughter."

He smirked and walked closer to her. She rolled her eyes as he approached, but stood and carefully transferred the sleeping girl into her husband's waiting arms. He sat by the fire, lying back, and placed their daughter on the flat expanse of his chest.

She sank to the floor, curling into a ball against his side, putting an arm around both him and their daughter.

"How did things go?" she asked quietly. Her husband reached his hand up and ran it soothingly along her arm as he kissed her forehead.

"Not tonight," he told her and looked at the little girl clutching at the folds of his shirt. He sighed. *"She's going to be beautiful, just like her mother."*

"And a handful, just like her father," she teased.

"Remind me to buy a shotgun when Kira turns thirteen," he mumbled as his eyes draped further and further shut. She let the mix of his breath and the crackling fire lull her to sleep and kept her fingers on the small of her baby's back, letting her breath mirror the rise and fall of her little girl's body...

When Kira opened her eyes, she was back in her own skin, in the starkly lit dungeon that shocked her eyes, which had become attuned to the gentle firelight. Pavia's hand slid from hers and Kira ached to clutch it, to never let it go. She didn't care about Aldrich's plan or saving the world. She wanted to be back in the warmth of that small cabin, basking in the love so clearly trapped within its walls.

"Please," Kira softly begged. "Just one more." She shuffled her outstretched hand, looking through watery eyes for the pale shape of Pavia's hand. But Pavia leaned away from Kira and sank back into her cell. "I'll get you blood...I'll give you mine," Kira said and started to pierce her own skin like some sort of junkie.

"Kira," a woman's voice said. It wasn't Pavia, who was still mute and staring at Kira with a confused expression. It was one of the female conduits. "You have a job to do."

"I don't care," Kira whispered. She had given up Tristan to follow through with this plan, but giving up her parents, the opportunity to know them—Kira couldn't do that.

"Yes you do," Pavia said, turning her glance on Kira, confusion gone. "How about a deal?" She shrugged, embracing the carefree attitude again.

Kira nodded. Anything, she almost said, but stopped when she realized how desperate it sounded.

"You get me out of here alive," Pavia said, "and I'll find you and I'll show you whatever memories you want to see. You get me out of here alive and free, and I promise it won't be the last you see of me."

Kira tried to focus on Pavia. She had made the mistake of trusting the words of another female vampire, a moment of weakness that had led her on a wild-goose chase that nearly cost Kira her life, not to mention Luke and Tristan's. Diana had tricked Kira, giving her the words she most ached to hear, but despite herself, Kira nodded to Pavia.

"Deal," Kira said. Her tongue felt heavy in her mouth, but saying it out loud gave her a quick sense of freedom. She wasn't turning her back on her parents, she was trying to be the daughter they hoped she would be—the one who would fight, who wouldn't let ancient myths seal her fate. The one who wanted to prove everyone wrong.

Kira took a deep breath, swallowing her emotions back down, before she turned a cold stare to Pavia. She could feel her eyes burning. "If you're lying, I'll hunt you down. There's nowhere you can go that I wouldn't find you."

"Now that is a threat I believe," Pavia said, leaning back with a grin. "I'm not in the habit of being indebted to people. You get me out and I'll keep my promise. After all, I'm immortal. Time doesn't matter a whole lot to me."

Kira looked down at her watch. All of her time had already run out, and with one last glance at Pavia, she took off at a run, zooming down empty corridors. Tristan and Aldrich were still nowhere to be seen, but Kira didn't come across her fake mother either. The absence put an extra ounce of energy into her steps.

Kira had waited too long. Her carefully thought out plan was unraveling before her eyes and it was all her fault.

Self-directed anger pushed her onward until Kira found herself skidding to a halt before the door. Her only way out. But it would be a blind exit. Aldrich could be waiting—fangs at the ready.

Kira clenched her fists and took a deep breath to force the nerves out of her system. Raising her palm, flames burst from her skin, sizzling against the black backdrop of the secret corridor.

After one final pause, she twisted the handle and opened the door.

Empty.

A river of tension flooded from her system and Kira snapped her flames back, pulling them securely underneath her skin.

Everything was fine.

"Kira?"

She jumped, slamming the door shut behind her as her heart leapt into her throat.

Her fake mother rounded the corner and her eyes narrowed as she sensed Kira's racing pulse.

"Is everything okay?" she asked, caught between her normal fake concern and suspicion. Her eyes shifted around the room, looking for something that seemed out of place.

"You scared me!" Kira laughed and put a hand to her throat, swallowing loudly.

"I didn't hear you…" She looked around again.

Kira walked swiftly to the counter and picked up her phone, shaking it in the vampire's direction.

"Must have been my music." Kira shrugged and scooped some oatmeal into her mouth. "Just a dash of cinnamon and it'll finally be done!" In reality, it tasted like mush in her mouth—totally overcooked. But, lucky for Kira, a three-hundred-year-old vampire didn't know what good oatmeal looked like.

"Come upstairs when you're finished. We have a lot to do before the ceremony." She ran her gaze around the room one final time, sniffing the air quietly, before turning around with a satisfied nod.

As soon as she left, Kira collapsed against the counter. Her hands were shaking. She swallowed, gulping the air in to stop the panic spreading from nerve to nerve, zinging down her arms.

There was nothing left for her to do now. No fight, no mission, no truth to uncover. The plan was going perfectly and all she had to do was play along.

But already, Kira could feel the ghost of a prick along her neck. Aldrich's fangs were there, haunting her, poised to bite.

And against all her instincts, Kira would have to do the hardest thing she had ever done—stay still. Stay still and let him.

Chapter Fourteen

Kira hardly recognized her reflection in the mirror. Her hair was piled high in a bun on top of her head, and a few stray curls fell elegantly over her forehead. Her skin was pale, lightened with fine powder. Her lips a deep red, slicked with rouge. Her blue eyes looked like great lakes in the middle of her face—they were so infinite and expansive. Her angular cheekbones arched gracefully up, defined by a few swishes of pink blush.

Kira smiled, almost surprised to see the girl in the mirror copy the movement exactly. But she kept the smile plastered on those foreign features as thin hands continued to coil her hair, continued to run lovingly through the curls.

Kira closed her eyes and pretended those hands belonged to the real thing. That her mother was standing behind her, lacing her fingers through Kira's messy tangles to tame them into something poised, something worthy of display—that the hands tickling her scalp were the same ones that had soothed her to sleep years ago.

"All done." Those hands patted her shoulders softly—a signal that Kira should open her eyes. But as soon as she did, Kira would remember that the woman behind her was fake, a mere shard of the memory playing in her mind.

Instead, she leaned her head against the woman's forearm and sighed contentedly. Kira wasn't ready for her fantasy to end.

Almost taken aback by the intimate contact, the vampire behind her took a step away, reacting to Kira's touch.

"I'll go get Tristan," she said softly, covering up her own mistake. When the door slipped open, Kira let her eyes follow suit. They found their way past her reflection to the red dress draped across the bed. The silk rippled over the sides of the mattress, turning to different hues as the candlelight bounced off the fabric.

Her dying dress.

At least, that was how Kira thought of it.

"Hi," Tristan said quietly after closing the door behind him. They were in the female vampire's room, an unexpected gift from Aldrich. Kira hadn't dared hope for a few minutes alone with Tristan before the ceremony and she was thankful for it. The room was soundproof. For the first time in hours—hours that felt more like weeks—Kira could speak plainly and honestly with Tristan. And he with her.

"Hi," she said, spinning in her chair, unsure of herself.

"You look…" He trailed off as he walked closer to her.

"Like a vampire?" Kira supplied. That had been her first thought.

"Yeah." The hint of sadness in his voice was undeniable.

"It's only makeup," Kira said, resisting the urge to wipe it off with her wrist.

"I'm not sure if that makes me happy or sad."

Kira turned toward the bed, searching for an escape from his analytic gaze. "Will you help me with this?" she asked and started to untie the knot holding her robe in place. She had her underwear on, but Kira still kept her back to Tristan. Maybe it was an unwritten rule of breaking up, but she suddenly felt self-conscious in front of him, in a way she never had before.

With her robe around her shoulders, Kira pooled the dress on the floor and stepped into it. She brought the smooth material all the way up around her waist before letting her robe drop, leaving only the arc of her back exposed. Tristan's cool fingers brushed her skin gently as they fiddled with the zipper. For a moment, he stopped moving. His thumb brushed down her spine, sending a shiver to the tips of her fingers. His breath kissed her neck, letting Kira know his lips were tantalizingly close to her skin. She closed her eyes, ready to lean back, but then the dress cinched tightly shut as Tristan sealed the zipper. Kira waited for it, but his fingers didn't touch her bare flesh again.

Instead of missing caresses that didn't belong to her anymore, Kira looked into the mirror at the other side of the room, wondering if Aldrich was watching them. Would even these few minutes of peace need to be a show?

The dress was stunning, Kira thought as she studied her reflection, but no matter how beautiful, it didn't match her. She looked like some sort of Grecian temptress in the deep ruby gown. Fabric bunched above her right shoulder, falling gracefully in tight pleats to her waist before cascading loosely to the ground. The skin on her left side was bare, open and waiting for Aldrich's bite. Even though the one-shoulder dress covered her body, Kira felt exposed.

The only thing giving her comfort was the chain hanging around her neck. Kira raised her hand, clasping her father's ring and Luke's charm within her palm. Somehow, they would keep her safe.

As if sensing her thoughts, Tristan stepped in front of her, blocking the mirror from view.

"Do you think he's watching?" Kira asked.

"Probably." Tristan shrugged. He circled her waist with his hands, drawing her closer. Kira slipped her arms over his shoulders, completing the embrace. Was this for them or for Aldrich?

"Do you hate me?" Kira whispered. She couldn't meet his eyes.

"No," he said.

"Do you love me?" She studied the opening of his shirt. The fancy cream buttons almost blended with his skin. His smooth chest rose in a deep breath, and his Adam's apple rolled out as he swallowed.

"Kira..." He sounded lost, like a little boy.

"It's okay," she said, looking up into his deep blue eyes. "I just asked because I want you to know that for me, that answer will always be yes. Part of me will always love you, and even if that's the only forever we have, I think it was worth it. All of it."

He leaned down, resting his forehead against hers, but he didn't speak. His sigh thickened the air around them, rolling down her body like a wave.

"Will I ever see you again?" she asked. He shook his head, but Kira couldn't accept the silent message he was sending her. She pulled back, willing him to answer her with words, no matter how hard they were to say out loud.

"I'm leaving," he said, looking past her face to the wall over her shoulder. "After all of this is over, I'm going to walk away and try my best not to look back."

Kira bit her lip to keep a murmur of protest from bubbling out. Instead, she simply said, "I don't want you to just disappear."

"You made your choice, please don't take away

mine." His lips brushed her ear while he spoke, making it hard for her to concentrate.

"What do you mean?" Kira tried to lean back, to look into his eyes, but Tristan held her firmly against his chest.

"Don't ask me to stay."

"But—"

"Kira," he interrupted, stopping her protest. "You chose being a conduit. I can't change being a vampire. It's better for both of us to end it here, now. But when you tell me you love me, that you will always love me, I can't even breathe for the thought of losing you. Let me be strong for once. Just let me walk away."

And he loosened his hug, finally letting Kira go just enough for her to look up into the somber features of his beautiful face.

He was right.

Kira lifted her hand, letting her fingers gently glide along his defined jaw line, moving around to the back of his neck to play with the small, soft hairs there. She pressed her other hand over his heart, feeling the steady thrum against her palm. His eyes were shifting, oscillating between a deep, melancholic navy and a contented, sparkling sapphire.

He brought both of his hands to her neck and cupped her head firmly, lifting her slightly closer to his face in a way that was possessive but caring at the same time. Kira knew what it meant. Part of her would always belong to him, and for the next couple of minutes she was still completely his.

It was Kira who moved first, rising onto her toes to close the last inch between their lips. Tristan welcomed her, easing her head to the side to deepen the kiss that she had started. His lips pushed hers open slowly, steadily. His movements were controlled, mirroring the deep desire they had always had for each other, proving to Kira that they were more than just a flash of lust. Her hand slid behind his back, pulling him closer.

Tristan gently kissed along her jaw, burning a path along her skin with his lips. As his mouth moved down to her throat, warm tingles shot down her spine. He wasn't marking her, but he was claiming her. That spot would always belong to him, no matter what Aldrich had in mind.

But thinking that just reminded Kira that they didn't have time, no matter what either of them wanted to believe. And this time Kira cupped her hands around his neck, dragging his mouth back to hers. The end was too close.

And Tristan understood. Their movements became frantic. Their kisses were no longer slow and purposeful, but quick and jumbled. Kira kissed his skin, her hands roamed his body, feeling the ripple of hard abs beneath her thumb while trailing her other fingers down the curve of his spine.

Tristan pulled her close, using his strength to lift her off the ground, kissing her lips, then her cheek, then her neck, back to her lips. His arms crushed her into his chest for fear that releasing Kira for even a second would make her vanish.

The door behind them opened with a bang, and like cloth being ripped down a seam, Kira and Tristan broke apart in a flash. The distance felt painful, even if only to her heart.

Tristan's normally pale skin was flushed pink and Kira knew if she touched it, his cheek would feel warm for the first time. His breath was heavy, like an echo of the ragged sounds coming from her own mouth.

"Plenty of time for that later," Kira's fake mother spoke through her grin, looking at them with knowing eyes.

As much as Kira didn't want to look away, she had to, because she knew Tristan never would. And when she did, the spell broke. He set her down on her feet and stepped away, distant and cold once more. Kira ran her hands down the front of her dress, smoothing out the wrinkles and trying to regain some semblance of composure. As far as goodbyes went, it was a short one, but it was all they would get.

"Sit back down," the female vampire sighed and pointed at the chair Kira had vacated only a few minutes before. "You, out." She shooed Tristan to the door with a tsk and walked behind Kira.

"I leave the two of you alone for a few minutes," she said, shaking her head and pulling Kira's curls back into a tame bun.

Kira sat quietly with her hands in her lap, trying to play nervous while all she really felt was sad.

Kira was so distracted by the image of Tristan walking away that she hardly noticed when high-heeled shoes were slipped onto her feet. A slender hand pulled her up to a standing position and led her out the door. Kira followed placidly until they reached the top of the steps and her nose was blasted with the scent of freshly cut flowers.

And then Kira finally took in the scene around her. The steps were lined with flickering candles that extended across the marble floor, forming a pathway into the dining room. At the threshold of the dining room, where reflections of flames danced along the polished floor, a pool of red petals began. Against the glowing light, the shadows between the flowers dipped and swirled, seemingly alive. The floor danced, rippling almost like warm blood.

As she made her descent, the rest of the dining room came into view. Kira hardly recognized it. Rows of candles circled the room, covering the plain white walls. Painted white antlers still hung in the background, casting finger-like shadows. The large china cabinet had disappeared, and the wooden chairs had been removed. But the glossy black table was open, bare, waiting to be covered by Kira's body. It looked like an empty furnace, glinting with fire but with nothing to roast.

Behind the table, Aldrich and Tristan stood side by side, close enough to touch each other. Tristan's arms were crossed, his face emotionless, but his eyes warmed when they landed on her.

Aldrich's though—Aldrich's glowed. His hands were clasped behind his back in a stiff posture only combated by the rigid line of his mouth. His body slackened almost imperceptibly when Kira came into view, but his eyes were unmistakable. The normally black holes lightened and his pupils narrowed with hunger, making his eyes appear almost completely white. When they slid from her face to her neck, Kira swallowed a gulp.

The fear suddenly clenching her gut made Kira think of Luke, of his warm smile and his laugh, of the way he always made her feel safe and protected but also strong enough to manage on her own. She saw his spirit in the fires set around the room—the glint of his hair and the warmth of his laugh and the heat in their kiss. Drawing on Luke, as well as the power gathering in her heart, Kira felt ready.

Help was coming and she would manage just fine until then.

When her thighs bumped the edge of the table, Kira stopped and waited for further instructions. Until Aldrich made his move, she would play by his rules.

"Kira," Aldrich said happily, letting a wide smile spread across his face. Somehow, it looked harsh rather than natural. He unclasped his hands and spread them out, motioning to the décor. "What do you think?"

"It's beautiful."

"Not too," he shrugged, "over the top?"

"No, it's perfect," Kira said.

"Good, because I want everything to be perfect. For you. For Tristan. For our new family." He stuttered over the word *family*, letting out a cough afterward to cover up the flub. "Excuse me," he laughed, "my excitement is getting the best of me."

Yes, it is, Kira thought, *but what exactly are you so excited about?*

"I think we're all excited," Tristan said, laughing with Aldrich and clapping him on the back like old chums. Kira lifted the corner of her lip, a small movement thanking Tristan for finally playing along.

"I know I am, so let's get started," Kira said and looked around, waiting for instruction.

"Lana, dear?"

"Coming," a polite voice echoed down the hall. Kira turned. She hadn't even noticed that the female vampire had left the room.

A second later, she walked back in holding a silver tray.

Once it was set on the table, Kira peered down, curious. A sharp silver knife reflected her blue eyes back at her. They looked fierce, hot and almost like fire except for the color.

Next to the knife were a pitcher of blood and an empty wine glass waiting to be filled.

Kira's throat went dry as the tension in her body rose. "Can we go over the process one more time?" she asked.

Her eyes were still focused on the tray.

"I think we should just begin," Aldrich said and leaned his hands against the table, smoothing out the area in front of him. Kira understood. His patience was at an end. There would be no more delaying.

Kira turned around and placed her butt on the tabletop, lifting the rest of her body. She fell back slowly, sinking against the flat surface as though it really were her deathbed. When her head touched back, the folds of her skirt swished over her legs. Aldrich used his mind to smooth them out so her dress fell over the edges of the table, cascading into the flower petals below. For a guy who didn't seem to like color, there sure was a lot of red in the room.

Kira stared up at the ceiling, waiting for more instruction. She traced the candle glows with her eyes, following circular lines as they intersected and maneuvered around each other in an endless pattern, broken only by the large black chandelier swaying gently above her head. The iron looked heavy, like it strained to escape the screws locking it in place.

A hand landed on her calf and her entire body jolted. Kira lifted her head reflexively, only to meet Tristan's gaze. He was trying to calm her, to stay connected with her as she ventured into the one part of the plan he couldn't partake in.

Further up, another hand touched her and this time Kira focused on remaining calm as Aldrich's cold fingers latched around her wrist. They felt like ice cubes against her rising temperature. Kira fought with her power, holding it tightly with her mind to keep it in place. Her control was getting better, but it still had limits.

Aldrich lifted her hand to his lips, placing what Kira thought was supposed to be a reassuring kiss on her palm.

"Are you ready?" he asked, squinting down at her. From her place on the table, he looked like a giant looming overhead.

He flipped her wrist, tracing her vein with the tip of his finger.

No. No. No. No. No.

Kira's mind was racing. Her heart was pumping and she knew all three vampires could hear it. She didn't care. It felt like bugs were crawling along her skin, and she wanted to run.

Her power coiled around her heart, extending down her veins and searing her blood, making it boil. She clenched her free wrist, keeping it contained—barely. It would be so easy to let it go, to blast Aldrich against the wall and get away as fast as she could without turning around. She could see it in her head, see the flames bursting out, see the boils exploding along his flesh, see the ash in the air as he fell dead.

But then she would never know.

She would never know what sort of evil she was really capable of, because that's what it had been about all along.

Aldrich's big secret, Kira knew, had something to do with her destiny of destruction—the one the conduits feared and the one Aldrich longed for.

Taking a deep breath, Kira let her fire lay like a blanket over her organs, circling her insides but not escaping.

She met Tristan's eyes and stayed there for one prolonged moment before turning to Aldrich.

"I'm ready."

She bit her lip and he bit her wrist. Fangs sunk deep into her skin to catch the blood pumping free and quickly out of her adrenaline-filled veins. Kira forced her mouth to stay shut to keep from crying out at the pain.

Tristan's hand tightened on her leg, keeping her grounded and on the table when she wanted to breakaway at a dead sprint. His fingers dug into her muscles as though he were staying grounded through her as well, as if she was his anchor. His eyes cut at Aldrich, harsh and angry, blazing a deep black Kira had never seen before.

Aldrich, however, had his eyes closed. Ecstasy played across his features as they softened and he gripped her wrist even tighter.

And Kira's power was screaming at her, burning her since it had nothing else to scorch. Lava and not blood was what Aldrich swallowed, lava that was melting her to the table, that would kill her if she didn't let it go. But she couldn't let it go. She had to hold on, to keep fighting for a minute, no a second, just a moment longer.

Behind Kira, a soft cough sounded.

Remembering himself, Aldrich slipped his fangs from her wrist and pulled a handkerchief from his pocket to dab at the blood dripping down his chin. Her blood—brilliantly red against his snowy face, brighter than all of the flowers around the room.

It was silent.

All Kira could hear was the rapid beat of her own heart as the seconds drew further on. It pumped in her ears louder than a drum, shaking her entire body.

Next to her, Aldrich flexed his wrist, waiting. Her blood needed to course through his body, needed to transform to match his vampiric composition, his cell structure, his evil.

No one moved. Tristan still gripped her leg. He hadn't even blinked.

And then a jingle sounded softly by her feet. The knife, gleaming silver with an ornately decorated handle, rose from the tray, slowly trailing over her body to settle over Aldrich's outstretched hand.

He let it rest, poised over his own wrist, and looked down at Kira with white eyes. This was it, the moment Aldrich had waited for, the moment Kira had needed to witness but had also dreaded. He was not even trying to cover the smirk on his face, the glint in his eyes reading only of success and power.

One breath.

Two breaths.

Three breaths.

The knife moved quickly, slashing a deep gash and blood dripped from the wound, landing on Kira's dress, her arm, her hand.

Aldrich smashed his wrist down into the wounds his fangs had created, and Kira felt it, felt the blood grip her veins, pushing back into the holes in a completely unnatural invasion. Sticky, like sap, it sunk into her, grasping for her skin, her arteries. As it entered her bloodstream, Kira felt her own blood change from the burning, fire-filled flames she was used to. Her blood caught on, transforming with this intruder, sticking to her insides and turning black like tar melting on the street.

Frightened, Kira tried to pull away, but she couldn't move her fingers. Her arm seemed heavy, like a rock had been placed above it, holding her down. When she lifted her head to look at the spot, nothing was there. Aldrich had already retreated and was closing his wound.

The blackness sunk deeper into her, traveling up her shoulder, weeding its way into her neck, and Kira's head banged against the table as her nerves fought and failed to keep their strength.

Above her head, Aldrich started laughing a high-pitched squeal.

"Oh, Kira," he whispered for her ears alone, leaning

down over her face, rubbing a finger down her cheek, "what a fool you are."

And try as she might, Kira couldn't get her mouth to move. Her lips were glued shut and her tongue felt as though it weighed one hundred pounds. Her eyelids soon felt heavy, and blinking became too much of a burden.

And that's when Kira started screaming. She couldn't make a sound but her soul ached, screeched against the black tar turning her body to stone. And Kira released her fire, let the flames go free, but they were weak against the dark cloud spreading through her veins.

Kira focused on the only thing she could think of, protecting her heart, her core, the place where the sun never seemed too far away. She gathered her flames, letting them grow and coat her heart, circling it like a shield.

And before she knew it, the rest of her went flat. She had no energy aside from the power boiling in her center.

Her eyelids sunk lower. Past Aldrich's face. Down Tristan's arm. Until her vision was nearly spent.

And the last thing Kira saw was a single candle flickering just past her vision, holding on for dear life.

And then even that was gone.

Chapter Fifteen

The sun.

All Kira could think about was the sun.

Somehow, against all odds, it managed to shine brightly in a sea of black. It managed to break through the darkness to survive.

Kira needed to be the sun. Her heart felt like the sun—rock solid, burning, exploding into the blackness around it.

But the dark coiling around her veins was relentless, and it fed through the small cracks in her protection, seeping through every gap, straining to break through her power source.

Protection was all Kira could think about, protecting herself from the darkness and repelling the evil struggling to break her. Using only those powers, Kira focused all of her energy on protecting her heart. She found every hole in her defenses and bottled them shut, weaving fire like yarn, encasing her entire being within those folds.

And when Kira finally felt calm for a moment, felt like the ash had stopped pressing forward, had stopped gaining ground, she knew she had to fight.

Holding her Protector powers secure around her heart, Kira delved into the other side of her fire, the deeper side. She focused on her anger, letting herself go to the place beyond control for the first time in a long time.

Kira focused on Aldrich, on his snide comments and sidelong glances that held promises of terror. The image of her mother's dead body being thrown to the ground like a play toy for a starving vampire boiled her blood, infusing her power with more strength and perseverance. Every moment Kira ever spent hating a vampire, fighting a vampire, resisting a vampire, popped into her head in an endless stream of clips, bringing her powers to a breaking point.

This thing would not consume her. Every fiber of her being rejected the very idea of becoming one of them, and Kira poured that belief into her powers as they burst from her heart in a relentless stream of heat.

At first, her fire slammed against the black liquid cooling her veins. The two powers crashed together, like two titans in a mortal battle, reverberating down her insides with a boom Kira was sure could be heard outside of her head.

Her flames singed the tar, burning it, melting the solid mass that was hardening her limbs. The blackness responded, shrouding her flames from the light like an eclipse inside her body.

But unlike the evil trying to consume her, Kira had passion and conviction on her side. She refused to give in, refused to back down, and for that her fire pushed through.

At first, the retreat was slow and Kira used all her power to chase the sticky rubber from her veins, letting her warm blood return. But soon, her flames melted the blackness further, until it was slick oil sliding out of her veins, oozing from her pores in as quick of an escape as possible. Her skin felt grimy on the outside, like a greasy residue had been left behind, like she couldn't get totally free of the substance.

But her insides were hot and light once more, and distantly Kira felt her senses return. Her back was cold against the table. Her joints ached from lying atop the hard surface. Sugary sweetness licked at her nostrils, and Kira remembered the flowers strewn across the floor.

Then hands were shaking her shoulders, bouncing her from side to side, and jerking her neck painfully. She fell back against the table again and a heavy body fell on top of her. It was trembling. Slowly, muffled sobs broke through her ears.

"Kira!" A deep voice cried. She recognized Tristan's agonized scream. She wanted to comfort him, to calm him, but her limbs still felt like jelly.

The pressure lifted and she heard the accusation. "What did you do?" Tristan hissed.

"I turned her," came the calm reply. "I did exactly what I said I'd do."

"But it's impossible," Tristan said. Kira, feeling more and more like herself with each passing second, began to wonder what she had missed. She was eager to join the fight, but too interested to see what information Aldrich would give up while he thought she was still under the thrall of the change.

"Not impossible." Kira could envision him shrugging in her head. He was only too happy to have the power.

"Conduits can't change," Tristan told him firmly.

"No they can't," he said gently, "but Kira is so much more than a conduit." Fingers brushed her hair from her forehead. "And soon, she will be so much more than even that."

"What do you mean?" Tristan asked, his voice more curious than angry, almost hopeful as if something he had stopped dreaming might still somehow come true.

"It is a common misconception that the mix of each conduit breed results in a mixed breed, a half-blood if you will. But they're all wrong, Tristan. It's the conduits that are less, that are divided. Kira is pure. She is the joining of two halves. Two conduits do not make a mixed breed, Tristan, they make an angel. An original."

"An angel?" Tristan asked. His voice was distant, disbelieving. His cool hand cupped her cheek. Behind closed eyes, Kira could imagine his face peering down at her, roving over the curves of her face.

"Yes, an angel. And angels can do what conduits can't." Aldrich paused and Kira felt a tug on one of her curls. "They can fall. And when angels fall, there is no one on this earth who can stop them."

Kira let those words sink into her still recovering mind. The Punisher had been right. She was falling, becoming an unstoppable evil, something no conduit could burn and no vampire could bite.

"What will happen when she wakes up?" Tristan asked softly. The glimmer of hope behind those words was unmistakable, and anger boiled in the pit of Kira's stomach at Tristan's response.

"She won't," the female vampire said from across the room. Kira wondered if she still looked like her mother. If when she opened her eyes, there finally would be a stranger in front of her, a stranger she would be happy to kill.

"But—"

"Oh she will wake, Tristan, but she won't be the Kira you remember," the woman continued. Her tone was spiteful, nasty. Her eyes flashed in Kira's mind, deep and full of loathing. "If the turning goes the way we hope, her soul will be broken, and she will emerge as a wild, uncontrolled beast."

"Kira would never let that happen," Tristan said, completely confident.

"She won't have a choice," Aldrich said calmly. "The change will drive her to insanity. When she wakes, only one thing will consume her thoughts—blood. And not just any blood—conduit blood. Kira will be our reckoning."

A rage-filled growl broke through the room. A huge crash sounded next to Kira's ear, and she heard Aldrich chuckle softly. By her feet, Kira heard Tristan curse at him and yell again.

She flexed her finger, testing part of her body to make sure it responded the way she wanted. Her finger obeyed, moving the precise way Kira had ordered it to. She was about to jump and show Aldrich he had been wrong, ready to kill him and any knowledge he had in his small head, but something else broke through her consciousness before she could order her feet to stand.

A sense of conviction and honor pulsed into her head. Hot pride and perfectly simmering love punctured the veins around her scalp, and words started whispering inside her mind.

"I'm coming, Kira. I'm coming. Just keep holding on. I swear, we'll be there soon. Just keep fighting. For you. For me. Keep fighting."

And the encouragement continued in an endless tirade that puffed her chest with hope.

Luke.

He was close, nearly here and projecting his thoughts to give her the strength he somehow knew she would need. The same golden warmth she had felt during their kiss began to spread from her heart, fixing her bruised soul.

Keep fighting, he whispered over and over in her head. Kira knew to listen.

"We have company," the woman said, and Kira snapped back to her surroundings, letting a sense of Luke continue to funnel through her body while she turned her direct attention back to the words being thrown around above her head.

"I hear them," Aldrich said roughly. "I had hoped it wouldn't come to this, Tristan. I really didn't think you would betray me."

"What do you know about betrayal?" Tristan cut. His voice was laced with pain, and Kira screamed against her instinct to open her eyes and save him from whatever trouble he was in.

"More than you will ever know."

And the front door banged open and heavy boots came storming in, pounding against the marble floors.

"Kira!" She heard the yell in her mind, her heart, and her ears. Luke was here. Finally, Kira let herself move as her lips tugged into a slight smile. "Kira!" His next yell was strangled, filled with hatred and fear.

And Kira finally realized what she must look like, fallen and unmoving on the slab of table like a fresh kill ready to be eaten. Could he tell that her dress was red and not blood stained? Was it both?

Kira turned her head toward the sound of Luke's voice, blinking her eyes to get adjusted. His golden head came into focus first, alight from the candles in the room. Relief flashed across his features when their eyes met, but it was short-lived as the doors crashed together, sealing the dining room off from the intruding conduits. Luke pounded his fists against the wood to no avail.

In one fluid movement, Kira slid from the table and jumped to her feet, bringing flames to her hands and preparing to fight.

The instant Aldrich's gaze landed on the fire dancing between her fingers, his mask fell. Gone was the confident bravado, the sophisticated arrogance. His eyes immediately turned into ebony pools, slick like the oil Kira had felt in her veins. His fangs popped out, still stained slightly red with her blood. Like an animal ready to pounce, his posture fell to a crouch and his head sunk lower so he looked hungrily at her under hooded brows.

And suddenly the table slammed into her legs, dragging Kira backward and pummeling her into the wall. Her thighbones crunched as they snapped and a wail unexpectedly broke free from the pain. Tristan's voiced screamed too, and Kira looked over to see him stuck against the wall, pinned by antlers sinking through his flesh into the hard plaster behind him.

Using her powers, Kira forced her bones back together, dulling the pain and reattaching muscles torn to shreds in Aldrich's rage. He saw what she was doing and pushed the table against her harder, so even her power couldn't totally heal the indigo bruises lining her skin.

"Stop!" Kira gasped, reaching for some tool to use against him. She stuck out her hand, aiming at the woman, and released her powers without looking to see if the face of her mother was still plastered dishonestly on the vampire's skin.

Immediately, Kira felt the familiar feel of a vampire bubbling beneath the onslaught of her strength. She forced the candles around the room to bend to her will and the fires burned brighter all around her, almost setting the room ablaze.

"I will kill her if you don't let us go."

"Be my guest," Aldrich hissed and slowly continued to push the table into her legs as the chandelier above their heads began to jingle.

Aldrich was immune and Kira would have to break through that, so she forced out everything she could, sending fire out through her palms, her hands and the skin all the way up to her elbows.

Kira could feel the strong barrier drinking her blood had placed around Aldrich, and her power rolled off him, practically bouncing from his skin. She was half-Protector and half-Punisher so he was immune to both of her flames, but Kira knew she could break through. She just needed time. The other vampire, however, was a different story. She had never tasted Kira's blood, and her fake mother's hair singed, burning off. Her skin flaked, made crispy by Kira's power.

Soon enough, she was just a pile of ash dusting the petals along the ground. And Kira felt no remorse at killing this vampire who had mocked her mother and tried to fool her. Part of her just wished the vampire had looked different, like anyone other than her mother, who Kira had already seen die far too often in her dreams.

Aldrich didn't even pause to give the woman, his supposed wife, a second look. Instead, he managed to pull the chandelier loose of its hold, and Kira looked up just in time to see it flying toward her face. Her hands rose instinctively as she shut her eyes, but the hit never came.

Tristan, using Aldrich's diverted attention to its best use, had managed to free himself of the antlers just in time to leap and catch the chandelier in midair. Using all of his strength, he threw the iron fixture back at Aldrich. Like a bullet, it sped blurrily through the air only to crash to the floor as Aldrich focused his attention on his own life.

How much could he control before his powers weakened? Kira asked herself, begging for some sign that they stood a chance.

A loud bang sounded from behind the door as something large slammed into it, breaking the hinges so

Aldrich's power was the only thing keeping them secluded in the dining room.

Something rammed into the door again, pounding against it, almost splintering the wood. Aldrich looked over, concentrating on the door, and Kira took the chance to continue bombarding him with her fire—all of it Punisher and meant to kill.

An antler rose from the floor, whipping around and cutting into her arm, twirling Kira to the side so her powers slid off of Aldrich. Healing the bruise quickly, Kira continued breaking through the hold of his immunity. She was close. She felt the ripple in the imaginary cover, the slight warping of the glass case around his body. It was about to break apart into a million pieces.

A spike broke off from the chandelier, an iron pole aimed at her heart. Tristan jumped through her flames, letting out a yell as the heat scorched his flesh, but he had saved her.

"Tristan," Kira called out, easing up on her powers just a little bit.

"Don't stop," he screamed over the crackling roar of her fire.

But Aldrich saw the moment of weakness and sent more pieces flying toward her head. Tristan deftly jumped, staying cautious of her fire but not completely clear of it, to catch the items and keep Kira safe.

And she was almost there. Kira could feel Aldrich's

protection thinning, like Saran Wrap about to reach its breaking point. One more push and there would be a hole.

Aldrich looked up. He felt it too. His features were slightly nervous.

Kira smiled.

And then the table lifted off the ground, smashing Tristan, pinning him, squishing him against the wall.

Kira ran to help, but candles bombarded her, pelting her skin like baseballs, leaving welts she could barely heal fast enough to stay on her feet. She pulled her flames back, forcing them underneath her skin to protect her body from Aldrich's merciless pursuit.

She yanked on the table leg, trying to free Tristan, but it wouldn't budge.

A set of antlers flew at her face, and Kira jumped to the ground, but not soon enough. One branch pierced her calf, breaking through flesh and lodging itself against her bone. Kira cried out and tried to yank the antler free, but it was like iron clamped to her leg. Holding back tears, Kira let out a scream—of pain and frustration.

From the other side of the door, Luke's muffled voice called out. His warmth surged through her, but it wasn't enough to keep the pain at bay.

The pounding on the entry began anew, and for one split second, when the door burst fully open, exposing the conduits behind it, Kira met Luke's warm honey-green eyes. And that was enough to keep her pushing on.

Aldrich forced the door closed again and the wood protested, splintering along its joints. With Aldrich turned away from Tristan, the table fell back to the ground. The second he was free, Tristan disappeared, running quickly across the room to latch Aldrich's arms behind his back. With one twist, he snapped his neck, knocking Aldrich out, and all the floating objects in the room dropped to the ground.

"Now, Kira!" Tristan yelled, looking pointedly at Aldrich.

Kira shook her head. "Step back!"

"I can't. He'll wake up at any moment." Tristan looked at her sadly, almost as if he had accepted this as the end. "Do it."

Closing her eyes, Kira let her fire free and felt her flames engulf Aldrich, licking Tristan's skin as well.

She knew exactly when Aldrich woke up. She felt his neck snap back into place, felt his power immediately surge to keep the other conduits out, but they were already inside. The table flew across the room again, barreling into all of them, slamming into the entry like a substitute door, but this wouldn't last nearly as long. And Aldrich knew that. Because he knew his time was almost up.

Just like that, the immunity shattered around him, and Kira's flames were sinking into his flesh, burning his skin and melting the black oil that slithered through his veins. She hated this man and finally, he would die.

Kira crept closer, forgetting about Tristan's proximity, forgetting about everything except Aldrich and everything he had taken away from her. A father. A mother. Her childhood. Her future. Everything.

And Kira realized she wanted more than death for him. For someone truly evil, death was not enough. She let her flames sear his skin enough to hurt, enough to cause him pain, enough to prolong the process. And part of her enjoyed hearing his screams. Part of her wanted him to beg for his life.

With those thoughts, a little black sliver of tar Kira hadn't managed to dislodge from her heart roared to life. She knew what she wanted—his blood.

Kira wanted to suck the life from his veins, to feed for the first time.

But no, she fought against it, letting her fire surge forward again. That was the last thing she needed. The last thing she wanted.

Or was it? The blood would be warm, it would boil through her heart, adding to her power, making her strong enough to kill him and make it hurt.

But it does hurt, Kira thought as she listened to screams sounding in her ear.

But does it hurt enough? An ugly voice rearing to life inside her mind questioned.

Kira licked her lips, lowering her hands just a smidge. Her tongue traveled over her teeth. They drew blood. Her own blood—warm and tasting like fresh embers.

No.

No. No. No.

Kira's real voice screamed in her head, pushing the blackness back once more as she fell to the ground clutching her scalp in her hands. What was happening to her?

Kira focused her flames inward, letting them burn her blood, letting the fire scorch her back to life, back to sanity. She healed her cuts, scrapes, and wounds, blaming blood loss for her mental break. But the little black patch over her heart wouldn't go away. It retreated, creeping back into the little crevice it had hidden in before, but Kira felt it staining her soul, waiting for the opportune moment to sneak up on her again.

"Kira!"

Someone was screaming into her brain. Someone was shaking her. Hands gripped her arms, but the pain was welcome, and it brought Kira out of herself.

Her vision came back, spotty at first, until a blonde head broke through the blur.

"Luke," she said lazily with a smile, as though she were waking up from a dream. But his face was filled with horror as he glanced at Kira, over her shoulder, and back to her.

Kira tried to sit up, but her vision fell away again, forcing her back to the floor.

"Luke. What's wrong?" Kira asked, watching his mouth open into a gape and his eyes widen, shocked. But he wouldn't speak. His eyes kept traveling back and forth, until Kira could no longer endure it.

She leaned her head back, peering over her shoulder, expecting to see the pile of ash that should be Aldrich's dead body.

Instead, there was something inhuman, a mound of charred flesh, burned black and flaky but not yet dead. Limbs curled in on themselves and Kira sat up, ready to finish the job.

"It's okay," Kira told Luke. "He won't be able to heal himself anyway." She brought a flame to her hand, looking at the steaming body behind her. Even vampires didn't deserve to die that way.

But before she could move her flames even a centimeter closer, Luke yanked on her arm, jerking her flames to the side.

"Kira!" he gasped. She looked at him confused. Suddenly wondering where Tristan was. Had he already left without saying goodbye? Did he already disappear from her life and walk away like he said he would? Was he just gone?

But, Kira sat up, he wouldn't just leave without knowing she was safe. Not after all of this. So Kira looked around the room, at the nervous and scared faces of the conduits around her. Why were they all looking at her so strangely?

She lifted her hands to her mouth, feeling for fangs. Were her canines slightly longer and sharper than before? They felt almost normal...almost.

"Luke, what's going on? Where's Tristan?" Her voice rose an octave as nerves took over.

"Kira," he said hesitantly—gently—placing a hand on her arm, "that is Tristan."

Kira followed his eyes, disbelieving, back to the pile of burning flesh behind her, still looking for Tristan beneath the broken remnants of the room. Wax had melted all along the floor and the wooden table was a pile of simmering embers, barely tall enough to hide a mouse. The flower petals had already turned to dust.

With nothing else to look at, Kira stared back at the burnt vampire curled in on itself against the floor.

A fist closed around her heart, squeezing her chest tightly, painfully.

She couldn't breathe.

He couldn't mean...

She would never...

And then, slowly, one charred eyelid slid open, revealing a midnight blue twinkling eye that Kira would recognize anywhere.

She screamed.

Chapter Sixteen

"Tristan!" Kira shrieked again. She pulled on her hair, begging for the pain to wake her up from this horrible nightmare. This couldn't be happening. Kira wouldn't accept it.

She had killed Tristan. He was dying, burning, because of her fire.

"Kira." Luke gripped her shoulder.

Kira shirked his hold.

"What have I done?" she asked herself, Luke, no one. "What have I done?" Kira whimpered.

"Kira, you have to end it," Luke said softly. Kira looked away from the mass of flesh Tristan had turned into. She couldn't bear to look at his blackened, scarred, burnt skin any longer.

"What?" Kira asked Luke, scanning his face for some other meaning in his words.

"Tristan—he's in pain. You have to end it," Luke said. His eyes were concerned, warm, trying to give her strength but also lost.

"I have to save him," Kira said, shaking her head at Luke's words. "I have to help him."

"You can't," Luke urged.

"I have to," Kira whispered and turned away from Luke. She crawled over the floor until her skin was close enough to feel the heat emanating from Tristan's body.

In some places his skin looked like melted rubber, bright red and stretched, bubbling with blisters. In other places, it was dark and charred, flaking into ash, already disintegrating. His knees curled into his torso like a child's, his arms were glued to his side, melted against the abs Kira had loved to touch. His fingers, his beautiful artistic fingers that Kira had previously seen blackened with charcoal, were now blackened by her fire. They had blown up to twice their size, swelling with blood that was just about to break free of his skin.

Biting her lip to keep from screaming, Kira finally looked up at his face. Wet tears fell down her cheeks, landing on his skin and instantly fizzling dry.

Aside from the one eye still looking at her, pleading with her, his face was unrecognizable. Gone was the black hair she always ran her fingers through, the long strands that fell over his forehead when he was really concentrating. His scalp was bald, an ugly harsh red mixed with black, like a cooling lava field. His ears were melted flat. His soft lips that Kira could kiss for hours were gone.

Kira looked into his open eye again.

Luke was right.

Tristan was in pain. He was begging for release, and Kira couldn't do anything to save him. She could only end it, end the hurt.

Kira took a deep, unsteady breath and brought a small flame to her palm. She put her hand over the center of his chest, knowing it would be the fastest way to end it.

Slowly, while his body jerked in pain, Kira sunk the flame into his heart, expecting it to already be black and broken.

But, unlike his skin, his heart was whole and healthy. It was red, pumping, full-of-life. It looked almost human, except for a shell of hard, black metal around it, sealing it off, protecting it.

Kira burned the shield, melting the black away.

And suddenly an idea came to her. What if she could push the darkness from his flesh? What if she could save him? Kira had protected herself, had managed to push the vampire out of her.

Kira changed her flames, letting her Protector fire flow freely around Tristan's heart. She could almost feel his soul hiding within its walls, something white and pure, silvery and straining to be free. It hadn't been burned. Only his body, and Kira knew she could fix that.

She encased his heart in her fire, protecting it from the dark shell it had been trapped in for more than one hundred and fifty years. And then she continued to burn Tristan, focusing on the darkness woven through his body. Slowly, methodically, Kira pushed her powers on, revealing pink flesh as the sticky, evil tar inside of him was melted away.

The further she moved, the more Kira expanded her protection, healing his wounds, healing the burns she had raised on his skin.

She kept her eyes sealed shut, too afraid that all of this was only in her mind, too afraid that in reality she would wake to a pile of ash and not a human, not Tristan. Could she be imagining her powers? Could she have gone crazy enough to live a dream?

Her flames slid up to his face, into his brain, restoring old nerves that had grown weak. Until finally, it was only the flesh of his face that needed to be healed, and she did so patiently, envisioning the curve of his nose, his striking hooded eyes, his soft almost pouted lips, the dimple that buried above his mouth when he smiled.

Kira brought her hands to his cheeks. Was the soft flesh she felt real? Could Tristan possibly be alive?

After a second, Kira felt warmth under her hands, felt blood pump through the cheeks below her fingers. A gasp filled her ears, the sound of a drowning man finally brought back to life.

Kira opened her eyes.

Tristan. Her Tristan.

He was alive. His pink lips were open and breath surged in and out of them. Kira pulled her powers back under her skin and roamed with her eyes instead.

His skin was tanned, not the pale white she was used to. His hair had returned, thick and falling over his forehead. His lashes were full, but closed, covering the eyes Kira was longing to look into. Mostly, his body was warm, brimming with life in a way Kira had never witnessed before. He felt human.

Tristan stirred. His limbs shifted, his arms stretched over his head as though he was waking from a long slumber. Finally, he blinked. His lids flickered open, quickly at first and then slower to reveal warm, milk chocolate brown irises.

He blinked again and Kira could see that his vision was fuzzy, blurred and unclear. One more time and there was more focus, but no recognition. His eyes locked on hers, confused.

"Who are you?" his hoarse voice scratched out. The deep rumble sent a shiver down Kira's body. It really was Tristan. But then, his words registered.

"Kira," she said, as though the answer was so obvious she couldn't believe he was asking it.

"Where am I?" he asked with aggression leaking into his tone. Kira didn't know what to say.

Tristan sat up, looking down at his body that was

naked except for Kira's dress, which had fallen over him during the healing. He looked at the ground, at the destruction all around him.

"What's going on?" His panic was clear. His eyes were widening in shock. "Where are my men? The commander?" He looked around the room again. "The last thing I remember is being in the woods, the men were moaning all around me. A stranger walked through the dead, sending blessings." He pushed Kira's dress aside, groping for his leg. "My wound—it's gone. I had been shot. I was dying."

His brown eyes met hers again. "Witch!" he yelled at her, anger clouding his words. "What have you done to me?" He reached for her throat and Kira was stuck, unsure of what to do. His hands gripped tightly, cutting off her air. "Witch!"

Kira tried to speak, tried to calm him, but it was no use against his strength. He pushed down on top of her, pressing her into the ground as her vision started to spot. Kira sucked for air but there was nothing.

And then, *whack!*

Tristan rolled off of her, knocked out, and Luke dropped the iron pole in his hand. "Man, I thought he was annoying before, but that was ridiculous."

"Luke." Kira sighed, massaging her sore neck. Things were happening too fast for her brain to process. "Is Tristan...?"

"Human?" Luke supplied. Kira nodded.

"Looks like it," Luke told her flatly. Kira scanned his face, which was carefully molded into a smile, hiding his real feelings. Kira was too spent to look past the façade and read his thoughts. Her powers were too drained. But she didn't need to. Kira knew Luke better than she knew herself. She could hear the pull to his words, the slight catch in his throat. His eyes were uncertain—gone was the confident gaze he had focused on her after their kiss yesterday.

Tristan was human and Luke's eyes were questioning her, silently asking her if that had changed everything.

Kira looked back at her feet to the spot where Tristan had collapsed. He looked vulnerable, like he needed her. Kira brushed the hair from his forehead.

"I don't think he remembers," she said softly, "any of it."

"Yeah, when he called you a witch and tried to kill you, I sort of got that impression." Luke shrugged and smirked at her. But this wasn't a joke. Luke knew that, he just couldn't think of any other way to deal with it.

Kira turned away from him, looking at the other conduits standing behind her. She had almost forgotten they were there, silently observing everything.

"The prisoners?" Kira asked, focusing on something tangible, something with a definite answer.

A man stepped forward, answering her. "They're safe. The female vampire, Pavia, ran too fast for us to catch her, but we did what you asked and didn't follow."

"Aldrich?" Kira asked, looking back at Luke who shook his head.

"Gone—vanished," he said sadly. "When we got inside, it was just you and Tristan. Somehow, he got away."

Kira remembered how.

She ran a tongue over her canines, relieved to find them nearly as dull as they had ever been. It was all her fault. Kira had hesitated. Part of her had wanted him to suffer, had called for his blood. She had slipped, had started to fall into the blackness gnawing at her heart. Instead of fighting Aldrich, she had needed to fight herself, giving him just enough time to run.

But Tristan had stayed. Why didn't he just leave, like they had planned? Why didn't he save himself?

Kira knew that answer too. He loved her. And when it came down to it, Tristan wasn't strong enough to let her go.

"Can we go home now?" Kira sighed, letting Luke pull her to her feet. The dress was destroyed, hanging around her body like a rag, filled with holes and shredded apart.

Tristan. Luke. Aldrich. Her own body. It was too much for her to handle right now, too much for her to figure out.

"Will you take him to the truck?" Luke asked someone over Kira's shoulder and two conduits walked forward, lifting Tristan between them. "Put him with the other victims. Make sure he gets a full medical check."

They nodded and Kira silently watched them maneuver through the wreckage, bringing Tristan's body out the door and into the night. The other conduits followed, leaving Kira alone with Luke.

He looked down at her, waiting for instructions.

"You didn't by any chance bring some clothes, did you?" Kira asked.

Luke raised his eyebrows, challenging her doubt in him. "Please—I've got jeans, a T-shirt, and my fuzzy worn sweatshirt waiting in the car."

"Thank god for you, Luke Bowrey," Kira said, taking his warm hand in hers, letting his strength funnel into her arm, surging up and around her heart.

With Luke by her side, Kira knew she would be able to face what was coming. His presence was like a drug, giving her strength she never even knew she had.

She didn't know what would happen in the future. She didn't know if Tristan would ever remember her. If he would wake with recognition in his unfamiliar brown eyes or if, like a child, he would be new to this world, struggling to make his way in a new century. Kira would be there, helping him, but she had been prepared for goodbye, ready for it even. And now even that certainty was gone. A door of possibilities had opened, hanging in the air like a question mark.

Kira didn't know what would happen with Aldrich. Where he had run or if he would come back. He didn't know how close he had come to succeeding, how close Kira had come to the turn. Or maybe he did and maybe he would follow her to finish the job.

And Kira didn't even know what she was. Her flames coiled in her heart, ready to break free at any moment, but there was something else there too, a little cloud of darkness that felt foreign in her body, something normally filled solely with light. It was teasing her, testing her, daring her to take that extra step away from the sun—demanding she fall, tumble down into the black hole it created. And Kira was standing on the precipice, looking down through the abyss, nervous that something or someone would push her over the edge, sending her flying so fast that she would change without even knowing it.

But Kira did know one thing, something so certain and binding that it took her fear away. Luke would be there to catch her, to save her from herself. He always was.

So Kira pushed her doubts to the back of her mind, forgetting everything except for the warmth emanating from Luke's hand. For once, she didn't want to think about the consequences or about whom she would hurt. She needed Luke and no matter what happened, she wouldn't let him go—not again.

Emboldened by the sudden thought, Kira looked up into his green eyes, at the flames dancing around the edges of his irises. He was already watching her, wondering what was going on inside of her head.

And before she could stop to think, could stop to worry about Tristan, Kira did exactly what she wanted in that instant. She leaned up and kissed him, quickly planting her lips against his.

In a heartbeat, it was over, and Kira was walking past him, out the door in search of a change of clothes, a way home, and a meal to calm the hunger knotting in her stomach.

Luke was stuck. His feet were planted against the ground in shock. His lips tugged into a wide smile and his eyes started sparkling.

Kira didn't need to turn around. She knew exactly what Luke looked like, because her face held the same expression—pure hope and happiness.

And like the last time they had kissed, her blood turned into golden honey, spreading warmth and tenderness around her body like a soft caress.

So for a moment, Kira forgot everything and let herself feel happy, truly and perfectly happy.

**Scorch (Midnight Fire Book Four)
is available now!**

Keep reading for a preview of the first chapter!

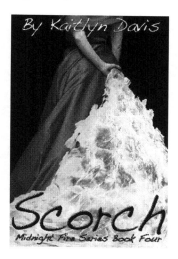

"All it did was remind Kira that time was running out. That she needed to choose. Or a lot more than a forest would burn. The whole world would crumble."

Aldrich escaped…again. Tristan forgot…everything. And Luke, well, Luke was getting more than a little impatient.
But those were the least of Kira's concerns, because something else happened in England—something she was trying desperately to forget. A wedge of evil had lodged itself in her heart, a little black hole had nestled into her flames, and it wasn't going away—not anytime soon…and maybe not ever.

Chapter One

From a chair in the corner of his hospital room, Kira looked at the steady rise and fall of Tristan's chest. His movements were in tune to the constant beep of the machines wired to his body. They were the only things telling her that he was alive, because every other part of him was still. His mouth was relaxed, slightly open to let each exhale escape. His eyelids were closed, his brows were flat, and the stress-induced wrinkles normally bunching his forehead were gone. He looked oddly at peace, floating between the realm of the living and the dead.

But it was time for him to wake up.

Two days had passed since the fight in Aldrich's castle—one long day of travel from England to Sonnyville and one long day explaining everything to the Protector Council.

Kira couldn't erase the pain in her grandfather's eyes

as she told him that his only daughter, her mother, was truly gone—that a vampire had stolen her memories, replicated her face, and pretended to be her just to fool Kira.

She couldn't forget the wounded look on Luke's face as she explained Tristan's miraculous transformation to the other conduits. His kiss still burned in her mind, playing on repeat, making her feel alive. Her love for Luke had been simmering in the back of her thoughts all this time, and it had finally broken to the surface, blossoming to a strong flame before she really even realized it was there. But looking at a human Tristan, now so fragile and new to the world, Kira wasn't sure she could let him go and make him face it alone.

But most of all, Kira couldn't loosen the knot in her chest, knowing she had let Aldrich free—knowing that somewhere out there he was alive and knew her secret. That was the worst part of it all, the darkness hiding inside of her that she couldn't share with anyone, not even Luke. A wedge of evil had lodged itself in her heart, a little black hole had nestled within her flames, and it wasn't going away.

She knew it.

Aldrich knew it.

And Kira didn't see Aldrich forgetting about that any time soon.

Which was why she had holed up in Tristan's hospital room, waiting with only her thoughts for company. After learning that she had been dating a vampire, the other conduits in Sonnyville started avoiding her. Her grandparents wanted to reconnect with her, but Kira couldn't stand the waves of disappointment churning in their eyes—after giving them new hope, she had failed to bring her birth mother home. Her adoptive parents had been furious when they heard about her trip to England, and Kira had hung up the phone to escape a lecture. And Luke, Kira's best friend in the entire world, was getting impatient. He wanted her decision and she wasn't ready to give it.

So, take away all of those people and who was left? Her comatose, once vampire now human ex-boyfriend who thought he was living in the eighteen hundreds. Oh, and who almost choked her to death when he woke up because he thought she was a demon witch.

Perfect.

Kira sighed, rolled her eyes, and knocked her head back against the wall. She really was in a corner—physically and mentally stuck. And she needed Tristan to wake up right now, before she actually went insane. She needed a distraction, and telling someone about the one hundred and fifty years of human life they had missed, well, that ought to take some time.

Antsy, Kira stood and walked to the foot of Tristan's bed just in time to catch his foot twitch. The conduit doctors had been keeping him heavily medicated for the past day in order to study his cell composition, but the twenty-four hours Kira had granted them was over, and Tristan wasn't going to be a lab rat any longer.

Farther up in the bed, his fingers bent into a fist and then flexed straight in a stretch.

Kira moved closer, stepping next to his face so she could put a hand to his warm cheek. His skin had a healthy flush and a slight tan, which, though natural for a human, seemed unnatural on him. The tips of her fingers brushed his silky black hair, and Kira studied the slightly curled strands for a moment before focusing on his eyes.

They blinked once and closed again, but Kira's heart stopped.

Brown.

She wasn't used to those chocolaty irises yet. And when he blinked again, Kira forced her breath to steady.

"Shh," she cooed while stroking his cheek. The glaze over his eyes began to recede, replaced by confusion and fear, both somewhat muted from his medication.

"Where...?" he began in a scratchy voice, but stopped mid-sentence when his gaze caught the fluorescent light blinking overhead. "What...?" His head tilted and an odd expression gathered on his face as he surveyed the room.

Oh right, Kira thought, *electricity*. It was easy to forget how long ago 1864 really was.

"Please try not to panic," Kira said. After thinking about this moment for the entire plane ride home from England, she had decided to leave their relationship out—to pretend they were never more than friends. It would be easier that way...for her at least. "I'm Kira," she said, "do you remember your name?"

"Tristan, Tristan Kent," he said with a deep swallow and locked his gaze on her, sending a little swarm of butterflies into her stomach.

"Nice to meet you, Tristan." Kira leaned back, letting go of his cheek to shake his hand.

"And you, Miss..." he trailed off, waiting for her last name.

"You can just call me Kira," she said. He had to be introduced to the twenty-first century at some point—might as well start now.

"Miss Kira," he breathed, letting the words roll off of his tongue while he reached for her outstretched hand. Unexpectedly, he brought her fingers to his mouth for a quick kiss.

Kira untangled their fingers, forcing more intimate memories out of her head. "What's the last thing you remember?"

"I was in a forest. Men were screaming all around me. I was wounded, the pain in my leg was worse than any other I've felt. I was a foot soldier in the Confederate Army and the Union had just delivered us a harsh blow."

"Good," Kira said and patted his hand. He didn't remember England at all—Kira silently thanked her good luck for that. "The thing is, Tristan, I have a sort of crazy story to tell you and I need you to just sit there, listen, and try to take it all in. Can you do that?"

"Of course, Miss," he responded before lifting his hand closer to his face. He tugged at the wire stuck to his wrist, the one monitoring his pulse.

"Leave that there," Kira said, covering the spot with her hand.

"But, if I may ask, what—"

"Just listen, I promise I'll try to explain."

Tristan nodded and set his hand back down on the bed. His movements were slow and seemed slightly disconnected from his brain, letting Kira know this calm mood would probably only last until his meds wore off.

"You don't remember, but we've been friends for a little while—good friends. I know a lot about you and I know how you came to be here, in the hospital. But Tristan, I have to tell you something that will seem a little scary." Kira squeezed his hand, trying to provide an ounce of comfort. "We're in the future. The Civil War happened one hundred and fifty years ago, and—"

Tristan jerked into a seated position, and the beeping of the machines grew to a frantic pace. He squeezed her shoulders, digging his fingers deep into her skin.

"What do you mean?" he said in a harsh whisper.

"Tristan, please calm down."

"What year is it?" he said a little louder.

"Tristan," Kira said, trying to escape his hold.

"How is this possible?" He shook her, hard enough to hurt, and an animalistic fear seeped into his stare. "Where are my men? What did you do?"

Kira slapped him across the face. The sound echoed against the sterile hospital walls and she stared at her red palm in shock. She looked up at Tristan, who looked back at her with an equal expression of surprise.

"I'm sorry," she said slowly.

"No, it is I who must be forgiven. Please excuse my abhorrent behavior, I am just... well, I can't quite explain it...confused, scared, lost...to treat a woman so—"

"It's all right," she soothed while taking his hand. "I understand."

"I do not. How did I come to be here?"

"Let me show you something first."

Kira stood and pushed the chair aside. Lifting her palm before Tristan's eyes, Kira lit a small and controlled flame above her fingers, suspending it for a moment. Tristan inhaled sharply, cutting the air. Kira sucked the fire back in and dropped her hand.

"There are a lot of impossible things in this world," she said before Tristan had time to regain his composure. "And I'm one of them, but so are you."

"Are you a witch?" he asked, unable to hide the current of fear and hatred traveling with that word.

Kira shook her head. "I'm a conduit, a vampire hunter, and you were my friend—a good person trapped in a life he never wanted."

"And what life was that?"

"You don't remember because I just cured you, returned your humanity, but for decades you lived as a," Kira hesitated, hating how crushing this word would be to hear, "as a vampire."

Tristan flat-lined.

His human heart had had too much, and it stopped as soon as she uttered the word. His chest fell back onto the bed, while his head banged painfully against the wall.

"Tristan!" Kira jumped and shook his shoulders, trying to wake him up. An alarm sounded from the side of the room and the intercom system started flashing.

"Help!" Kira yelled, hoping the lightly staffed conduit hospital still had some nurses available somewhere.

Leaning over his chest, Kira listened for a heartbeat but there was none. Forming a fist with one palm over the other, Kira pumped on his chest to the count of three. She widened his lips and forced her own breath down the opening, praying he would wake up.

She pumped again.

His lashes slipped open to reveal nothing but the whites of his eyes, and Kira screamed.

"Move, please." A doctor charged through the door, pushing Kira gently to the side. He put his fists on Tristan's chest, pumping, while a nurse jammed oxygen into his lungs.

"What happened?" the doctor asked.

"We were just talking, I was just trying to explain..." Kira trailed off as the doctor continued to work. After another round of CPR, the machine picked up a heartbeat again, and Kira instantly relaxed, trying to slow her heart to the same beep beep beep of Tristan's restored pulse.

"Give him another round of relaxants," the doctor told the nurse, who jotted a few scribbles on Tristan's chart and reached for a shot of fluids. "Now." He turned to Kira. "What did you say exactly?"

"I just..." Kira walked closer to the bed, lightly running her fingers over Tristan's still forearm. "I was just trying to explain how he got here, in this time period. He's so confused." She winced as the nurse sunk a needle deep into his skin. "He doesn't understand any of this."

"It's all right." The doctor, blond and so obviously a Protector, placed a hand on her shoulder. "It's not going to be easy for him to adjust, but these things take time."

Kira let out a loud exhale. "Have you ever dealt with something like this before?"

"Vampires returning from the dead?" He chuckled softly under his breath. "No, not in this lifetime. But I have seen people with amnesia and memory loss, and they recover eventually—forever changed maybe, but people have a way of adjusting to situations that may seem insurmountable at first." He squeezed her arm reassuringly.

"Yeah, I know about that—believe me," Kira said. If

she could overcome the changes in her life—the truth about her parents, her heritage as a conduit, and her role as a half-breed or potentially some angel meant to fall into darkness—Tristan would figure it out eventually. "Thanks," Kira told the doctor as he walked out the door.

"He shouldn't wake up again for a few hours," the nurse informed her before following the doctor to the exit.

Kira eased onto the side of Tristan's hospital bed. Even though his skin had darkened and his eyes had lost their striking blue hue, her Tristan had to be in there somewhere. He would look at her with warmth and love again, and not as a stranger or a threat.

"He looks pretty good, you know, for someone who was dead three days ago."

Kira recognized that voice instantly and turned to welcome Luke with a grin. He stood in the doorway with his hands lazily resting in his pockets and his shoulders slightly shrugged as though he were mildly uncomfortable. When he stepped into the room, he looked down toward the floor, avoiding the bed.

Kira thought the green in his T-shirt made his eyes shimmer like dark emeralds, and she resisted the urge to run a hand over the soft cotton. "Does he still think you're a demon witch? I myself thought the description was uncannily accurate."

Kira rolled her eyes at the playful jab. "You don't want to know what nicknames I have for you."

"Prince charming? Knight in shining armor? Love of my life? You're not that original, Kira." He smirked, looking at her piercingly under his hooded eyebrows.

Kira breathed deeply, releasing a shaky breath, and subconsciously slipped her hand off of Tristan's. "And you're no Disney prince."

"I know," he said and slipped closer to her, gaining confidence with their easy banter. "Being two-dimensional would totally cramp my style."

"Yeah," Kira started but her breath caught when he reached his hand out to run his thumb along her lower lip. Kira swallowed. "You don't want a perfectly packaged princess to run off with?"

Luke moved his hand along her cheek, stroking her skin until his fingers rested at the base of her neck. He tilted her head slightly upward and forced her to meet his stare. "I prefer my pain-in-the-butt demon witch." He leaned down, arching her head up farther.

"Luke," Kira murmured, shifting her head to the side so his lips landed on her cheek. Even if she wanted to kiss Luke, which she did, and even if Tristan didn't remember who she was, which he didn't, Kira was too conscious of his body lying still right beside her.

Luke sighed and pressed their foreheads together, taking a deep breath before retreating a few feet away to the empty chair next to the bed.

"So how is he actually?"

Kira appreciated the genuine concern in Luke's tone, even if it were more for her sake than for Tristan's. "Well, I told him he's been a vampire for the past hundred or so years, and his heart stopped beating and he passed out...so, yeah, not great."

"He still doesn't remember anything?" *Or who you are?* Kira finished Luke's question in her own mind.

"No, nothing. But he seemed a little more in control, at first at least. The nurse gave him a few more meds..." Kira trailed off as she traced Tristan's body with her gaze.

He was fast asleep and not waking up anytime soon, but what she couldn't help noticing was how serene he looked, even with all the confusion. His features had never appeared so relaxed to her, not in all the times she had seen him sleep. It was as though some invisible weight had been lifted, as though he had been freed.

"So what did you really come here to talk about?" Kira looked over at Luke, catching him mid-stare.

He opened his mouth, ready with a witty reply, but closed it again. "The council," he said and let his eyes slip away to the window.

"Which one?" Kira sighed.

"Both." Luke leaned forward, resting his forearms on his knees, clearly stressed out.

They both were. The past two days had been taxing on everyone, but Kira thought she and Luke had taken the brunt of the heat over the failed mission in England.

Everyone forgot that Luke had managed to save all of the locked up conduits in the dungeon just because he had let a single vampire go free—Pavia. He refused to put more blame on Kira by telling the council that it was her demand to let Pavia escape and instead let everyone believe she had slipped away.

But the real stressor, for both of them, was the Punisher Council. Never in Luke's lifetime or in his parent's lifetime had the two councils met in full. Whenever cross-conduit business needed to occur, one member from each council would travel and make the necessary decisions. But a full meeting of all seven members of each council was almost unheard of—and they were meeting today to discuss Kira's fate now that she had completely changed the game by bringing Tristan back to life.

Kira swallowed.

Her hours of peace stowing away in Tristan's hospital room were about to come to an end. It was almost time to face the world and its consequences again.

"When are they supposed to get here?" Kira asked.

Luke didn't need clarification. "Soon, really soon."

"And what did the Protector Council say?"

"They won't let anyone hurt you—I won't let anyone hurt you. But they are concerned about how the Punishers will act, what they'll demand. This goes against everything they know. For hundreds of years, Punishers have been fueled by their belief that vampires can't be saved, that their humanity is gone, and what you did completely negates that."

"And there's more," Kira said. Luke continued wringing his hands together and looked at her questioningly.

"More than that?"

"Well, that's their argument for why Tristan should die—that the evil will still call for him. But what's their argument for me? I told you what that Punisher in the dungeon said. About how he thinks I'm an angel that's falling and becoming an original vampire, an unstoppable force. They'll want to put an end to me before I have the chance to make that transformation."

Luke leaned back and waved his hand unconvincingly in the air, dismissing the idea. "Come on, Kira, that's insane. Anyone who looks at you can see what side you're on."

"Anyone who looks at me can see my blue eyes, or are you that used to them now?"

Luke scooted his chair closer so his knees touched hers. "I see them. I see two bright and beautiful and warm cobalt blue eyes that look like the sapphire heat of a burning flame and nothing at all like the dead cold eyes of a vampire."

Kira looked away, her heart melting a little under his scrutiny. "Yeah, well, too much sun exposure might have affected your brain cells. Besides," Kira continued, not letting him retort with any more compliments—she could already feel the blood rush to her cheeks a little, "they'll say

I'm too sympathetic to vampires because I was with Tristan. Maybe they'll twist it around so it seems like I wanted Aldrich to go free. I don't know."

"But you've never once acted like one of those things or felt any sort of calling like the Punisher described, have you?"

"Of course not," Kira retorted, trying to look angry that he even asked and not at all guilty.

Because, of course, she had.

During her fight with Aldrich, Kira had lusted for the kill, a prolonged painful death, and maybe even for Aldrich's blood. And that was why he had slipped free—why he had the moment he needed to escape—because Kira had started battling the demon inside of her instead of the one burning at her feet. Since leaving the castle, nothing new had happened. But still, she felt the change within her, the slight taint her flames now carried.

"So that's that." Luke slapped his hands together, jolting Kira out of her thoughts. "They have nothing, no argument that makes any plausible sense against you."

"I'm just nervous, I guess." She shrugged.

"The Flaming Tomato is nervous? I'm shocked!"

Kira smiled. "I haven't heard that one in a while. I was sort of hoping you had somehow forgotten about it."

"Forget the Flaming Tomato? You can't just forget the Flaming Tomato—it's too good." Kira raised her eyebrows in his direction and he responded by raising his hands up. "What? I'm just saying."

"So I have Demon Witch and Flaming Tomato? I seriously need some new nicknames...or some new friends." Kira muttered the last part.

"Would you prefer something more normal like...Kiki?" Luke asked, his face a blanket of innocence.

"Call me that again and I may kill you." Kira sent over her best death stare.

"See, that might have actually scared me when your name was Demon Witch, but with Kiki it's just not nearly as menacing." He folded his lips together to keep from grinning.

Kira launched herself across the room, going right for his ribcage with her hands. The benefit of being best friends was that Kira knew all of his vulnerable spots, and it took about two seconds to have him rolling around on the floor begging for mercy.

Tickling—it was totally underrated.

"Kiki...come on...I can't breathe," Luke gasped between giggle fits. Kira pushed even harder.

He grabbed her by the wrists, finally using his strength and size to overcome her. Without her hands to ground her, Kira's balance slipped and she landed on his chest with an *oomph*.

When she opened her eyes, the laugh had disappeared from Luke's face and in an instant, the air felt thicker. She licked her lips, unable to look away.

"Ahem."

Kira rolled off of Luke immediately, jumping at the sound of an unfamiliar voice in the doorway. She looked up to see a well-dressed blond man who she remembered seeing around Sonnyville before.

"The Punisher Council has arrived. We request your presence at the council dais immediately."

"Thanks," Luke muttered while he stood up and brushed his clothes off.

"I'll meet you there in a minute," Kira said, looking back at the still unmoving Tristan.

Luke nodded and dragged the protesting Protector from the room.

Kira walked back to the corner of the hospital room where she had left her handbag and took out the shabbily wrapped present resting inside. Hastily, she scrawled a note on the blank card.

"Dear Tristan, I'm sorry I won't be here when you wake up again. Remember what I said and please try to stay calm. Here's a history book I think you'll like—it'll get you caught up on everything you've missed. And there's a little extra too. I couldn't find the charcoal you like, so I got some soft graphite pencils instead. I know how much drawing relaxes you. Please don't worry, I'll be back soon. Love always," she erased that, "yours truly," she erased it again, "your friend, Kira."

Kira left the package at the foot of his bed and

walked out of the room, hoping she could keep them both safe from the Punishers now waiting just a short walk down the street.

About The Author

Kaitlyn Davis graduated Phi Beta Kappa from Johns Hopkins University with a B.A. in Writing Seminars. She's been writing ever since she picked up her first crayon and is overjoyed to share her work with the world. She currently lives in New York City and dreams of having a puppy of her own.

Connect with the Author Online:

Website:
KaitlynDavisBooks.com
Facebook:
Facebook.com/KaitlynDavisBooks
Twitter:
@DavisKaitlyn
Tumblr:
KaitlynDavisBooks.tumblr.com
Wattpad:
Wattpad.com/KaitlynDavisBooks
Goodreads:
Goodreads.com/author/show/5276341.Kaitlyn_Davis

50409642R00171

Made in the USA
San Bernardino, CA
22 June 2017